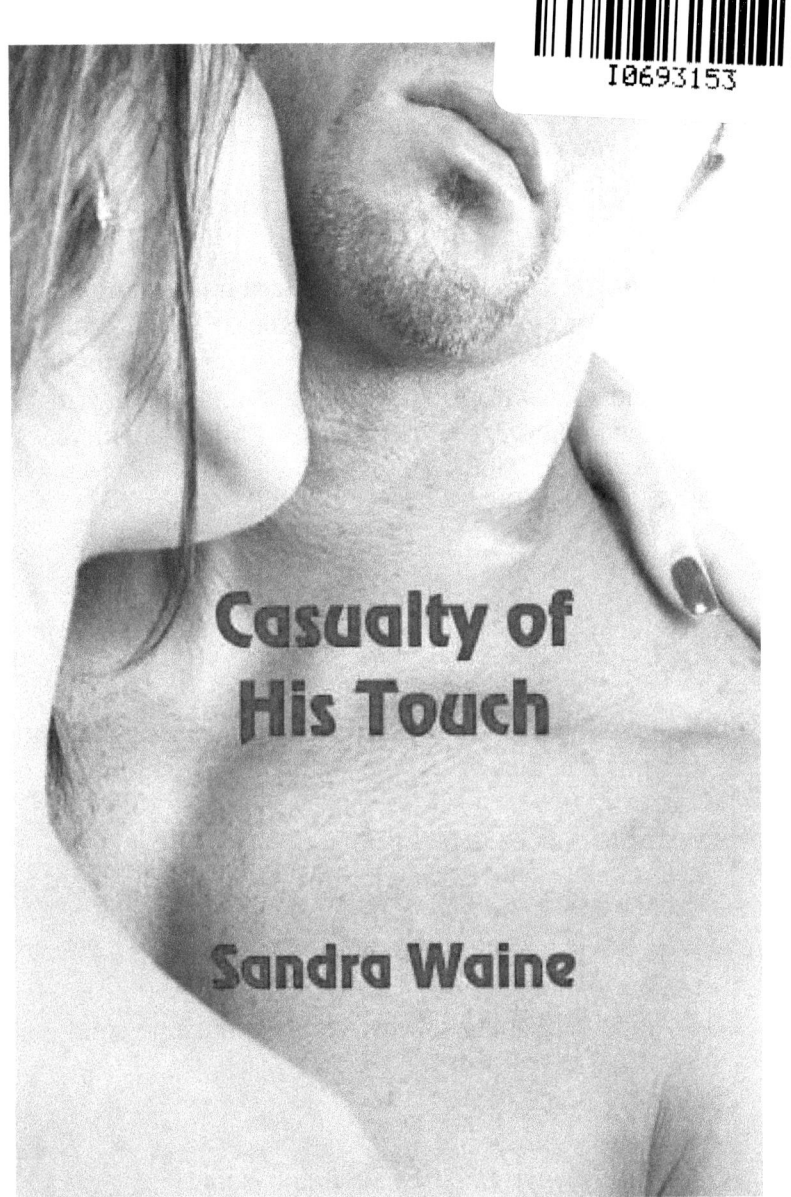

# Casualty of His Touch

## Sandra Waine

Cover Art:

Publisher's Note:

This is a work of fiction. All names, characters, places, and
events are the work of the author's imagination.

Any resemblance to real persons, places, or events is
coincidental.

Solstice Publishing - www.solsticepublishing.com

# Hostages of Love Series

# Book One

# Casualty of His Touch

# Sandra Waine

To Nick and Tyler. Two very special guys who always supported me and still do in all my crazy writing adventures and all else. I love you both.

# Chapter One

Commander Benzamin Gazeer stood glaring up at the television monitor inside his heavily protected office at Mossad Headquarters outside of Tel-Aviv. Clearly, he was agitated by what was appearing. "Hand me that remote," he barked, to a pain in the ass aid that had been in his shadow way too long. Assigned by the prime minister's office and had caused the commander plenty of irritation. Increasing the volume on the remote, he listened intently to a BBC reporter live on the scene in Al Minya, Egypt.

"Just minutes ago, a series of unexplained explosions rocked the interior of Cairo Capital Institution. We are still awaiting word on who is responsible. Our sources have speculated that HAMAS is involved. But positive confirmation has not yet been disclosed."

The BBC reporter stepped back bringing an eyewitness into view. "Tell me what you saw."

The woman's voice was shaky. Cuts and scrapes seeping with blood marred her pretty face and neck. "I was just inside with my cousin. She was making a deposit when a loud explosion knocked us both to the floor. It was not like anything I have ever seen. A bolt of lightning tearing in from one of the side windows. It happened so fast. Glass and debris flew all around us. It was awful. I saw a woman and small baby just lying there. The child was not moving."

The reporter gave her only a brief second to gain composure as he glanced anxiously around. "Then what happened?"

"We were grabbed roughly, pulled to our feet and brought outside by two special forces officers."

"Did you see anyone exiting the building? Anyone suspicious?"

The reporter was relentless not caring that the woman was close to tears and clearly distraught. "No. But," Her reply was halted as a heavily protected police officer came between them. The reporter swung abruptly around. "Do you have any updates? How many dead? Has it been confirmed it was HAMAS? Why this institution? We have learned that it has financial ties with Israel and the prime minister's office. Can you confirm?"

The commander's blank, stoic face changed too grim. One eyelid twitching as he watched on.

"We will have a statement as soon as possible," the officer gruffly replied. Then nodded at the witness to follow as he turned away from the camera and strode off.

Commander Gazeer hit the mute button throwing the remote onto a tabletop, glanced out of a thick-paned glass window then resumed pacing. Completely aware his assistant stood close by awaiting orders.

"Athol, get Zamir on base now."

"Yes sir, I'll locate him. Last disclosed he was on holiday and no one knew his exact position. Not even the prime minister."

Internally the commander could give a fuck. Everyone liked to pull that shit around here. It made no damn difference with him. "I said get him in here. Page him. If he ignores it, you personally get your ass on the road and locate him. You have one hour."

The assistant slammed the door muttering as he walked briskly down the long-carpeted hallway and entered the communication command center.

Several sets of eyes locked on him. "The commander wants Zamir paged. Stat. I don't care how you reach him. Just do it. I'll wait right here."

"Sir, he is not wearing a tracking device, so we have no fixed location. The satellite will be unable to pinpoint a locale."

"Not good enough, soldier. Do you want to go back to the commander and advise him of this?"

"No, I sure as hell do not."

"What's your name?"

"Casson, sir."

"You have thirty minutes to locate him or we'll be visiting the commander together. No doubt following our negative results, he will transfer us to some dank and dark location. We are intelligence. Find him and get this request done. Now."

"I'm on it."

Athol knew if anyone could locate Zamir, Casson was the guy. Sitting back, he knew the clock on the wall had become an enemy of state watching the large black hands tick. Deafeningly loud and irritating, it was a constant reminder time indeed was melting away. Finally, the secure phone's indicator glowed red as Casson accessed the line.

"ID yourself."

Casson nodded, listening, as a grin formed knowing the language on the other end was not suitable for speakerphone. He spoke up while choking back a laugh and interrupted the caller on the other end.

"Stand by for the prime minister's assistant."

Casson glanced over toward Athol.

"We have him, sir." He picked up the receiver and handed it over while disengaging the call from his headset.

"Commander Gazeer orders you to base immediately. You have one hour." Athol stopped to listen. "Excellent. I will advise him myself. But possibly choosing my words more carefully."

He handed the phone to Casson and left the command center continuing back to the commander's office. Knocking on the door, a sudden wave of unease enveloped his body.

"Enter."

"Sir, I just spoke with Zamir. He's inbound now and expected in less than one hour."

"Good work, Athol, now use my secure line and call in the joints of staff and get me a list of who we have out in the field and where their current locations are. Focus on Algiers, Morocco, Spain, France and the U.K. I need that before they all convene here. Open access to SATCOM. Then you go about your business and bring the prime minister up to date."

Piss on him, Gazeer thought. That would keep him busy and out from beneath his highly polished black shoes for at least an hour. A resentful respect was truly all they housed for the other. "It reeks of HAMAS. I need an assessment of damages and if their systems were compromised. Contact the special police and have them transmit their congregated report and any additional information straight away."

"Yes, General, I will take care of that."

They both glanced back out the windows contemplating what mood their special agent would be in when he arrived.

***

Zamir shifted down to first grinding to a halt at the high chained fence outside the perimeter's guard shack. A hand held out the ID as the guard quickly scanned it then gave it back along with a salute while the gate was lifting. Shifting, Zamir drove onto the expansive area. "Damn," He muttered inside the car's interior. Only two weeks had passed since exiting the base.

Disrupted by this bullshit and having to leave the warm embrace of a certain lady friend in Petra, he was pissed. It was clear by how fast he shifted through the gears in an area of the base where several were walking. Many took a sideways glance toward him as the car sped by. He could care less.

He knew the commander would be ornery as all hell that it took much longer to arrive. *So, what*, he internally thought. *They needed him and could wait.* Delaying his departure from Petra was necessary. Just like pushing his foot down on the pedal and using his special license plates as a shield. A reason to speed and get away with it.

Parking the car, he pressed the auto lock button and used his ID card to enter headquarters. Soldiers were scrambling in and out as he examined each of them, nodding to a few. His shrewd eyes recalling the large assembly of bulletproof black sedans parked further away from the building. They all flew the Israeli diplomatic flag. His stride gained purpose as he entered the command center.

"Casson, what the hell is going on?"

He pointed the remote to one of several large wall-mounted television screens and hit play. Zamir slid his hands into side pant pockets stepping closer and watched the pre-recorded BBC broadcast with minor interest.

"This is what brought me in?"

"You know I can't discuss this with you. The general will see you right away. As in now, Zamir. He is fully aware you have checked in and on base. You'd better get in there or the prime minister's assistant will be on your tail. He is a thorough freaking ass."

Zamir grinned not giving a damn. "Think I want to hear a briefing from you first. They can wait. Go on."

Casson's lopsided grin worked into a broader one as Zamir shrugged that knowing look off.

"We have a team on site now interviewing the special police and those inside the building. We did find one person that managed to keep his calm while the shit was hitting the fan. He was positioned at the exterior of the bank. When he was brought to questioning he presented blurry but usable cellphone footage of the rooftop just opposite the bank. Just before the third and fourth explosions rocketed in."

Zamir froze as Casson enlarged the rooftop image. Three faces came into clear enough view. His blood turned to ice. Stepping closer he took in the scene.

"Zafir."

"Confirmed."

"We found their abandoned van approximately two klicks from the area."

"Prints?"

"No. But a second team is on it. Sweeping for explosives and relative evidence."

"Do we have ID on the other two? How many in all?"

"Five or six we guess. But not confirmed. We do have one confirmation back from INTERPOL. Amis Davide. A known operative with HAMAS. The others we are still collecting data on."

"So, we have no fuckin' idea?"

The grin evaporated from Casson's features. "No."

"Keep on it. You know how to reach me. I'll head into the lion's pit and see how the pissing match is going on. Do we have intelligence on how they entered Egypt?"

"Yes," Casson clicked the remote. "Surveillance tapes from the Taba Border. Unfortunately, we are waiting for a positive ID from the manifest."

"Good. Deliver all files to my cellphone."

"Roger."

Amichai Zamir was hands down the best Mossad operative the Israeli Government had, and Casson knew it.

"Casson, I need you to be my eyes and ears here. You know what I am asking?" His hand was poised on the door handle as he turned it and started to walk away already knowing the reply. Closing the door, he continued down the long hall.

Zamir opened the commander's door and closed it soundly as several sets of eyes focused in his direction. Pacing bodies halted. *Damn*, Zamir thought, *these pompous dignitaries, military men, and politicians liked to argue.* As a grin formed on his handsome, tanned, weathered features.

Commander Gazeer rushed toward him speaking loudly. "Zamir, good. We have just received INTEL that Zafir and HAMAS are responsible for the bombing. Upon closer evaluation, our team has reviewed some of the shattered remains suspecting this has all the signs of '*The Engineer*,' Daniel Levy. We had previous information he was out of the country in Afghanistan. Unfortunately, this has not been confirmed."

Zamir knew he could speak his mind amongst this group of high-ranking military officers. "Commander, time is not going to stop while all the INTEL is gathered. I need all the important details now. The rest can be sent via a secured network. I need to move out."

Gazeer glanced at the stout old faces gathered around the room and could feel the shift in the atmosphere from previous bickering to one of acceptance. Motioning to Zamir and moving to a back table, the general continued.

"One operative in Cairo has obtained secured information to confirm the five have transported by rail to Algiers. Further INTEL is being gathered out in the field. We strongly suspect it is the Al-Qaeda training camp where they will suspend their journey temporarily and regroup for their next destination."

"Commander, is this a reliable source?"

"Affirmative. We have a mole who's been undercover for eighteen months. A Brit with established contacts on both continents."

"Has their purpose been disclosed?"

"Sleeper cells. It is suspected their destination and the safe house to be used will be in England. Deploy and await further information. Their normal process will be to descend underground until additional training can be provided and orders are received. We are monitoring all activities closely now."

"Objective?"

"You have clearance to take them out using whatever means you need. MI5, MI6, and the SAS are at your disposal. Your liaison between them all is a retired Lieutenant Colonel Douglas Hawthorne."

"Hawk." Zamir's eyebrows raised.

"You know him?"

"I do."

"Care to elaborate?"

"No, Commander, I do not."

There were not too subtle grumbles around the room. "We can establish a point of contact upon your arrival."

"Don't bother. He will find me."

No response ensued as Commander Gazeer stared at Zamir for several long seconds. Then, seemed to reach a conclusion, nodding.

"Passport name."

"Use any of the ones we've provided. No issues there. We can follow your trail on any one of them."

Suddenly up on the monitor a face appeared as everyone in the room turned to listen in on new developments.

"Commander, we have positive ID they have departed Algiers. Our source confirms information received. Their destination is England. The city of Bristol."

"You are sure it is not London or Manchester?"

"Yes. MI6 suspects a known safe house currently under surveillance is their prime location. They have a joint agent underground at this premise that will contact Zamir by code. Awaiting your orders, Commander, so I can reach back to MI6. The mole in question is with MI5 as they closely monitor all events."

"Reply back their contact is on the way. Use Zamir's code name."

Commander Gazeer glanced about the room. One could hear a pin drop if it fell. "Gentlemen, are we in agreement?"

Everyone nodded.

Zamir saluted his superior officers and exited closing the door behind him. Re-entering the command center, he proceeded directly over to Casson. Towering over his sitting form he watched with interest as thousands of coded pages filtered on screens.

"You are my sole contact. I don't care if an order comes from the general. Do not post out any assignments. Keep this one close to your shirt. Understood?"

"You bet."

"Do you have a photo of the mole in Bristol and what code is being established for contact?"

"The photo will be transmitted by MI5 when you are in Bristol as well as all the other details."

"Sex?"

Both men laughed. Casson knew what he meant. "It'd a female. Ironically your sequence is *heat*. Don't take that literally."

"Fuck you. What else?"

We have a person of interest that INTEL has verified as a possible non-combatant but requires confirmation. Margaret Cohen. Resident head librarian at the University of Bristol."

Both men never took their eyes off the monitor. "Her department allows the use of their facilities after-hours for all types of groups to meet. Including radical. But it requires investigation while you are there. We are not assured she is not a mole as well. MI5 and MI6 cannot find anything of use on her. All likelihood her past has been covered up. So, the red flag has been raised on this one. It appears she is entirely clean or well secured beneath an internal source."

Casson clicked the mouse and brought her picture up on the monitor as Zamir felt a brief flicker of something buried deep inside. Then it swiftly passed away. His training did not allow for feelings to get in the way. Ever. But silently admitted to her being extremely attractive.

Wavy dark brown hair pulled back, blue eyes and a very appealing smile loomed before him while he absorbed every detail to memory. He knew someone else that would immediately take a preference to her.

"I need the particulars."

Casson smiled knowing Zamir as a deadly killer but all-in-all was still a man. "Single, twenty-nine, just completed her masters at the university in her field and has a large family expanding out to Wales, England, and Italy."

"Ever been married?"

"No record of that."

Casson swiveled his chair around but did not stand. "Whatever you come up with for a cover, let me know and I'll make sure it is all in synch. You know the procedure. Anything else I can provide?"

"Negative. I'll be in touch." Turning abruptly, Zamir exited the room, strode with purposeful steps outside then got into his car and drove off in a flash. At his apartment in Tel-Aviv, he opened the safe encased inside the closet beneath wooden shelves and removed a British, French and Egyptian passport along with credit cards and cash.

Jamming them inside an internal pocket on his carry-on, he showered and changed into business clothes and sat down at his desk to book flights on the laptop. His British passport would be needed along with bogus documents. The other items were just in case he required a swifter way out of Britain. Flights booked and confirmed, he finished packing and rang a reliable source for a quick taxi transfer.

Outside of London in Reading, Zamir kept a flat neatly paid for and in the ready stocked to the nines with gear and necessities. He fully anticipated that was where Hawk would find him, that ornery bastard.

His cellphone vibrated as he removed it from his waist holder and scrolled through the contents from Casson. Glancing outside seeing the cab pull up to the curb, he grabbed his bag, set the alarm, then pulled the door shut. Adrenaline coursed through his veins as he entered the elevator. Yeah, he liked this. Was born for it with no wife or kids to hold him back. Just mistresses. That was all he had ever needed as more interesting horizons beckoned.

The transfer was fast as he moved through security at Tel-Aviv airport, boarded the flight and soon enough was touching down at London's Heathrow Airport. His eyes examined every single face upon exiting through passport control and immigration. He had no delays. None had been anticipated.

"What is your destination, sir?"

"Forty-four Shinfield Road, Reading, off the A327."

His British accent was clear, voice strong.

"Okay, very good."

Zamir lifted his bag and walked outside into a brightly lit day and slid an expensive pair of Oakley's over his eyes walking toward the next cab in line. Placing the bag into the back seat and closing the door, Zamir nodded he was all set as the cabby swerved out into heavy traffic. Exiting the airport, he glanced up periodically at the highway signs to keep track of their location. As the cab driver pulled too close to the curb, he glanced in the rearview mirror but never uttered a word as Zamir slid his credit card through the reader, paid and got out slamming the door.

Close in proximity to the University of Reading, his flat was just as he left it several months ago. Setting the keys down on the table he swept the room for any unwanted listening devices then rolled the bag into the middle of the living area. Removing a small key, he maneuvered out of the way a large, heavy, woven rug. Then pried up three-floor boards and inserted a key into the lock of a submerged metal case.

Immediately a cover sprung open as a digital display appeared on the panel beneath. He pressed in the code as the box lifted out of the floor, top expanding open.

Viewing the contents, he removed small wire, potently effective explosives, pistols, suppressors, and a razor-sharp knife. Standing, he gathered the arsenal.

Mossad operatives rarely proceed like this. Then again Zamir was outside the normal box and he knew it. With full governmental backing. His primary function to eliminate all hostiles. Then slip back to his country and rejoin the ranks of his countrymen. Journeying amongst them until needed again. In the volatile world of today, Zamir knew it was never long before his service would be required once more.

He threw what was necessary into a duffle bag and grabbed motorcycle keys satisfied that no rain was in the immediate forecast. The bikes grip was always suspect when the roads were wet. *Then it could always be slowed down and not driven so damn fast*, he thought to himself, smiling.

Lifting the garage door, he began the short ride to Bristol as his mind began weaving in intricate detail what his next maneuver would be. Then laughed into his helmet. *Hawk*. He had been wrong. Now, where the hell was he? That was a first. One hand balancing the bike around an S-turn, Zamir reached into his side jacket pocket and pulled out his cellphone and checked for messages.

Nothing.

Damn.

Accelerating, he increased well over the local speed limit and continued.

# Chapter Two

"Shalom, Miss Cohen, last night provided an excellent turnout. I have come to thank you for allowing us the use of one of the library conference rooms. I hope our attendees were not disruptive? It may have sounded that way if anyone was listening. Like an angry mob had gathered."

Without warning a sudden tremble weaved up Maggie's spine as his eyes bore into her own. Scrutinizing for what seemed like an eternity before a slight movement closer to her desk brought her back around.

"No worries, Michaez. I will admit it was a bit rambunctious at times. But you appeared to have it all under control. I could not hear the discussion. Sounds were muffled and I had my door closed listening to classical music. I did, though, see arms moving in very animated ways." She grinned. "But I suspect it was due to such a diverse crowd."

She watched with open curiosity now as his face displayed what Maggie thought was a flicker of something. Was it he was anxious? She evaluated him closely now while he resumed speaking.

"Everyone is using the word extremism abundantly these days. I know we all need to be diligent and cautious, but I wanted to set a precedent. Open the floor up to a proactive discussion about the difference between Muslims, terrorism, terrorist acts and the gross, abusive behavior toward our women."

She genuinely smiled. "Well said. That certainly is an expansive topic and an empowering reason. You are completely correct. Many make false statements with pure intent to dissuade others from their cause. I agree. The public needs to know to form a more accurate opinion. I applaud you. Now, I presume you are here to book another time slot for next week?"

"Yes, Friday at six o'clock. Is that open?"

"Indeed, it is. I'll put you in. I understand you have gained a member that I know. One of my associates, Susan Perkins. She's an excellent teacher in our journalism department and an outstanding writer. I've read some of her reports and articles."

"Ah, yes, Miss Perkins. She joined us two weeks ago and again last night. Perhaps she will ordain our group by attending on a regular basis. I believe she is the right voice to present our points and lay all falsities to rest. Her style is just what we need."

"She's a great resource, I agree, and a true professional."

He smiled. "I have to meet friends now, Miss Cohen, or I will be late. See you next week."

"Goodbye, Michaez."

Maggie thought it peculiar that he never mentioned what classes he took there at the University of Bristol. Assuming he was probably a political science major by the sounds of his activities. He seemed to be older than most of the kids on site. But his usage of the English language was excellent with a somewhat formal middle-eastern accent. *Then again*, she thought, *one is never too old to attend any learning institution.*

Taking a pair of sneakers from a tote-bag, she slipped them on and tied them up just as her cellphone vibrated. She picked it up. "Maggie here."

"Mag, it's Patty. Are you almost through? You probably forgot it's Friday night. If you get your ass out of there and home, you have time for us to pick you up for a few pints of beer at Goldbrick's. Can you make it this time?

Do we have to come and force you out of that damn office?"

"Shut up. I'm logging off now and heading out. I'll be ready in an hour. Does that work?"

"It does. Hey, meet us outside. The parking at your apartment building can be hell on a Friday night."

"See you in a bit."

Maggie grabbed her bag, shoes, keys, and cellphone then logged off the computer. Flicking the light switch on the way out of her office, she shut the door and twisted the handle ensuring it was locked. Across the hall her assistant Caren's office lights were on but she was not in there. So, Maggie kept going.

It was a gorgeous late summer night just perfect for a short cycle ride to her flat as she veered the bike behind the Radisson Blu Hotel. Enjoying the proximity to the waterfront and overall area. It was right in the hub of it all. Bristol to her was an amazing lively city. Not far from London by train and wonderful for hiking and cycling in the national parks just short drives away. She loved it here.

Entering the flat her eyes drifted fondly around the quaint living space. Small, yes. But, it was hers and a far cry from having to share a room with her sister inside their parent's house years ago. Someday she'd look south and buy a cottage. Get a cuddly cat. For now, this suited her single life and professional purpose just fine.

Standing in front of her dressing closet, Maggie dropped her work clothes to the carpet having no time to hang them properly. Wiggling into a tight pair of jeans, she threw on a soft rose lacy top, socks, then slid on and zipped up a pair of brown leather boots. Dabbing perfume at her neck, she barely had time to change out her bag, grab her keys and jaunt off at a fast clip while shutting the door behind.

The 'out of order' sign hung across the elevator doors as she hustled down four flights of stairs and arrived slightly out of breath at ground level. Outside, she started to laugh as the Range Rover came curbside and held up traffic. Pissed-off motorists honked horns stuck behind the vehicle as Maggie climbed in.

"People seem a bit impatient tonight. I don't understand why unless they want to get alcohol into their bloodstream before we do." They all laughed as Maggie glanced at each of her friends always glad when they got together.

"Are you in another one of your strange moods, Mags? Do I need to lower my own alcohol intake tonight and keep a keen eye on you?"

"Don't know what the hell you are talking about, Sasha. And you," she pointed a long finger at Ahmad sitting next to the other door, "Don't give your opinion just to suck up to your girlfriend. Not tonight." Maggie's tone was friendly, but her eyes relayed a straightforward message.

Suddenly Patty perked up. "I told Mr. O'Malley that tonight I may match him drink for drink. Feeling like this Friday could not come quick enough. It was a tough week with Susan, the paper, and those damn groups you book at the library."

For a split-second, Maggie's mind disengaged from all her friends in the vehicle to the brief conversation with Zafir.

"Mags?" Her eyes refocused back to Patty. "Can we not talk about them tonight? If not, I may be forced to drink you all under the table."

Sean was sitting beside her, and Maggie knew what a solid Irish drinker he was. "O'Malley, I don't think I could ever consume what you do. But match me up against your girlfriend, I'm sure I can."

"Now wait a minute." Patty tried in vain to get her voice heard but it was no use. Everyone broke out in laughter as Maggie spoke up just as they arrived jabbing

Sean in the ribs. "No one in this vehicle can drink like he does. Unless they are fresh off the boat from Ireland."

Ahmad skidded to a halt in a front parking spot nearly sending them all forward inside the vehicle. Doors opened and slammed shut as Sean grabbed Maggie's arm tightly with Patty on the other.

"Hang on just a second there, Mags. You look different tonight. Expecting anyone?"

Everyone laughed knowing how Maggie did when it came to relationships.

"Shut up."

"Come on," Sasha grabbed her arm. "I see a table open with enough chairs." A waitress hovered back waiting for their group to sit before the rounds were ordered while the noise level escalated rapidly as the bar filled.

Maggie slugged back her beer first, looked at them all, then slammed the mug down on top of the rough wooden table top. "Asses. My grandmother can drink faster than the lot of you. I'll go and find that waitress and order up another round." Reaching under the chair for her bag she stood and headed toward the bartender as her dark blue eyes honed on two men very deep in conversation leaning against the bar. Scanning quickly, she had no choice but to try and gain the bartender's attention over their shoulders.

Halting in mid-sentence, they simultaneously stepped aside to allow her to slide in between them. She smiled at them both.

"Thank you."

The one on the left spoke with a crisp and deep British accent. There was something about the way he sounded that caused a very pleasant tingle to weave up her spine. Followed quickly by a somewhat sensuous warming. *Hmm*, she silently thought.

"Our pleasure. Clearly, you'd be the rose between two thorns."

Maggie laughed softly as golden, brown eyes locked with blue.

"That's pretty good I must say. But I apologize if I am interrupting your conversation. I can step aside. I just came up to order drinks for my group." She turned and pointed at their table then held one palm up over her lips to cover a laugh. They were watching intently.

Then it was as if they all woke up, stopped staring and began hurling remarks that drifted over the loudness in the room as the other man spoke.

"All your friends?"

She knew right away he was from Israel. She dealt with faculty and students from various areas of the middle-east.

She smiled. "Yes. If I don't order their drinks soon, they will descend upon us and whatever conversation you two were having will have to be postponed indefinitely. They can be extremely distracting."

He laughed as his friend threw in what Maggie thought was a very well-worn, highly used remark.

"You look familiar." But his next statement halted a snide remark. "You're the librarian at the University of Bristol in the media section, correct?"

Stunned, she stammered out, "Yes, I am. When have we met?" She scrutinized him closely as his eyes held her momentarily hostage. "If we have, I apologize. I can't recall."

She saw out of the corner of her eye the Israeli wave over to the bartender who was finishing up with the waitress.

"No, I was at a program in one of your conference rooms hosted by Michaez Zafir."

She could feel the appraisal.

"Ah yes, Michaez. He stopped by tonight to see me. Nice enough student although he does seem to be older than his group of friends." She caught the quick exchange between both men.

"Who can I get drinks for?" The bartender was tapping his fingers on the dark mahogany bar top. But more in time with an AC/DC tune blaring from the house speakers than from impatience.

"Oh, yes. Five local brews sent over to that table, please." Maggie turned to point and noticed an addition to their party. "Oh, make that six." It was Suzie Perkins who had joined Maggie's friends. She handed him cash including a hefty tip. "Thank you, guys, for letting me step in." She turned but not before noticing as she left how quick their gap closed, heads bent deep in conversation.

***

"Interesting we met up here by chance, eh Hawk? Then right beneath our nose the lovely Miss Cohen appears along with Miss Perkins. Just how convenient is that? Good start, old chap."

"Damn convenient. I agree. Just a word of advice compadre. I saw the way you looked at her. Don't you have enough women left to conquer back in Tel-Aviv?"

"You are not speaking about her, are you? Both men glanced back toward Maggie.

"Fuck off."

"I can see for myself your retirement has not improved your disposition at all, my friend. By the way, what the hell happened? I fully expected your sad ass on my sofa when I arrived in Reading."

"Sorry to disappoint you, Zamir, but I figured if I had to see your face again so soon, it better be over a pint to wash away its ugliness."

Both men laughed out loud.

"It's not that I need to '*get to know her better*' if you get my drift."

Michael did indeed. They both knew INTEL was needed to get her off the watch list, so they could focus on parties of interest.

"It's your call on this one, Hawk."

Recently in then out of retirement, Lieutenant Colonel Douglas Hawthorne looked back over his right shoulder toward the group in the corner and grinned catching a glance at the librarian checking him out. Yeah, it was time to mix a little business with pleasure. As the sweet scent of her perfume lingered beneath his nostrils.

He glanced at Michael who was looking over eyeing the pretty Miss Perkins. Both turned toward each other, raised glasses in a mock salute and swigged their drinks back as Zamir signaled to the bartender for another round.

Leaning sideways Hawk watched things unfold rather to their advantage. It seemed the entire room polished off two more rounds and bordered on drunkenly disorder in a hurry. "We should be in a seedy side alley somewhere in Lebanon, my friend. This is reminiscent of other times. Other countries."

Zamir laughed as both men turned abruptly toward a loud noise behind them. One of the women at Maggie's table pounded her fist down and yelled loud enough for both men to hear. "Mags, you are up again. Go and get another round. It's on me."

Standing, Maggie laughed just as the waitress appeared balancing a large wooden tray. On top were several mugs of beer. Sitting down, she looked up glancing into his brown ones once again as a devilishly handsome smile hovered on his lips. Maggie seemed spellbound. Unable to look away.

*Oh fuck.* She mentally concluded. *One more drink may put me under.* Then her mind digressed in a hurry. *What the hell*, she thought. *After tonight she'd never see him again*, while a hand simultaneously tugged a vacated seat closer to her own as her brain started to register exactly what was going on.

Hawk's grin grew as his eyes swept over her entire appearance. He knew full well what he was doing. Knew how to control his emotions. Years and years of hard military practice. But something did stir, he could feel it. A slight tug in the gut. Ignoring it, he moved even closer to her. No glance towards Zamir was needed. He knew he sat next to Perkins.

As Hawk spoke into Maggie's ear, voices around them quieted sensing her friends were trying to listen in.

"I hope you don't mind the intrusion?"

She turned slightly as their jean-clad legs touched. Even in the dimness of the room he could see warmth spread up her cheeks. Then something else took hold. Danger. It was danger. Followed in hot pursuit by desire.

"Nope, not at all."

Extending his hand, she clasped it and noticed how small it was in comparison to his own.

"Douglas Hawthorne."

"Maggie Cohen."

"So, who are your friends?"

She laughed softly. Are you sure you are ready to meet this lot? They are quite a handful." He nodded, grinning, caught up in that engaging smile of hers. His own expanded while lowering his gaze to her full, pink lips. Hawk was having a devilish time removing his eyes from them and the temptation they provoked.

"Okay, but you have been warned."

It did not take much to get their attention. "Everyone this is Douglas Hawthorne. To our left is Sasha Lewis, Ahmad Sollam, Patty Robertson and, Sean O'Malley. Watch out for him." Her friend's all started to laugh. "He can drink any living soul not already in bed with the devil under the table. Oh, and on the end next to your friend is Susan Perkins."

He raised his glass and saluted them. "Besides Susan is my friend Amichai Zamir. I call him amongst many names, Michael."

Maggie watched the smile pass between her work associate and Douglas's companion.

"What do you do for a profession?"

"Call me Doug. I teach a criminal justice class at the City of Bristol College and fill in as my department needs me. I have a law background." He chuckled, as their shoulders touched, watching the astonishment on her face. But her response really surprised him.

"I had expected you to be ex-military or something like that. Did you ever serve in the forces?"

Great, he silently thought. *What a way to begin having to lie right up front.* "Nope, why would you suspect that?"

"I don't really know. A hunch. There is something about your tone and stance up at the bar. I don't know."

He grinned. She was perceptive as caution flags went up. He would have to be very careful. "So, what do you do in your spare time away from the library? Are you a private detective by chance?"

They both laughed.

"If you ask my friends, co-workers and even my family they'd tell you I would not be a good candidate. They all seem to think I am too nosey for my own good. A nosiness that lands me in trouble at times."

"Interesting. So, what do you do besides work?"

"I hang out with these guys a lot, often we cycle, hike and take trips. Things like that. Do you like to ride?"

"Yeah, I cycle but truthfully prefer my motorcycle. I've done plenty of hiking over the years. Have you ever been to the Alps?"

"Which ones?" She smiled, as those internal warnings intensified. "I've hiked the Dolomites with these guys earlier this summer and near Lago de'Como in Italy. It's gorgeous there. Have you been?"

Indeed, he had, winter training nearly had a third of his men hospitalized due to harsh wind, weather conditions and extreme cold. "Yup. Hiked there a time or two during the winter. But I prefer the summer months now."

For a few seconds, an uncertain pause came between them before he switched gears.

"Do you like classical music?"

"Oh yeah, very much. It was always on when my Pops was home and I was a young girl."

"I know what I'm going to ask is straight out of the blue. But hell, why not. I have two tickets to tomorrow night's venue at Colston Hall. Would you like to go? I know it's really short notice for a Saturday night."

He watched an interesting play of emotions cross her features and instantly assumed she would think he had plans with someone else and that person had bagged on him. Her hesitation continued, and he found growing amusement in it.

"They were my sister and brother-in-law. They can't attend and were placed in my hands. I wondered what I'd do with the other one. How about it, you free? Otherwise, my possibilities are grim." He paused, directing a look toward the end of their table. "I'd have to take him…"

She glanced over at Michael and broke into a giggle.

He studied her carefully as she started to form a reply, then both their heads swung around as her friends seemed to yell in unison, "She will go!"

"Hey. Mind your business." Maggie tried to chastise them but had to laugh. "Go back to your drinks," was all she managed to get out. Then turned back toward Hawk. "Why not. What time? Where do you want to meet?"

"I'll pick you up. Seven-thirty if you live in the city. After the performance we can grab a bite to eat."

"Ok." She took out a piece of paper and jotted down her cellphone number and address then placed it into his open palm. His gaze penetrating deep within as she raised an eyebrow. He graced her with one raised of his own as they broke out in laughter again.

"What the hell was that all about?" Patty hollered from the other end of the table. "Have you two met and been secretly dating? Mags, you been holding out on us?"

"No, I can assure you I've never met this lady before tonight. My word on it."

"Fine. If you say so. Did she agree to a date?"

"Indeed, she has. All I ask is that none of you disclose any dark secrets about her. I want to discover them myself."

Patty let out a sigh while attempting to stand. Weaving suddenly, Sean reached up and tugged her back down. Her bottom hitting the wooden chair with a resounding thud. Just then the house lights flickered signaling to all who could still think that it was officially last call.

"Who's driving you home?"

"Sean. The Rover will see us safe. It knows what way to go. Joking aside, he can really hold his liquor."

"Just the same I'm headed out. Do you want a lift? Then I'll know where your place is."

"Okay. Yeah, sure. I think that would be fine."

He stood and repositioned his chair back to the other table and pulled hers out as she stood.

"Hey. Where're you headed sunshine?"

She glared at Sean. "Home. Doug's going to drop me off." Knowing it was coming Maggie held up a hand, palm facing toward them all. "Save your speech. I'm a big girl. Even if I am slightly drunk."

She grabbed her bag and quickly hugged all her friends and then smiled at Doug who was already holding the outside door open. He nodded over his shoulder to Zamir then touched her arm briefly. "This way. I am down the street a short walk from here. I hope you don't mind riding on the back of my bike?"

She stopped. "Motorcycle?"

"Yes."

"Do you have an extra helmet?"

"I do. Shall we?"

She continued in stride chancing quick sideways glances at him as he caught those looks and managed to suppress a grin. Then she halted a few feet short of reaching the motorcycle.

"Are you okay? You look a bit peaked."

She seemed to disregard he had even asked a question as he watched her eye the bike closely. "Hey, if you prefer, I can get you a cab."

Her reply nearly threw him for a loop. "I think you are lying."

He rested one hand against the extra helmet not entirely sure what game this was. "Because?"

"This bike is customized. I mean really customized."

He removed the helmet and handed it to her. "Here put this on. See this button? When the strap is secure engage it and we can communicate while I drive."

"Really? That's very cool. It has been years since I've ridden on one of these." She clipped in the chin strap and pressed the button. He could tell the cobwebs were now clearing and with it, her full attention focused on him.

"Can you hear me?"

"Roger that."

He hesitated before pulling out. Concealing the urge to turn around and look at her. To see if she meant that or was joking around. "Okay, which way?"

"Bang a right and head down toward the Radisson Blu Hotel. I live behind it on Baldwin Street, number six. It is a small apartment complex."

He almost said, '*Roger that*' back then caught himself. "Hold tight."

"Are you going to pick me up on this tomorrow night?"

He laughed as her hands tightened around his waist.

"No. I have a proper vehicle for that."

The bike jerked a bit as Maggie clutched him even stronger. He felt those fingers move over his abs.

"You still back there?"

"Can't you feel my hands? Hell, you must be kidding."

"I sure can. I was just teasing you."

"I gathered as much."

He pulled over to the sidewalk and shut off the bike. Kicking the stand down he removed his helmet and got off extending a hand. She grasped it standing while he undid the strap and then took her helmet off.

"Right location?" They both simultaneously glanced up at the neon lights of the Radisson Blu and back to one another laughing.

"Spot on. Thanks for the lift. I really could have walked. It is so close."

"No, not a great idea this time of night. But you are welcome." In a rapid perusal he evaluated the layout of the building and area around it.

"Call me just before you arrive," she handed him a card that had her personal number written on the back. He nearly reminded her she had given him details back at the bar, but refrained.

"I'll meet you down here. Parking is difficult on a Saturday night. Everyone comes into the city."

"Want me to walk you up?"

She eyed him suspiciously, quickly, he could tell. Then seemed to decide something. "No, but thanks. I'll see you tomorrow night at seven-thirty." He watched her move up onto the curve, turn and give a slight wave. Then headed toward the front of the building away from him. He waited until she was inside before he put the helmet back on, started up the bike and pulled out and headed home.

***

"Yes!" She chimed into the vacated lobby. "The damn elevator lives again." Happy that it was working. She punched in the fourth floor and once inside her flat the shoes came off as she locked the door behind. As total silence engulfed her. It was deafening. No sound of another person. No cat or dog to greet her. When had this life she so loved, become bleak? *Yeah,* she thought, *perhaps this guy would stick around and liven things up. If I don't mess it up. Again.*

It always seemed that her penchant for being invasively nosey always brought along with it the guy ditching her within a few dates. Even with all those past screw ups and her parents and sister's warning, she still could not help it.

Maggie turned on her computer and Googled his name and wasn't surprised that zilch came up. Her intuition was rapidly generating warnings. While an overactive mind pondered as she softly spoke into the empty room. "Stop it. Don't do this. Give the damn bloke a chance."

Sighing loudly into the night, she wondered if this was just her past creeping up again. Playing with her mind? Hadn't she gotten into enough trouble in her twenty-nine years to last a lifetime? *Probably not,* she thought, grinning. *After all, do leopards truly ever lose their spots? Do Jimmy Choo shoes ever go out of style?*

But then again life for her was never truly boring. Not long after she'd make promises to her Pop and family to keep her nose clean, she'd be knee deep in shit and looking for help to get out. Isn't that the meaning of family? Sticking by your side through thick and thin?

As she readied for bed and finished brushing her teeth, she glanced up at the reflection in the mirror staring back. A broad smile appeared. Yeah, she knew it was time to have some fun. Real fun.

***

Back at his temporary pad, Hawk accessed INTERPOL and found Maggie's dossier, examining it carefully. It didn't appear she had any involvement with this sleeper cell. But who knows. One can go from normal to radical overnight. He negotiated that idea for a few moments recalling those arms holding tightly around his waist. "Ah shit," A smile creased the corners of his mouth. "I'll investigate her a bit longer before I send in my report.

Grinning, silently admitting tonight's events were more interesting than he had thought, and perceived there was nothing common about Margaret Cohen. Tomorrow, Zamir would report his findings. They would compare and then formulate the next move. Everything else could wait until then.

# Chapter Three

Her Gray Tiana B dress was indeed the right choice as it fell just above shapely knees. Which were covered by woven gray tights and matching high-heeled shooties. *These in their own rights,* Maggie thought, *were easily accessible weapons,* as she glanced at the wall clock knowing she had to get a move on. It was nearly seven-thirty.

Picking up a clutch and soft, ivory wool wrap, she closed the door. Twisting the handle to ensure it was locked. Not even bothering to check if the elevator was working or not, she rushed down four flights of stairs. Just as she entered the interior corridor her cellphone rang. Fumbling, she reached it just before it went to voicemail.

It was Doug.

"Hi, I'm on approach. Should be there in less than two minutes."

"Great, I'm in the lobby now and will be outside when you arrive."

She was standing at the curb when he pulled up in a pristine, golden brown, antique convertible. He stopped the vehicle as Maggie skimmed fingers gently up and over one side in complete awe. Hardly noticing he was out, car running, door open.

Patiently he watched as complete enjoyment enveloped her features. "We can certainly stand here all night appreciating it, but eventually it will run out of gas."

She laughed. "Sorry." She got in as he shut her door and came around. Shifting, he had them out in traffic straight away.

"Is this yours? It's an MG, right? What year? I always wanted one of these. My father was adamantly against it. I'm a bit envious right now."

He chuckled at such enthusiasm and barrage of questions. "Let's see if I can answer you in proper sequence. Yes, yes and nineteen thirty-five. Born in Cowley, Oxford and was my granddads. It sat beloved, covered and tendered to until my father took it out of storage in the seventies and worked on it himself. I used to enjoy tinkering with it. When I turned forty he presented it to me. It now has a new home. How'd I do?"

"Very good." She smoothed a hand over the leather seats and up onto the dashboard. "Does it shift hard?" Their eyes caught briefly as a sweet blush swept up her cheeks.

Doug shook his head slightly then refocused toward traffic. "Used to be, but not any longer. I had to search high and low for parts I could incorporate into the drive shaft. Now she handles like a kitten."

Maggie grinned. "Isn't it difficult to find the right petrol for it?"

"Nope, no issue. I have access to all the bases and fuel."

"Ah, got you, Doug. You are in the Military. Aren't you?"

They had covered the short distance between her flat and the hall when he pulled over and parked the car. Hands clenched on the steering wheel. "So, you are a detective after all?" Pitching in a different direction he averted the question but knowing full well it would not end there. "Shall we?"

He moved around opening her door as she smugly lifted one shootie then the other onto the pavement. Hand extended, she clasped it looking briefly up at the sky. "Hope it won't spot us with a touch of rain. The forecast tonight seemed to favor a warmer night."

*So*, he thought, *we've turned to the weather now?*

"How ironic is this? I live such a short distance, yet have never been here and no clue who is performing."

"It's the Bournemouth Symphony Orchestra. There should be plenty of classical music tonight."

As they walked side-by-side up the walkway, others were gathering. Doug knew by the look on her pretty face questions were forming. Damn though, it didn't take long before she probed deeper much to his irritation.

"Why would you not want to admit you have a military background? It's something to be proud of. I'm beginning to think you have duped me, Doug. Playing me for a bit of a fool. Now, why would that be?"

"Your imagination runs all over the place, doesn't it? I said I have access to bases. But, it could be for entirely different purposes that I am allowed entrance to them. Perhaps I am an engineer. A contractor. Did you think about that?"

Maggie glared at him momentarily as he nearly missed a step wanting to laugh out loud. She was indeed someone he needed to be on full alert with. He had hoped to relax with her tonight. Catch *her* off guard. Now it was *his* that was up.

As their eyes engaged he could practically read what was going on behind them in that smart ass brain of hers. There was little that could be done now, he knew. She was entirely too perceptive and quite sneaky in her approach. Not your typical nosey woman that he was becoming astutely aware. Doug motioned her ahead toward an empty table and chairs.

Seated outside at the Bistro, Maggie looked around. "I've no idea why my friends and I have not come here. This place is fantastic. The views of the city and channel are nice. Funny, isn't it? You live someplace for a long time and don't bother to truly explore." She leaned toward him smiling, "Makes no sense we've not hit this bar up.

You may have gathered how much we enjoy a good cocktail now and again."

He grinned, nodding. "Yeah, I kind of noticed that. So, what would you like?"

"Pinot Grigio, please."

As the waitress took their order she dangled a bit of flirtation with it then left their table as the grin on Maggie's face grew.

"Don't go there," He threw out quietly. "Shows she has good taste."

"Damn good thing I wasn't drinking, I may have spewed it out right onto you. I see you are not short on ego. How refreshing."

Momentarily, without knowing why or any sort of reasoning, she reached over and surprised them both. "It would appear she does have good taste. I did the same thing when we were in the bar the other night."

The waitress set Maggie's drink down without a word but leaned toward Doug exposing a bit of cleavage while placing his down.

"Okay, that was blatant."

"Yeah, no kidding. Write down your number on a piece of paper and I'll slide it into her bra on our way out."

They both broke out in laughter. "You are pretty damn feisty, Maggie. You and all your friend's. I hope Michael is in safer waters than I am right now."

A flush crept up her cheeks softening to a pretty pink as she sipped on her wine. "What's he doing tonight that may put him in danger?" Her eyes twinkled as one eyebrow rose.

"Nosey wench, I'll tell you. Susan and Michael are out on a date tonight. Dinner. Seems they hit it off as well. I thought you may know that since she's a friend of yours."

"Nope. Well, not terribly. We've met at faculty meetings and have become a bit more than acquainted. I really don't know her all that well. She and Patty work on the same campus paper and appear periodically at some of our evening events. But I like her. Tell me about Michael. He seems a bit mysterious."

"Ah, there's nothing mysterious about him. Regular dude. One that tends to date more than commit. His job keeps him away from home much of the year.

"Well, they did seem well suited, I think. When I stood between both of you at the bar, I wondered why two good-looking gents were out together. Women missing."

"So, you were waiting for them to appear? Is that why you kept glancing toward the hallway over where the ladies room was? Be honest."

Her laugh was light. "Honest?" Her mind fully engaged, thoughts running rampant as the battle of their minds took hold. "Now that is an interesting thought. Okay, yes. I was looking for them to appear and further, glad when they didn't and you two joined us."

"Any regrets so far?" His eyes bore into hers. Unrelenting and questioning. As she thought about it further, it was in a rather prying manner. Interrogating manner. Suddenly, she felt like a hostage. Tied up with no escape route in sight.

"No, none so far. But I admit I think there's more to you than then meets the eye. Continuing to omit important details. Causing me to keep my true thoughts under review."

"What do you think I am hiding, Maggie?"

"Your background. I heard what you said earlier. I think you are sliding the truth."

His eyes never left hers for several long, hard, contemplating seconds. A strong emotional struggle was taking place inside as Maggie wanted to jump to her feet and run. Run as fast as she could away from this intriguing, yet handsome stranger. Finally, the silence drove her nearly over the edge.

She waited. Then could stand it no longer. "Wow, was it that loaded of a question?"

"Yes."

"I get it. Don't bother answering with just some random crap. Why don't we finish our drinks and you can bring me back? I think I've been played for a fool. Knowing your answer is not important."

Her tone was so factual Doug momentarily didn't know how to reply. But he did need her to stick around. A bit longer anyway. The next words out of his own mouth even surprised him.

"You are correct, Maggie, I am retired. What clued you off?"

"Words like affirmative, roger, extract. Is Doug your real name?"

"Indeed, it is. For those that know me well, it's Hawk."

"Why the ruse? I'm not daft. Are you undercover and I am part of your," she stopped, hesitated, glancing around at others deep in their own conversation. "Mission?" She leaned slightly in. "What do you need? Just ask."

Perfectly glossed pink lips tried to smile but he could tell by the look in those beautiful blue eyes her confidence waivered.

"Do you want something stronger before I answer that?"

"Yeah, you read my mind. I'll have a Patron."

He signaled the waitress over and ordered a shot and another scotch for himself.

"Are you going to continue to ask me questions that I will feel obligated to answer?"

"Yes and no. This is a two-sided sword and it's up to you how you do it. If I overstep your hidden boundary just let me know. I detest lies. But know sometimes they are absolutely necessary."

Only a few inches separated them now as she sprang up from the stool. He thought for a quick second she was just going to bolt right on out of there.

"I'm going to the lady's room. I will be right back."

He sat down and lifted the glass of scotch to his lips, tipped it back and polished it off. He knew several more could be had before his tolerance would be met. Then contemplated what his level of tolerance would be toward her. Charming, smart, strong and astute. Yeah, he knew. He had to draw the line between them and keep it there as he monitored her return. Admitting silently, she was indeed a handsome woman. Period.

*Fuck it,* he thought. Eyes focused intently on every curve she possessed with mind just imaging his hands on each one. No, he knew this train of thought had to stop right now. Dead in its tracks. There was no time for a dalliance with her. There was work that needed to be done.

She sat down and swigging back the Patron. Glass empty, she set it down as he watched determination rise on her face, in her eyes. Doug squared both shoulders prepared to embrace what was surely coming.

"What was your rank?"

"Lieutenant Colonel."

"Ah, a commissioned officer. Did you attend Sandhurst?"

He was surprised she knew about that military college. "I did. Your knowledge is a bit interesting to me, Maggie."

She liked how her name sounded on his lips. Yes, the Patron was working. "I wonder what your real mission is. Are you retired and brought back for a special assignment?"

He could not waiver here. "I cannot disclose that information or I will have to take you hostage."

She grinned unwittingly ramping up the game between them. "Handcuffs are for local officers. What do you use, soldier?"

Maggie had no clue what had gotten into her. Oh, but she sure did. It was that maddening alcohol. Her own delicious poison. It always spelled trouble. For her and anyone else within the vicinity.

"If that's the case then let's bag the music and head back to your place."

She stared at him for the longest time before realizing he had left his stool and was grabbing her by the arm, smiling. "Come on. The performance is about to begin." He could not keep the laughter from rising.

Consciously, Maggie recognized there was indeed a need for caution by these careless flirtations with him. He may corner her, and she'd be offered no outlet for escape. That would be a first! He certainly had not answered her direct question. Was she part of his mission? Was he using her to gain something else? Her friends? All the bells and whistles rang loudly in her ears. But the potent combination of wine and stronger spirits caused her to throw caution and common sense directly into the wind. *The hell with it*, she thought. *I may as well have fun now. It's all going to end soon enough.*

She was then brought back to reality in a flash feeling his hand against her backside. Then, to her shock, it wandered a bit south as he ushered her to their seats.

Side by side they sat, shoulder to shoulder and watched the beautifully dressed musicians perform with perfection. As the alcohol relaxed her further, an overwhelmingly strong temptation took hold as she nearly allowed her head to rest against one of those strong shoulders. Shaking slightly, Maggie caught herself just in time.

"Can you see alright?" His head moved close, breath warm against an ear as it penetrated against her skin.

Hands clutched tightly against the armrests, Maggie felt it, felt him. As a quake took hold, eyelids drooping until at last it passed. Not daring to glance at him, she prayed these raging emotions would cut it the hell out.

"Yes, enough. But no worries. It's the music I want to hear more than see the orchestra."

"If I doze off, feel free to jab me."

Tilting her face closer to his, their lips nearly met. *Damn*, she thought. *These seats are close. Cozy.* It was too much as she raised one hand to inflamed cheeks. Yes, he had somehow managed in a short period of time to penetrate her wall.

Having no escape route, Maggie closed her eyes completely and allowed the music to transport her far, far away to lands she had visited and loved. Eastern Europe. Lands filled with ancient ruins, beautiful people, and lively customs. Then before she even realized it, without the normal customary intermission, it was over. How could that be? It seemed as if only thirty minutes had passed, but clearly two had. As the lights slowly came on she could feel the heavy intent of Doug's perusal well before daring a look.

"What did you think of the music?"

"Wonderful and I applaud you. Not once did I hear a snore."

His crooked grin wreaked sudden havoc on her senses as she realized the wine and Patron had worn off. Her mind engaged a plausible explanation why she was so attracted to this guy. He was different than any other she had gone out with. Tall with dark, handsome looks and confidence that comes from being a hardened soldier.

They rose from the cushy chairs as he caught hold of her arm. Then moved them through the large gathering leaving simultaneously. At one point he was in front and her hand in his. It was strong, large and oddly comforting. As she tried to pull it free, his grasp tightened.

The crowds converged clustering at the final exits when Maggie found she was now in front of him. One hand clasping her own and the other possessively on a hip. He halted her progress so quickly she found herself pulled up against the wall of his chest. As they stood there, a cute little old couple passed nodding appreciation at being allowed out ahead of them.

Maggie nearly crumbled to the carpet below when she felt his chin on the top of her head as the old woman stopped, smiling at them both.

"What a nice couple you are, thank you."

When had her breathing stopped? Feeling stifled and the need to be outside and put distance between them, ideas formed in Maggie's mind. Space. Yes, she needed space from him as soon as possible. Not completely understanding what the hell she was feeling, but she knew it bordered on discomfort and fear. A deadly combination.

Outside in the fresh air she gasped in quickly then expelled it slowly allowing taught nerves to calm. At last, her mind started to make sense of things. She knew from the look on his face that he was keenly aware of her sudden withdrawal. But she had no choice. This was protective mode taking over and she was glad for it.

Silently, she prayed something would come up. His phone would ring with an urgent request. Then she could just walk home and put this all behind her. Right away.

At the MG he stopped to open her door just as his pager vibrated. He pulled it from inside his jacket and read the message, glancing up at her for a few seconds before speaking. "Maggie, I know I promised dinner, but I have to go. Something of a very urgent matter requires my attention immediately."

She glared up at him. Momentarily stunned that her very deepest wish to bug out on him was granted that quickly. As she grinned, more at the powers of the mind and universe, she could tell he mistook it as relief.

There was no lingering doubt now that it was better this way. She was totally sure. "That's okay. I'm fine from here. I'm close to home and it's a busy night with plenty of people out on the street. I can see myself there without any worries. You go and take care of matters. I enjoyed the music. Thank you."

In the far recesses of her mind, she wondered if he was married. Was that why it went off? Then realized married men do not wear pagers. Military men on assignment do. She knew that one-hundred percent. Stepping back a few feet from the curb, she did not bother with further conversation. Instead, turned and headed off in her own direction.

***

Dismissed. Just like that she had formed a plan, thanked him and dismissed him. He shook his head as a laugh sprang out while applauding her quick wit and polite tact. Thus, avoiding any type of hassle that any other woman would have seized upon.

*Good job, Maggie*, he thought. Scrutinizing her carefully as she walked up ahead on the sidewalk. He got in the car and started it up, shifted and drove by her slowly giving a wave. He knew what that would do. He watched her in the rearview mirror then his eyebrows shot up as he realized she had flipped him off!

***

Maggie was grinning boldly knowing he saw it and did not care. *Asshole*, her mind reeled. But she got what she wanted. Time to herself for the rest of the night doubting their paths would ever cross again while muttering softly, "Whatever he wanted from me, I hope he got. Sure, as hell wouldn't be a second date. I'll not see the likes of him again."

Hailing a cab three blocks from the hall, it stopped as she climbed into the back seat. "Oceana please." She'd head to the nightclub area of Bristol to see if the gang was around. If not, then have a drink and call it a night. Frig him and frig these damn ass crazy emotions. They could all ride out together on the next tide.

*How rude*, she thought. Not being able to shake off that he hadn't even attempt to secure her a cab home. Jerk, her mind reinforced. He seemed to have gentleman manners enough when he wanted something. "Oh hell." She muttered again, "Screw it. I'm done."

Instead of going into throngs of party-goers at the Oceana, she diverted and walked down the boardwalk stopping at a favorite dockside haunt. It was always quieter with less fanfare at The Shore Café and Bar. In seconds she was seated overlooking the harbor and ordered an apple martini.

Sipping, it was tasty going down and relieved some of the stranger emotions that had grabbed hold earlier. Glancing out over the half-moon lit night, Maggie sighed watching the swells of the tide swallowing up then releasing the city's shadowing lights as they danced on the bay. Her eyes shifted left and caught the hazy silhouette of a man that she instantly recognized.

But what the hell? Who was the woman he was talking with? So close too? Their bodies not touching but heads bent in private conversation. He was clearly calm, no deep angry tones made it her way. But the woman appeared to be very agitated. Maggie's eyes were transfixed, wishing she was closer to overhear the conversation.

As her mind drove on down the crazy lane, it reached a conclusion that Doug was indeed a womanizing cheater. A true bastard. But still, Maggie's mind wanted to rationalize. Know more as heart and brain fought an intense duel. The conclusion came when her heart backed down and brain won. Screaming internally inside her head, *just let it go!*

Furthermore, should he turn this way he'd see her. She found some comfort realizing there was a rail separating the tables from the walkway. Feigning any further interest, she tipped back her martini glass and stood knowing her best and safest choice would be to go back inside and out the alley entrance.

Standing, hunched slightly, Maggie began her exit knowing the staff in the kitchen would hardly notice her passing through. It was one of her most used and infamous escape routes. It always worked. Yet, often the best-laid plans are the first to go amuck. The woman Doug was with began to walk away as he turned, looking down at the cellphone in one hand.

Mesmerized and perplexed, Maggie was unable to continue. Glued to the very spot and just kept right on staring. Why the hell had her expensive boots not moved?

Then he turned and saw her.

Finally, paralyzation relinquished its hold over her legs as they began to move backward step-by-step. Irritating voices inside screamed at her to just turn and run. Anxiously glancing around, she knew the safest place and headed straight there. The ladies room.

Sitting on a closed, cold plastic toilet lid with legs crossed, she mumbled to herself. "Interesting move. I could have just confronted him or been an even bigger girl and said whatever and moved on. Now, what do I do? Stay in here until they close? Climb out a window?"

Placing it all neat and tidy into perspective she stood and opened the stall door and stared at her reflection in the large, well-lit mirrors. *Crap*, she thought, examining the sad eyes reflecting back. There it was. The truth. She *was* hurt by tonight's turn of events.

The door creaked as she peered out noticing him at the far corner of the bar near the door. Leaning down, she swiftly removed her high-heeled boots and walked with stocking feet across the room. Well beneath his visual range and exited.

Leaning one palm against the cold brick wall of the alley, she placed the boots back on, stood straight, gazed around, then headed out into a side street and hailed a cab home. Great, she realized. Tomorrow was Sunday. She detested Sunday's if she didn't have something planned. Paying the man, she climbed out of the cab, ignored the elevator and took the stairs. In no time she had disrobed, washed up and climbed into bed. The night's events had taken its toll. *He* had taken a toll on her as well. It didn't take long before she drifted off.

As darkness turned to daylight, Maggie stood and lifted a drape back and glanced outside toward the sky. The day was bright and clear with no rain in sight. So, a quick decision was made. There was no way she was going to stay put and brood about last night. Dressing, grabbing her cycling gear and supplies, she placed the bike up on the rack attached to her BMW and took off. In a few miles she was headed south out of Bristol exiting off the motorway toward Exmoor National Park. There she would cycle the anger right out of her body and at the same time exhaust her mind.

The beauty of that area would soothe any soul regardless of circumstance. Then, she'd have a light dinner in the ancient medieval village of Dunster and head back. Arriving and pulling off the single-carriage road, Maggie took the bike down, placed her water bottle in the holder, slid on a small backpack and immediately started pedaling straight up a nasty little hill.

She felt invigorated by the smell of fall in the air, the green grass plumped up by recent rains and catching glimpses of rabbits hopping about. This was truly an area she loved spending time in. When she finished the loop, and arrived back at the car, her spirits were lifted tremendously.

Wiping the sweat from her brow she unclipped her cycling shoes and in stocking feet lifted the bike back up on the rack and secured it. Just as she moved toward the door unlocking it, her cellphone rang.

"Where are you?"

"I'm still in Exmoor and headed shortly to the Dove's Break. Planning on food and a pint. What's up?"

"I stopped by and saw your car gone. Why didn't you tell me you were riding? I would have come along."

"Thanks, Patty. I was in a foul mood and just needed to exorcise some demons."

"How long was it? Did you do the coastal path?"

"Thirty-one and parts of it. I maneuvered in and out of the park."

"Well, hell, don't hiss at me through the phone. You know I need to ask. Did your date not go well?"

"Let's put it this way, it did until some woman called him on his cellphone after the performance and he left me on the sidewalk taking a cab home."

Maggie closed the book on those nasty emotions and thoughts that raged through her last night. Which prompted such an unscrupulous retreat from the bar. But today was a new day. Last night was officially placed in a mental box and sealed. Forever.

"He did what?"

"I don't want to talk about him again. It's over before it ever began."

"You okay? I can drive down and we can drink the night away."

Maggie had arrived at the Dove and parked, got out and locked the car walking around the back to make sure the bike lock was engaged. "Nope. After I finish here I'm headed home for an early night with Masterpiece Theatre.

But thanks. I'll ring you in a few days. Hey, have you heard from Suzie? Do you know how her date went?"

"Interesting you ask. I guess Michael had to cancel last minute and she ended up hooking up with Michaez. You know that guy that's been holding those radical meetings in your conference room."

"Yeah, I know. But I thought they were just acquaintances. Hmm, interesting. What else do you know?"

"Not a damn thing that I'm going to share. That's if it's going to land you in hot water and me in trouble with your Pops."

"Come on."

"I know she's home. Why don't you give her a buzz?"

"Nope. I'm sure to bump into her sooner or later. I'll wait. Thanks for being concerned, Pat, I'm going in now and shutting off the phone. Talk with you soon."

Later that Sunday night while gazing out of the living room window at the harbor in the distance, Maggie grabbed her pad and pen, opened it up and jotted down some notes:

Retired Lieutenant Colonel Douglas Hawthorne – Army, she surmised.

Michael Zamir, an associate but from the Middle-East.

Susan Perkins, faculty at the U. and has made an association or relationship with both Zamir and Zafir.

Michaez Zafir hosts a new meeting nearly every week but not sure he's a student.

The first call to order tomorrow she would head to the registrar's office and delve into his background. Also inquire about Suzie. Being a new employee and all. Perhaps her friend in that office would help with some private information that would help clarify some questions Maggie has. Put her mind at rest.

Softly adding, "I wonder where Zafir is staying?" While adding that to the growing list. Picking up the notepad, she slid it into her crossbody bag. If this didn't disclose what she wanted, a quick call to her Pops may be in order. But only as a last resort. It was just a bit too soon after the last incident. One that left a very lasting impression on them all. Maggie had been forced to eat crow.

Oh, how she hated crow.

*** 

On the other side of the city a different type of event was taking place.

Two men and one woman were meeting in a secured campus location. "Why didn't they tell me you were the mole? You were with him tonight. Did any of his friends show up?" Hawk glanced briefly at Zamir then back to Susan.

"Yes, one." Suzie stopped talking and pulled out her cellphone and opened a file then transferred it to both their devices.

"Have you sent this to headquarters?" Zamir moved closer to her.

"I have. Amis Davide is confirmed. He traveled with Zafir. Both have strong ties to HAMAS."

"What about his passport?"

"Si, Espanola."

Neither men found amusement in her open attempt at a joke. Faces remaining stoic.

"Are there any others?"

"No. At least not that we are aware of right now."

"Have you contacted airport security for their tapes?"

Susan looked perplexed for a moment. "No, great idea. I'll get that right away."

"Good. Exit the way you came. You'll get a text for our next meeting."

Hawk was leaving the area when she turned to him, Zamir remained behind.

"Did you write a report on her?"

He stopped, not turning around. "Maggie? Yes, she is clear." He kept walking then slammed the door behind him.

"Zamir, what the hell is wrong with Hawk?"

"I think he started to take a fancy to our Miss Maggie. Anyway, you know how he is. Over before it even began. It's all par for the course with him."

She grinned heading out in the opposite direction, never glancing back.

# Chapter Four

"Hey, Maggie, what's up? Are you on lunch break?"

"Yes. Sorry to barge in like this. I need your help, Maureen, and I am a bit rushed. I've got to get back to the office for a meeting."

Maureen eyed her skeptically but could not refrain from being interested in what Maggie was involved with now.

"There is a student scheduling a weekly program that has me a little concerned. I'm actually not positive he is a student here. Before I blow any whistles, can you see if you show him registered? His topic is gaining momentum and I need assurance, well, that I'm not be overly suspicious."

Both ladies grinned.

She slid the piece of paper with Zafir's name on it toward Maureen and waited.

"Actually, he is not. Is the spelling correct?"

"Can you try it with Michael instead of Michaez?"

She clicked away on the keyboard. "Yes. From Spain. Enrolled in the political science program. First year. But this is unusual. He is twenty-five. I guess he started a bit late."

"Do you have a location of residence here on campus?"

"Hmm. Well, this is bizarre too. It is a building currently closed for renovations. All those registered to stay have been relocated to different housing. I don't have one listed for him. This must just be an error. A simple clerical error."

Their eyes locked for a moment.

"Want me to email you?"

"Yeah, but no names. Just send the location." Maureen stopped again and eyed her carefully. "Do you suspect anything? You know we are required to report on concerns. If he is running any kind of a radical movement we should let campus security investigate."

Maggie held both hands up to her, to halt further inquiry. "I know. I will keep you posted. It could be nothing. Just a human error like you said. A glitch or delay in updating internal details. Probably someone at data entry is just sitting on this. Can we keep this between us for now?"

Maggie rose as Maureen nodded.

"Thanks a lot."

Then on an afterthought she halted and leaned down. "Can I check on a faculty member? Privately?"

Maureen swiveled her chair back and twitched her head in a clear indication that said, "*Follow me.*"

"They'll have my ass on a platter if this is discovered. But I have the registrar's codes in the event anything happens. I can access all records and today is your lucky day, Maggie. I have updates to run. You can't breathe a word of this, understand? Do you have your laptop?"

Maggie patted her bag and kept in stride.

"I want you to connect to the hard drive. Then you can maneuver off the set while I let the files update. When you see the name of the person you want to '*review*' follow these two steps and be fast. Or, you will lose the chance. I see you brought a flash drive," They smiled at each other. "You are always prepared, which scares the shit out of me. You ready?"

They were behind closed doors in the registrar's office with blinds pulled shut. Maggie connected her laptop to the professor's hard drive and winked at Maureen. Time was ticking at such a slow pace. Maggie could feel the perspiration forming on her upper lip. Believing at any moment someone would just barge on in and realize something was amiss. Catching them both in such a compromised spot.

Thank heavens she saw whom she was looking for and grabbed the details. She nodded to Maureen. Finished, she walked behind her out of the office unseen and exited the building. Suddenly, she felt like all the friendly faces she'd seen all day long looked suspicious. Back inside the arts and social sciences library, a burst of air finally expelled out from her lungs.

*I'd never make a good spy,* she thought.

"Ah, Maggie, there you are. A surprise was delivered to your office. I hope you don't mind, I unlocked the door, so it could be placed on your desk."

Maggie jumped, clearly startled then quickly gained composure. "Really. What is it?"

Caren Abbott, her smart and perky assistant, seemed extremely excited about something which immediately peaked Maggie's curiosity. Swiftly they moved side-by-side. One anxious to see it and the other anxious to see her reaction to it. Opening her office door wide, Maggie's lower jaw dropped.

A very large and seemingly expensive Waterford crystal vase held the most amazing late summer bouquet she'd ever seen. The Queen's gardens at Buckingham Palace could not produce finer. Roses in soft yellow and pale pink were nearly overshadowed by purple heather sprays, gold and blue Larkspurs with a complement of happy white daisies. It was positively lovely as Maggie reached for the card pulling it off the spiked clear plastic post.

It read, *"Don't pass judgment on the other night until I have explained further. DH."*

Her mouth gaped open.

"Maggie, who is it from? A new man? They're gorgeous."

Maggie moved around and plopped down into the oversized work chair. Dropped the bag to the floor then stared at them in total astonishment. "No, nothing like that. Just…" She then stopped talking briefly to gather her own thoughts. "I don't know what. Sorry, Caren. I'm a bit dumbfounded right now."

Both women laughed.

"You sure are, Mag. Which makes me wonder who *he* is."

"Probably someone I'll never see again. But they are lovely. Now, do I have any messages?"

"Just a few. I emailed them to you already. Nothing was urgent."

"Good. Well, I had better have at it."

Caren closed the door as Maggie leaned in inhaling the bouquet's sweetness. It was a nice gesture but one that she wished he hadn't done. It was not going to work between them. But all the same, the pain in the ass voices inside her head were causing havoc as her heart thumped wildly.

"Damn." She softly mouthed.

She clicked on the icon for the removable drive and pulled up the information on Susan Perkins. Journalism degree from Oxford University that looked impressive on paper: single, thirty-four, parents, siblings, blah blah, nothing of real interest. Quickly realizing she could check this out on her own, Maggie found and rang the Communications Department at Oxford and in swift order had a clerk on the other line.

"Yes, this is Margaret Cohen from the University of Bristol. We are finalizing our synopsis on one of your Alum's. A Miss Susan Perkins. I am hoping you can fill in one or two blanks for us?"

"Yes, Miss Cohen, I can assist you if the information is in her database is not marked confidential."

"Excellent, we are just looking for her former professor's name and one or two pieces we can review for our own internal article being created."

"How do you spell her name?"

"Perkins, Susan Perkins."

"Please hold the line."

Maggie glanced over at the digital desk clock as time ticked away.

"Miss Cohen?"

"Yes, I'm here."

"I need your details. How you can be reached. Would you provide that?"

"Margaret Cohen, Assistant Librarian, Arts & Social Science Library, University of Bristol, Tyndall Avenue, Bristol, England. Do you need my phone number?"

"Yes, I will."

"0117-928-8111."

"Very good, please hold on the line."

She was tapping her pen on the desk feeling the pit of her stomach constrict. Something was drastically wrong being kept waiting all the same. This was not a good sign and she knew it.

"Miss Cohen, I have dispatched your information to the link on Miss Perkins site. Someone should be back in touch with you about the information you seek."

"Do you know who this person is and when that will be?" Maggie could not keep the anxiousness at bay.

"No, it won't provide me with a name. Just that any access to Miss Perkins information is restricted and all parties that request information on her must be registered with this source."

*Shit*, her mind screamed. *What have I done!*

"Thank you." Maggie threw her headset down on the desk and hit the disconnect button. Fuck. This was not good. She stood pacing frantically about the room. She glared over at the phone half tempted to ring her Pop. Then hesitated just as a hand was about to pick the receiver up. No. More information needed to be obtained first. To wait on Maureen's findings. Her eyes roamed to the flowers. Thankfully, she thought, there was no way to get in touch with him. Plus, what kind of trouble would that bring? From whom?

She sat back down in her chair and rested her face in her hands as her stomach muscles squeezed so intensely it felt like a sumo wrestler was sitting on it.

\*\*\*

At MI5 the data was being transmitted to an in-house operative who quickly stored and relayed it directly back to Hawk. His pager vibrated just as class ended. Waiting until the last student left his room, he dislodged it and reviewed the details: *Request for information has been lodged on Perkins by Margaret Cohen at the University of Bristol. Your INTEL report stated not a concern. Investigate further then report.*

Damn. *What the hell*, he thought. Then it dawned on him, quite pleased with himself for sending those flowers. He'd give her twenty-four hours. Hopefully, she'd not get further involved in that time. If she was just inquiring into Perkins background now, then she was beginning to piece things together. He clicked on the access to her building and waited. The planted cameras worked as he watched a tall man head into her office. *But fuck*, he thought, *the audio is not engaging*. Sitting down, he had no choice but to gather what he could.

Maggie was pacing around her large office when her boss knocked on an outside wall. "Maggie, you got a minute?" Her stomach lurched believing he had already discovered from some unnamed source that she was snooping again.

"Sure, Seth, come on in."

He sat down. "As you know we need to send a representative up to Edinburgh. To install software and train staff on our new software package for their art and library department. Unfortunately, the board has transitioned me to another location during that time and with my schedule, I can't cancel at this late stage. I know it's last minute. But I need you to go. It has already been cleared with upper management." He leaned down and nonchalantly smelled the bouquet.

"Can you secure your calendar with Caren and go up tomorrow? Take what flight you want from Heathrow Airport. The use of the guest apartment on campus has been offered. Or, if you want something lower key they can also set you up at The George Hotel. Return any time on Friday. Or spend the weekend. It's totally up to you."

"Seth, this is great news. I'd love to go. I can clear my calendar. I'll book my flights now and will probably return on Friday. Just in case things need my attention here. I'll email you my itinerary when it's confirmed. I'd prefer The George. I don't need the extra fluff of an apartment. Can you let me know who to advise on that?"

He moved toward the door. "Sure enough. I'll pop them details. If you need anything you can text or email me. I will be off-site, but will check them periodically."

"Thanks, this means a lot to me."

He left her office as Caren stuck her head in. "You're going?"

"Yes, does your hearing extend all the way from your desk to my office? Or, perhaps you have this room bugged?" They laughed. "Do you want me to book your flights?"

"No, I'll take care of them. Would you please refresh the water in my vase in a day or so? I am headed home. I'll send you my itinerary from there."

Maggie was already reaching around and logging off her computer removing the flash drive, picking up the necessary files.

"Make sure IT is on backup in case I need them. But, I suspect this install will go smoothly. Can you email me the adobe manual, so I can have it?"

"Right-o boss. What about the guy? Did you call and say thank you?"

"Oh, now you've become my conscience as well? You and my mother would be great friends."

"So, you've blown him off?"

Maggie shut off her light while gently pushing her assistant out of the office, closing the door and locking it behind her. "I've no mind to discuss this with you further," she was grinning. "Now get off with you and find someone else to harass. Remind me when I get back to speak with human resources about a replacement for you immediately."

Caren grinned on her way back to her smaller office. "What about the group coming in on Friday to use the conference room? I've seen their log of names. The list is growing. I may have to shuffle them around and use the larger one."

"You have a list of names? How did that come about?" Maggie had stopped abruptly at the stairwell, the door kept ajar by one black high-heeled Manolo boot over the threshold.

"I joined their informational website and can view all the names that have hit the system. It may not be an actual tally of those attending. But if it is an indication, then his little gathering has turned into a large group."

"Can you email me the link today and the name you trailed them too?"

"Maggie, what are you up to now? Remember the last time your Pops had to bail you out. You nearly lost your job here."

"Thanks for that reminder and yes, I must replace you as soon as I get back. Making it a top priority." She let the door close and left the building.

Maggie and Caren shared a unique relationship. Professional as well as a nice friendship. She glanced up at the window and could practically read Caren's thoughts even from down here. Maggie housed no doubt that she wondered exactly what she was up to now. More than once Caren had told her she should've been a detective instead of a librarian.

How they had laughed. Maggie glanced up again, waved, then continued along to her vehicle and headed to her flat. Parking and locking it suddenly a weird sensation weaved around her and continued until she was up the stairs and inside. With her phone in one hand talking with the airline, her other hand was busy pulling things out of the closet and drawers tossing them into a bag. Disengaging from the call she had just finished zipping it up when there was a buzz from below. Her taxi for the airport had arrived.

The driver had her there just in time as she rushed, got her electronic ticket and passed through security to the gate with seconds to spare. She was one of the very last people to head down the corridor to board the plane. Shoving the bag in the overhead and the other beneath her feet, Maggie sat back, released a needed breath then settled in for the short flight up to Scotland.

She had to smile at the handsome man standing there upon her arrival outside the airport who was holding a sign with her name on it. He stowed her bags as she got into the sedan and in less than an hour, she was standing there looking up at the stairs to the main library. Maggie was so pleased that Seth assigned her to this project. Gathering up momentum for the tasks to be completed, she walked up and halted at the guest desk. Quick enough a badge was inserted into plastic and around her neck as she was shown through.

A tall, bookish, but well-dressed lanky man in his early fifties was poised to shake her hand. "Miss Cohen, Maggie, we were all quite pleased to learn from Professor Litchens you would be coming in his place. Shall we begin?"

"Hello, Malcolm. It's always good to see you. I trust the wife and family are well?"

He nodded. "Indeed," sweeping a hand toward the mainframe. "Will you need IT to do anything prior? They have the main computer ready for your software install."

"No. Are all the other systems down so I can begin? We estimate this will take about six hours to run during the night. Then tomorrow I will train your key users. They, in turn, can do the same with the remaining staff. I will stick around until Friday morning. Then return to Bristol."

"Excellent, get yourself comfortable. This ID badge is your security pass, so you can come and go as you please at any hour. The department has been apprised of your clearance. By the way, did the professor mention our special event on Thursday evening?"

"Yes, indeed he did. I will be happy to schmooze the room with you. Right now, I don't have plans to depart until Friday later morning. But, if you needed me to stay on longer I can certainly arrange that."

"Thanks, Maggie. You never know who else may be interested in this new software program."

"Sounds great. Well I'm ready. I'll buzz you if anything comes up."

Maggie booted up the mainframe and inserted the first of several drives. Then monitored the loads while she worked on her laptop using the school's wireless connection. Something of importance arrived from Caron. The list of names she spoke about earlier. Scanning, she stopped with sudden alarm. Three names glared out immediately:

*Susan Perkins, Amichai Zamir, and Douglas Hawthorne*

Now, why the hell was Doug, a faculty member, and teacher at Bristol College, inquiring about a program not associated or housed on his campus? What was he up to? Glancing periodically at the monitor she started pacing inside the room. Then stopped and took out the notepad.

Reviewing what was previously written she could not connect any dots as the familiar ping signaled a new email had arrived. Throwing the pad down on top of the desk, she saw it was from Maureen. This was it. A start. It housed just a pair of words, but she knew how important they were; *Stonefield House.*

Accessing the internet with her netbook she started running a special library report on who had media out beyond the extended date of return, and if any names matched up to residents at Stonefield.

While that ran, and the school's computer continued being updated, she stood and stretched resting a hand on her stomach suddenly feeling quite hungry. Grabbing her purse and replacing the security card attached to a Lanyon around her neck, Maggie shut the computer room door making sure it was locked and followed the signs to the cafeteria. It was way beyond time that she put food and tea in her gut.

***

Meanwhile, Doug set his hand on one of the large glass doors to the library, pushed it aside and strode toward the reception desk clerk.

"Yes, sir, how can I assist you?" Doug assessed her in seconds. She really did look like a dowager. A tough old bird with hair wrapped up in a tight bun.

"I'd like to see Miss Cohen if she is free?"

"I will ring her assistant to inquire. Your name and do you have an appointment?"

"Douglas Hawthorne and no I'm not expected."

He started pacing as she rang up to Caren. "There is a Douglas Hawthorne here to see if Miss Cohen is available. He doesn't have an appointment. Would she be free to see him?" There was a pause while her cold accessing eyes locked with his inquisitive ones.

He suppressed a grin. Yes, his first assessment had been accurate. She was solid as a brick wall.

"I will advise, Miss Abbott, thank you. I am sorry Mr. Hawthorne, Miss Cohen is out of the office until the end of the week. Shall I take a message and leave it with her assistant?"

He stood sliding both hands into pants pockets. "No. I'll get in touch with her when she returns. Friday, right?"

"No, I said the end of the week. I am not sure if that will be Friday or Saturday to be exact."

"Okay. Thank you." Tapping the top of the counter Doug turned and strode from the building. Once outside he inserted a small wire in his ear and halted, leaning up against one exterior wall of the building. Glancing around, he took out his cellphone and listened hoping the long-range bug planted in Maggie's office was now working properly. He could hear shuffling, then a voice.

"Maggie, here."

"You have no idea who just stopped to see you. But never made it by Attila in the lobby. Who would not let him up before ringing me."

"Caren, focus, you are rambling. Who has done what?"

"Douglas Hawthorne." She let that dangle in cell space for a few seconds.

"Doug? He was there?"

There was a lengthy pause.

"Yes, and damn I should have gone down to speak with him. But I didn't react quick enough."

"He would have charmed you into telling him where I was. Caren, you have no backbone at all. I'm glad you stayed put. What did you tell her to relay?"

"That you were out of the office and would be back at the end of the week."

"Good. Actually, very good. Thanks."

"Anything else?"

"No, I have to ring off. I'm starving, and all the programs are running while I am out of the office heading to their cafeteria. I've got to get some food and get back in. If something of interest crops up, email me, will you? But if it's urgent you give me a ring. Keep me posted on that meeting Friday night."

Maggie took a breath. Doug could hear it just like he was right there next to her.

"Hey, there is something else. Contact Paul Ashton. He's *that* student that spends every waking moment in the video lab. See if he can live feed that meeting and digitally upload it when they conclude. Have him send the attachment to my netbook. He already has my computer details."

"What do you want me to say?"

"I want you to talk with him in person. Privately. Tell him I want to make sure all cameras remain hidden and check the audio. He should go in there on Thursday and run tests to ensure the equipment is prepared. I don't want any correspondence except when he sends the attachment. Understand? Oh, he must leave one camera visible. That is crucial."

"Okay. Fine. But Maggie, this sounds familiar. Yet, more serious than the last issue you were concerned about.

"Nicely said, Caren, but I can't tell you now. I will when the right moment presents itself. Don't worry. I'll be fine. Got to go now. Thanks a bunch."

Then there was silence. Doug removed the earpiece, placed it in a pocket, slid his cellphone in a back one and walked on. *"Oh, Maggie,"* he thought, *"You are too predictable. Glad you did not pitch those flowers."* He broke out in a whistle all the way back to his parked car.

# Chapter Five

"They are scheduled for Friday. Perkins, will you be at the meeting?"

"Yes, Zafir asked me to attend to continue writing for the next article about profiling Muslims. He is requesting I not outsource. I've agreed. I feel it's important since he seems to trust me."

"Have you secured any of the other names besides Davide?"

"Negative. I'm looking for a way to get inside of Stonefield. Intelligence advised today they believe the sleeper cell is growing. For months this building has been monitored with little to show for it. They are masters at going so deep underground little can be traced. We need more. Perhaps this next meeting will get us closer."

"Hawk, what do you think? You've been quiet. Are there additional concerns? Issues with Cohen?"

He glared at Zamir. "No to both."

Zamir let it ride. Now was just not the time. "I think we are through here. Anything else either of you has?"

"Yes," Susan replied. "I need to go and meet with a few students tonight. Hawk do you want me to spend a bit more time with Cohen and see what's up?"

"No, I'll handle it from here." The sternness of his reply closed off further comment.

Exiting from the cellar of the Beggar's Inn and Pub to the busy waterfront streets of Bristol, they strode away from each other with not so much as a backward glance.

\*\*\*

West of the city center across the street from the Regent Waterside Hotel people were coming and going focused on their nighttime affairs. Zafir stood back from a street corner leaning against a building. A small group clustered around him including a fresh recruit.

"Thomas, are you ready?" Zafir's dark orbs penetrated deeply into his eyes, unrelenting. "I see the fear in them. That is good. Fear and determination. A martyr you will be after this, my friend. Your soul will quickly rise to heaven. Walking along that golden path to Allah. So, let's do this. It's time."

"I'm ready." Thomas's sweaty palm and fingers held gingerly onto the explosive device detonator tucked inside his jacket. "Tell me the plan again."

"You'll proceed inside through the lobby and up to the second-floor conference room. The one we all viewed two days ago. Open the doors and walk into the center amongst them all. What will you say?"

"That Allah condemns the killing of his people in the middle-east. Their souls are doomed and will go directly to hell. I will then press the button and be in the hands of God."

"Do you feel peaceful inside?"

"I do."

"Then go and do his work and be with our other brothers and sisters."

Zafir stood back and watched as Thomas left them and walked as if in a drug-induced stupor. Across the street he went. Directly into the hotel and disappeared. Minutes passed when a severely massive explosion rocked several city blocks. Shards of windows spewed out striking many of the people in the area. Smoke filled the air, billowing up into the sky as high-pitched screams of terror rose.

Zafir's small clustered group grinned sadistically patting each other on the back. Then moved, disappearing into an alley toward Stonefield. "Come," he said. Speaking nonchalantly as if they were all just hanging out. A casual conversation amongst friends. "We have more plans to make. Bigger ones."

They stopped outside a large local electronics store to watch the carnage unfold as a local television reporter was first on the scene. They clustered around one another to hear him speak.

"In that conference room were Americans and Israeli's joined for a meeting. All completely ignorant of what was about to occur. We have received word that this was in retaliation for military action taken two years ago in Afghanistan."

The grin on each of their faces grew as the reporter continued.

"The great injustice in this act of terrorism for these injured and dead souls had been their nationality. This gathering had nothing to do with bad decisions made by military and government officials. It was a peaceful setting. A peaceful conference. More to come as we follow this tragic breaking news."

The following morning the Bristol Register's lead story blasted in bold red print across the top of page one:

SEVENTY DEAD AND SEVERAL INJURED AS EXPLOSION ROCKS AN AMERICAN – ISRAELI TOURISM CONFERENCE AT THE REGENT CITY HOTEL.

HAMAS CLAIMS RESPONSIBILITY.

The City of Bristol was under lockdown as MI5 swarmed in engaging with local law enforcement to begin clearing the carnage inflicted by the suicide bomber. While at Stonefield, people came and went to their classes with no due alarm, care or concern. It was just another day and a fresh opportunity to do it all over again.

Susan Perkins was in her office putting the paper down when Hawk strode in.

"Of course, you know."

"Shit, yes. I've been called into HQ. What about you?"

"It would be a benefit if my clearance matched yours in this situation."

He shrugged his shoulders not responding.

"Have you had contact with your friend?"

"Don't go there, Perkins."

"She's in Edinburgh installing new programs for their libraries. She's not just attractive but brainy as well."

"Mind it."

"Have you seen or heard from Zamir?"

"Yes. There is a meeting scheduled shortly. He has something to take care of right away. Edinburgh, you say. Do you know exactly when she'll be back?"

"Friday morning. I know she will be at the bar with the gang on Friday night. Patty asked me to join them. I begged off. I have that meeting to attend with Zafir's group."

"Good Move." He replied absently. "We'll be in touch."

She watched him go wondering what the heck was going on in that man's mind.

\*\*\*

Hawk was thinking the same thing about Maggie as he strode out onto the busy streets of the northern campus and walked right into her building. He was fully aware of some of her external attributes. But smart as well. Just fucking terrific he thought just as his cellphone rang.

"Hawk."

It was his Officer Commanding, Colonel Blair. "You secure?"

"Affirmative."

"It's time to step over MI5 here, Hawk, we need more, and we need it yesterday. We've received INTEL I've not passed along yet that there will be a series of bombings in strategic locations in England and Scotland. We believe the next one will be in Edinburgh. Right now, I have sources reviewing all cultural and business events planned over the next several weeks. Honing on if there is an American-Israeli gathering and where. We need you on the spot. Gear up. I have a high-ranking official up in Edinburgh considering issues stat."

"Roger, sir, I'm on it."

He sat on his motorcycle for a moment then started it up. Quickly, he weaved through traffic ignoring red lights and arrived at his pad. Inside he called the base and set up an airlift from Bulford to Edinburgh by helicopter. He pulled his gear bag from the locked closet, threw some extra clothes in then headed down to the car park. Quick enough he had his Rover out on the motorway and was headed to the base.

Hawk flashed his ID to the MP at the guard shack and drove beyond the gated area to park the Rover. Grabbing the bags and closing the rear door, the vehicle locked as he viewed a soldier standing at attention waiting to be recognized.

They both saluted.

"Lieutenant Hawthorne, HQ contacted us. We have been expecting you. The bird is prepared and out on the flight deck ready for departure. You are cleared through."

Saluting, he walked out to the tarmac and boarded the helicopter signaling the pilot he was ready for take-off. Removing his cellphone, he reviewed all the data being transmitted while on the short flight knowing he was probably twenty-four hours or more ahead of MI5. Who would be pulling agents from the area and sending them to Edinburgh.

This would be a quick trip. A hit and run. Before they even could regroup and deploy personnel he would be out of there and back in England. He'd not share space with them if his officer commanding didn't mandate it. Then suddenly a vital detail appeared. *Fuck*, he thought, openly pissed while reading about a special upcoming event at none other than the University of Edinburgh. A middle-eastern gathering this Thursday. It now became apparent. He had to locate Maggie.

Texting INTEL, he provided the full details of her name and waited for confirmation on her means of transport. Received, he reviewed it. She had flown up on British Airways. All the details including where she was staying were included along with the return flight.

He stared momentarily at her cellphone number. Shit, he concluded, this was going to get ugly real fast. She would be bloody pissed as hell at him accessing personal information. At least she would not be suspicious of him using her cellphone number. That, he already had. Shaking his head, he knew the deed had to be done and done now. He sent the text.

"Hey, I heard you bugged out of town. When do you return?" Time ticked on as he awaited a reply Thirty full minutes turned into an hour plus, as the pilot landed them on base. Hawk glanced and saw an awaiting vehicle at his disposal. He opened the trunk and placed the gear bag inside when his cellphone finally vibrated.

Glancing down, he let out a low chuckle at her clipped reply.

"Friday."

He typed away while getting into the vehicle and started it up. "Where are you now?"

"Work."

He stopped at a light and replied. "More specific."

Then she threw shit right into his face as he broke out in laughter. "You have INTEL. Find me."

He nearly rammed into a woman and little tyke crossing on the pedestrian walk. She was right. He could locate her spot instantly if he transmitted her cellphone to HQ. They could have her satellite location back to him in seconds. There'd be no frigging way he'd use funds for that. He opted to find her the good old-fashioned way.

"A bit angry, are you?"

He waited not knowing what would come back at him and was more than surprised at what did.

"PISS ON YOU!"

He roared with laughter handing the keys over to the hotel attendant waving off assistance with his gear bag. He glanced down at the camo bag just as the attendant did. Doug's eyes relayed an instant silent warning as he removed it and the attendant drove the vehicle to the guest parking location.

"Want to meet for drinks?"

"No."

Raising an eyebrow, he realized she was very upset and felt a momentary pang of guilt. But it quickly evaporated. Remorse had no place in his world.

"I'm in Edinburgh on business." There. He hoped that would peak her curiosity. Or, so he thought.

"No."

The front desk reception clerk seemed agitated waiting as Doug finally glanced up.

"Yes, sir, your name?"

"Hawthorne, Douglas. By chance could you ring the room of Maggie Cohen and let her know I'm here?"

The clerk seemed to know exactly who she was which surprised Doug right away. "No, sir. Unfortunately, she has gone out for the day. I can leave her a message on the house phone." His smile to Doug blended with a mixture of arrogance and politeness.

"No, I'll see her this afternoon. Thanks."

"Here are your room cards. Can we take your bags?"

"All set there." Hawk took the cards from the marbleized countertop and walked over to the elevator taking it up to his floor. Sliding the bag beneath the bed, he sauntered over to the window and gazed out upon one of his favorite cities, Edinburgh. Although he had never been here on anything other than business since leaving home at seventeen, he often thought about returning. Visiting old haunts. The Military Tattoo. Recalling many interesting teenage nights spent on drunken rampages with his brothers. Always ending by them stumbling home in the wee hours where his father would cover for them. His mother was warm and sweet, but at times her wrath was as strong as their father when they had crossed the line too often.

He chuckled into the empty room.

It was mighty tempting to give the parents a ring. They were not far from the city. But he knew his mother would be upset with him knowing he'd have no time to come over and hang out. That thought would have to be suspended until another time. Sooner or later there would be one.

He glanced down at his watch. It was three o'clock. He surmised Maggie would be out of work in the next couple of hours. So, he sat down at the desk and poured over the full intelligence report. A knock sounded at the door as he quickly looked in that direction, then down toward his bag. When the door opened he relaxed.

"Hawk."

"Zamir, you just arrive?"

"No. Have been here since this morning."

"Just reviewing all the shit."

"What do you have?"

"Two locations are the prime targets for HAMAS. The main library, and the square. Both are holding events on Thursday night. Which do you want to cover?"

"Square. Is she at the library?

"Yes, but I've not made contact. Have you seen her?"

"Affirmative. This morning. I viewed her leaving pretty as ever from the lobby walking up to the university."

Hawk was confident Zamir remained out of her sight.

"Head out to the square and scope the location."

"You headed in search of her?"

"Negative. I'm awaiting specs on the library's security. I have suspicions their bomber is already in place. We are working silently on this Zamir. Black six. We need to find out who those other three are that arrived with Zafir. Now. HQ advised no contact with MI5. Where will you stay?"

"Down St. Georges at a small bed and breakfast. Text me when you want to meet." He exited the room as Hawk's cellphone vibrated and reading the message indeed it was a surprise.

"Tempus Bar. Seven-thirty."

He knew better. It was not a safe location. "Negative. Not secure."

"Advise."

He had to grin at that reply for she was beginning to sound like she had military training as well.

"Meet me at the entrance to Princess Gardens."

"Roger, that."

His laughter filled the room as the cellphone was placed in its holder. Oakley's on, he left and exited the building. Inside the library, he flashed his clearance card and was allowed entry into the security office.

"Mr. Hawthorne, I've been instructed to clear the room while you work. If you need anything I remain located just outside this door." Hawk nodded as the dude left. He scrolled through all the points of entry and exit, rooftop, stairwells, parking area and located all the cameras positions. He would have those repositioned just for this event then they could relocate them back.

Three points of entry were easy enough but what would they be using for scanners? He stood up and went over and opened the door. "Come in."

"Sir?"

"What type of search operations are in place for this event?"

"None, it's open to the public. Similar, to a theater or local sports event."

"Bags of all sizes can be brought in?"

"Yes."

"Okay, thank you." The guard maneuvered to the opposite side of the entrance and closed the door. Hawk got up and exited the large room nodding to the officer and continuing down the hallway, into the stairwell, then up three flights of stairs. Entering the large meeting room, he noticed two sets of double-wide doors along with two on the opposite side.

*Good*, he thought, *attendees will be more contained*. Glancing down at his watch he noticed it was six forty-five. Exiting the building he stopped and glanced at throngs of people coming and going. Thinking like the trained killers of HAMAS, Hawk knew this would be a prime location for a suicide bomber to take many casualties. It would be interesting to hear Zamir's assessment regarding the Square.

He showered quickly and changed into casual brown dress slacks, a dark olive long sleeved silk dinner shirt, then slid his feet into soft Italian shoes. Grabbing his wallet, cellphone and room card, he headed out. Arriving first at the Princess Garden's main entrance. Where he stopped and focused on passing faces while leaning against a dark wrought iron fence.

He spotted her across the street and noticed straight away she was walking with purpose. As if she was still very angry with him. He suppressed a smile as she neared but it grew of its own accord as she halted in front of him.

That worked.

\*\*\*

Maggie couldn't help it. She liked the looks of this man. Quickly forgetting his pompous attitude and callous treatment of her and smiled back. A honking horn brought them both back to stark reality in a split second.

He leaned close inhaling subconsciously that gentle scent that was now familiar to him. As she moved closer placing a light touch on his buttoned shirtfront.

"I needed to see you. I have some information that you'll find interesting. Where can we go?"

Not really wanting to move away from her, he had no choice and held out his arm for her to grasp. "Why don't we walk up The Royal Mile and see if we can find a good spot to stop for a pint. Now, what's troubling you, Maggie?"

It was his caring tone, the strength of his forearm where her hand rested, the penetrating stare of his gaze and when she finally admitted it, later, just being near him. It was all just as simple as that.

Dammit, she hated with a passion having to say this. Her hesitation brought his other hand to hers in a comforting squeeze. She finally got it out. "I need your help."

"Go on."

"While I've been working with the main library, there has been an influx of people swarming around preparing for this special Israeli-Muslim-American exhibit opening Thursday night. I'm positive you are aware of it. During the event, the conference area will be opened to cocktails and hors d'oeuvres. I wandered down to watch while artifacts were being unveiled and caught sight of someone I recognized. That I've seen with Zafir. I managed to snap off a shot of him on my cellphone. I can show you."

He waited patiently knowing she was gathering thoughts.

"When I saw the BBC report and read the papers I realized one thing," she reached inside her purse and unfolded a newspaper article. Then handed it to him while they stopped walking. He glanced over the print and looked at the large picture in color while she took out her cellphone and handed it over.

He was clearly surprised. He spotted the man right away in the background with a group of others in motion as the shot was snapped. He matched her picture of the man she spotted at the library. She had done the work of several people and had no idea how important this was. Or, did she?

"Let's go to my room."

She eyed him hesitantly.

"Now." His tone afforded no argument.

She released his arm and walked beside him keeping up with his brisk pace. But couldn't resist a retort. "If you break into a run you will have to drag me along, understand?"

He heard the tartness underlying the joke but did not grin. He was in a rush not knowing who may notice and ID them both. He could not take that chance. Her life may already be in jeopardy.

# Chapter Six

Outside the main lobby doors of The George, she halted so fast he nearly knocked her over as she turned, directly out of breath, and straight into his arms unwittingly. "You are staying here too?"

He maneuvered them swiftly along. Not wanting to take any chances someone may recognize either of them out in the open in the large lobby. Quickly, Hawk directed them into the awaiting elevator relieved no one else got on.

"I am."

"Did you know I was already here?"

"No, not until I checked in."

"You are spooking me."

"Yea, well you are not spooking me, but are causing me immense concern, Maggie."

Inside his room, he took her newspaper photo and set it down on the copier. Then faxed it right off. "You wouldn't happen to have your cable for your cellphone, would you?"

"Yes, but not on me. It's in my room. I'll be right back. I'm on this floor." She left the door ajar and was back in less than five minutes. Closing it soundly she bolted it using the security lock.

"You so sure you may not want to exit this room in a hurry?" He was grinning until her whitened features wiped it away.

"I just saw Michaez Zafir go down the hall. I don't think he saw me. Doug, I am sure it was him."

"Positive ID?"

"Absolutely." She handed him the cable as he inserted both ends, uploaded the photo, then transmitted by the scanner. She was leaning up against the front side of the large mahogany desk as he sat down and waited.

His cellphone went off, "Hawk."

"Excellent." Came his reply while Maggie could hear a man's voice on the other end but nothing more.

"Perfect, Maggie. INTERPOL and HQ have confirmed it is Amis Davide. Pretty thick file on him too. Extremely dangerous. He has the dubious distinction of being on Interpol's top twenty-five most wanted list."

Turning away from her, Hawk began pacing over to the window running a large hand through his dark brown hair. She had noticed at this close distance the strands of white appearing and knew without a doubt how handsome he'd be when older. Knowing someday a very lucky woman would share his life. A man that attractive, smart and strong would not stay single too long in retired life.

He turned and walked back towering over her.

"How much do you think you know about what I am doing? It's important you tell me."

He stood so close she could easily have moved forward a foot and felt his rock-hard chest. Leaned against his body. Then her mind flashed back to his hasty departure the other night. Her internal wall grew thicker.

"Hunches only, Doug."

"I need more than that," he folded his arms across his chest and stood to his full six-three frame. She crossed her arms and legs as silently war was declared between them.

"This is not the time to be stubborn. Don't you understand?"

Feeling like an ass she let the wall drop a bit. "I think that you, Zamir and Perkins are working on a special assignment that somehow involves these men from Israel. I know Zafir and his friends are housed at Stonefield and rumors have been hot, this location is a safe house of sorts. I believe you and Zamir have known each other for a long time. But somehow, I doubt he works for the Ministry of Defense. I think he is with Mossad. A damn scary operative."

"You know I am retired from the British Army. Do you have an assumption on what Perkins does?"

"MI5 or 6."

He placed both hands on his hips, brows raising. "What did your father do for a living, Maggie?"

"British Army. Retired seven years ago. I'm surprised you had not made a connection, Doug."

He stared at her a bit taken aback by the tone of her voice. Then it dawned on him. "General Mark Cohen is your father?"

"Indeed, he is and if you keep pissing me off and ditching me for all your various reasons, I'll make sure he knows how angry at you I am." She was grinning now to take the bite out of that rebuff.

The distance between them evaporated as he moved closer forcing her chin to stretch up on its own as her soft blue eyes were absorbed by his brown.

"It seems we need to get this out of the way now. This is what you really want to know. I left you to meet Perkins. You must not have been close enough to see us. We had details to share. When my pager goes off and I'm with you, I expect you to understand now why I abruptly leave your presence." He ran a hand along the back of his neck adding as an afterthought, "I know I gave you one signal and then ditched you. Now you realize it had to be done. The thing is I don't want you involved in this at all and it's now unavoidable."

But he was not finished. Not by a long shot as his eyes lowered to her lips causing the breath to catch in her throat.

"That is irritating me. You seem to like involvement. I noticed it in your dossier. You've a bit of a rap sheet. Have you ever seen it? But interesting enough there was no mention of your father's name or rank on it. I wonder why?"

She blushed, nodding, having seen that crap they wrote about her knowing Pops covered up a ton of it. Maggie could barely breathe now. He was way too close. But what was to be done about a pounding heart?

Scrutinizing her closely, Hawk watched her stunning blue eyes turn so soft he was mesmerized. But it was her full lips parting so invitingly that brought his down on to them with no thought that this was not the right moment for an exploration.

Inviting as hell he could not just kiss them, their softness. Instead, he lingered, as she responded by placing both hands on his chest allowing them to glide up and clasp behind his neck.

She should not have done that.

He pulled her tightly against him. His manhood hard against her stomach. But Maggie could not stop as a deep sigh of longing found its way out.

He moved slightly separating them by only a few inches as her mind began working again.

"That was your way of an apology?"

"Nope. Not in the least. Was just something I needed to know that could not be found on a dossier."

"Oh."

He released her and moved away. "We have to get focused. Have you told the general about any of this?"

"No, not a word. I was going to see what comes up in the next few days. He did ring me to ask how I'm doing because of the bombing back in Bristol. He was quite relieved I'm up here in Edinburgh. Do you know him?"

"Yes. He's one of the Army's best. I had a few assignments on his watch. Don't mention me at all,

Maggie, it may compromise others. When it's time, I'll reach out to him"

Her tone changed abruptly. "You have my word. Are we all through? I need to do some work and eat. I'd like to go back to my room now."

"Ok," he handed her back the cellphone. "I'll walk you." She was already at the door. "No, that's not necessary. I'm only going down five doors to four-fourteen."

"Maggie, I want to walk you and check your room. Stop being so damn stubborn."

"Stubborn? I hardly think you know me well enough to know that or anything else. That damn dossier can't tell you who I really am or how I feel." She opened and closed the door leaving him standing there with mouth agape, anger mounting.

On the way back to her room she did an abrupt about-face and deviated taking the elevator down to the bar. There she knew she would be able to order food quicker and have a glass of wine. After that, she would tail it back to the room and retire for the night. She had lied to him. She didn't really have a damn thing that needed attending. But hell, he didn't need to know that.

The Tempus Bar was busy. Glancing about, Maggie located a small secluded table in a tight corner next to a large tinted window facing one of the crowded streets outside.

"Can I get you a drink before your order?"

"Yes, Pinot Grigio please," Maggie replied while taking the menu from the waitress hand. Glancing out the windows she noticed Zafir and Davide waiting to cross the street with three other men close behind. Immediately Maggie recalled seeing them come to Zafir's meetings as well as other locations on campus.

Quickly she assumed these five were the underlying connection to the Bristol bombing. *But*, she silently wondered, *what are they all doing here*? As a cold, menacing shiver ran up her spine.

It was appalling to her that they had no issues with their warped conscious by killing innocents and convincing recruits into believing their martyrdom would be to God's liking. She was not one to judge the movement of others, but this was insane. Maggie felt surreal as if such things could not be happening in her world. This was more frightening than anything she had been involved with in her past.

The drink was set before her. As she raised her eyes they were met with angry dark brown ones. He sat opposite as Doug's pint of ale landed with a thud on the wooden table top, liquid spilling over. He didn't seem to care.

"So, you have work to do?"

"Are my comings and goings to be discussed with you beforehand for approval?"

"You have a sharp tongue, woman."

"Did you join me for a reason? I can assure you I'm safe right now, right here. Look around. Do you see the harm in all these bodies? Danger lurking in all those eyes?"

But he did not take her rant.

"You never know, Maggie. Have you ordered?"

She sighed letting her shackles fall taking the boxing gloves off. For now. Wondering how the hell he could bring out the worst in her in mere seconds. *Damn*, she thought, *they mixed like oil and water.*

"No, she's on her way over here. Look at my menu."

The waitress arrived. "Are you two ready to order?" She waited patiently for Maggie to respond. "Grilled chicken salad with house dressing and another glass of wine, please."

The waitress looked down at Doug and smiled, leaning closer to expose a clear view of aging cleavage.

Maggie nearly groaned at such brazenness.

"Angus, medium rare with the steamed vegetable platter." He handed her the single menu. "Thank you."

He picked up his pint of Guinness and took a swig while Maggie polished off her wine. "When do you leave?"

"Friday, I fly out at nine-forty. Why?"

"Is there any possible way you can leave here tomorrow afternoon?"

"Thursday? No, I can't. I am in training all day until five. Then representing the professor at a cocktail reception while the event commences."

He frowned.

"Zamir and I are covering both locations. Maggie, I can't guarantee your safety. Your father will seek me out personally if anything happens to you."

She hated the reference to her Pop and the formality behind his sentence. She wondered what he'd think if he knew what she had that student doing back at the university. She needed him off her scent for a bit.

"I'll see if I can perform the perfunctory tasks and leave as soon as possible. Will you be visible to me during the events?"

He eyed her suspiciously knowing she was up to no good. One hundred percent sure of it. It was her M.O. That devious mind was concocting something when she readily agreed and gave him the response she thought he wanted to hear.

"Yes, but it may be hard to spot me in such a crowded venue."

"Are you working with locals as well?"

"Negative."

"Do you have a backup at all?"

Agitated, he replied. "Yes."

She exhaled, frustrated. It was worse than having a root canal. How the hell did her Mum put up with this for over forty years? Because she loved her Pop and her Pop loved her Mum. That's why and she knew it.

She stared him straight in the eyes with open contemplation while pushing her plate to the side resting the fork and knife over the edge. She did not waiver and for nearly one full minute she did not twitch, move nor speak.

Neither did he.

"Did you find what you were looking for?" His voice was deep, a bit on the rough side and reached to the very well of her being.

"Yes."

"Would you care for dessert or an aperitif?" The waitress had suddenly appeared as Doug spoke quickly, not moving his eyes from Maggie's. "No. Add this to my room. Hawthorne four-ten."

"Yes, sir, thank you." She slipped the check before him, he signed, added a tip and handed it back.

He stood and walked over pulling out her chair as she reached down to the wooden floor taking her bag. There was no way to avoid him now, so she turned tactics. "How can I let you know if I see anything you need to be aware of?" He had pressed the elevator button to the fourth floor and waited as they both got on along with a few other people. He moved closer, placing his hand on the curve of her back and let it rest there just above her butt while she glared up at him questioningly.

To Maggie, his smile was nothing short of roguish.

The door opened to their floor. "I assure you, LC, I can manage from here." He smirked at the shortening of his rank. Normally only his men in the field did that. *Smartass*, he thought. But continued toward her room smiling smugly at the consternation written all over her face.

Once she slid the key card out he opened the door flicking on the lights as she gasped, voice barely above a whisper. "Doug, someone's been in here."

He had her wait in the hall while he cleared the room and came back grabbing her by the arm, roughly, then pulled her in. "Get what you need. You're staying with me tonight. Don't argue, Maggie. You need to get your ass in gear and do it now."

With such force, she threw her bag onto the bed fully understanding the gravity of this situation. But not liking his damn tone at all. Rapidly, she collected things scattered around then finished with toiletries from the bathroom.

Thank heavens she had her netbook in her bag. She nodded glancing about making sure she had not left anything behind. Lifting her bag, Doug nearly dragged her the short distance down the hall to his room.

She sat on the bed as he placed her bag on the floor rack. "I'll have a team in there in minutes to lift prints. But, I have a strong suspicion nothing will be detected."

Maggie jumped at the loud rapping at the door anxious about who was on the other side. Doug glanced at her once before opening it to admit Zamir.

"Good, you were quick."

He sat beside Maggie on the bed. "Crazy woman. You were seen dining in the Tempus from across the street. I was monitoring the group of men and heard them point you out. It was one of them in your room looking about. Making sure you are here on business for the university and not with any counter-terrorism unit. If they felt compromised by you, Maggie, house no doubt you would be dead right now. I am confident you are safe. But as a precaution, you will stay with Hawk tonight and I will sleep in your room."

Zamir got up, nodded to Hawk and left. Maggie's mouth stayed open the entire time realizing Doug put this in motion. Having Zamir come and talk knowing she'd never believed him even if he had tried. *Damn*, she thought, *he knows me too well already. Arrogant ass.*

Suddenly he was kneeling before her and gently closed her lower jaw with a forefinger.

"Do you guys all operate like this? Appear and disappear all the time? I'm more and more appreciative of my Mum having put up with so much with my Pops. Doesn't he need my room key?" Then she broke out in shaky laughter. "Of course not. He is Mossad. The door probably just swerves open for him."

Hawk just listened, watching closely. He had seen this before. It was something she had to work through. Maggie knew it. He knew it. But he remained close. Fingers gliding over her smooth satiny skin until he cupped her face in his large, rough hands.

She slid off the bed then and right onto his lap. Legs wrapping around his waist while he held her close.

"I won't let anything happen to you, Maggie, I give you my word." His tone was soft, reassuring and comforting. She rested her head on his shoulder feeling his fingers run through her long hair. He stood as her legs slid down the side of him as his grip tightened.

She glanced at him and muttered out, "only one bed?"

He let her go patting her backside. "That's right, sunshine. You afraid to share it with me?"

Her mind was a torrential storm. Wind, rain, hail, snow, it was all happening inside it at one time and she had no freaking clue how to make it stop. But it needed too. Right now. She didn't care at all that he was behind her, watching closely. His penetrating gaze searing holes in her back.

Unzipping her bag, she removed a silky lilac nightgown. Softly groaning, her hands clutched it tightly to her breasts as she continued into the bathroom. Once behind the safety of the door, she washed and changed. A slight quivering smile appearing. "Yes," she mouthed softly, "I am not ready for this. For him."

Squaring shoulders, she picked up her clothes, opened the door and flicked off the light switch.

He was sitting in a chair over by the window. The room darkening shades were drawn and only the light beside him was lit. Her courage rose as she instantly became aware he was watching. For the heat of his stare penetrated thoroughly through her bones nearly exploding the skimpy gown off her already sensitive body.

She turned catching him by surprise. "Which side?"

"Door. You're on the inside."

She walked to the bed and pulled back the covers, no more than an arm's length from him. The shaky smile of previous was replaced by an all knowing one. Both knew what she was up too. His legs were extended now, crossed at the boots, arms wound up around the back of his head latched as he watched her nestle under the covers.

"Thanks for the show. I can honestly tell you I enjoyed it."

"My pleasure, soldier. Anytime."

He closed his files shutting down his netbook securing it for the night in the bag on the floor. Prepared to move out in a hurry if necessary. Once he finished in the bathroom, he came out only wearing boxers. It was right then that Maggie threw caution and propriety to the wind and thoroughly examined every single inch of him. Head to toe.

Tall and strong, if she had to create the perfect man he would be it. Absently she closed her eyes while shaking her head. As the mattress creaked, she knew he had settled next to her.

"Are you comfortable?"

"Yes, thank you."

Simultaneously they turned toward the other.

"If you have any questions this would be the right time to ask. After this, I can't predict where I will be."

"I want you to know that if Pop finds out, I will tell him you had no choice. I'm known for getting others involved who have no wish to be so."

"No worries, Maggie, I can handle the general. We do go back a few years."

"Were you drawn out of retirement for this? For me? Where do you come from? Where is home?"

"Back to Wales, I have an apartment there."

"Will you stop working at the school?"

"I will. Yes. I plan on full retirement. What about you?"

"I think I'll try harder at keeping my nose clean and out of other people's lives. It's time. Time for me to move out of my flat and buy a home."

"Where?"

"Exmoor I think. Or someplace quiet and peaceful so I can cycle, walk, make new friends. Well," she paused noticing that crookedly handsome smile appearing at the mention of new friends. "I like the ones I have. Wipe that grin right off your face. Anyway, maybe I'd like to get a cat."

"In theory that sounds perfect. But a cat? They like to get their nose into things. Sounds familiar, Maggie. Perhaps a birdfeeder or rabbit would be better suited for you."

She lightly punched his arm as he caught her hand placing a soft kiss on the top. "Can't see you keeping your pension to explore all the world has to offer at bay."

Maggie got it. She knew what he was saying. He doubted she would ever stop meddling in other people's lives. Besides, she housed no doubt that after this was over and they parted way, he would return to Wales. She, long forgotten.

Shuffling onto her back, she put a bit of mental distance between them. "Good night. I know if my Pops knew he'd thank you for keeping an eye on me."

The temptation to tug her right into his arms was strong. *Hell*, he thought, *I know she would not refuse*. But as her breathing settled his own eyelids dropped as he fell asleep. Realizing this was a first. A beautiful, smart and spunky woman to his side, sharing a bed and they were not making love.

It was during the darkest part of the night that Doug felt her head rest on his shoulder. His arm instantly moved around her hip as silky hair fell upon his chest. He was fully aware of what her presence was doing to other parts of his body as he smiled into the quiet, dark room.

# Chapter Seven

Hawk maneuvered his body slowly, untangling himself from her warm suppleness. Opening the drapes, he squinted from the grayness of the day. No sunshine streamed in. Rain loomed over the horizon as it seemed ominous that dark clouds would follow even darker events. As he glanced at her still sleeping form, thoughts of her father loomed.

Picking up his cellphone he sent a text to his OC at Central Command requesting permission to contact General Cohen. Hawk knew what chaos would ensue. But what the hell. Setting the phone down on the bedside stand he gently shook her by one soft exposed arm. Eyelids fluttered then began to open slowly, seductively, he thought. Grinning, his mind wandered back to last night when she'd wrapped her legs around his waist.

"How long have you been up and what time is it?"

"Not more than thirty minutes and it is half-past six."

"Six thirty? Holy cow it's early. Did you even sleep?"

"I did and quite well." He'd omit her sleeping on his shoulder most of the night. Apparently, she had no clue. "What time do you need to be at the library?"

"Ten. I have just two more clerks to train and then I will be free by mid-afternoon. I plan on coming back here to dress for tonight's event. What are you and Zamir up to today?"

"Maggie, you know I can't advise you on that. But, I want your cellphone, so I can program both our numbers in it. If you see or hear anything of suspicion, I need you to advise us immediately."

She threw the covers back. "Because you rise with the devil, do I have too as well? I don't like that policy at all. You won't have to remind me not to invite you overnight. It won't happen if you can't sleep after seven in the morning."

He laughed stepping aside allowing her petite feet to touch the plush carpet then watched her sway across the bedroom to her bag, removing the cellphone.

Then she returned holding it in one hand as his smile grew watching her cheeks turn a slight shade of pink.

"Douglas."

He smirked, took the phone, entered the numbers then handed back.

. "We'll remove Zamir's when this concludes."

"Well, maybe I'll keep it programmed in case you do something bad to me. I think he would find great pleasure in exterminating you."

"You mean assassinate."

She was grinning like the very devil. "No, I mean exterminate." She walked off grabbing work clothes and went into the bathroom. He heard the shower running as steam started to waft out from the slightly ajar door. She was saying something as he moved closer to hear.

"Are you going to order breakfast or eat downstairs?"

"I think we should order in. There is time. What do you want?" He leaned against the doorframe and tested his will by not looking inside. "Eggs, sausage, the works, I am famished. That salad last night hardly filled my stomach. Oh, and tea, lots of tea, please."

When she came out dressed in a tightly fitting brown skirt resting above shapely knees and an ivory silk blouse, Hawk realized how sexy professionalism looked.

Pinning her hair back while engaging him in conversation, he was barely listening as the need to rip those clothes off, throw her down on the plush feather bed and have sex with her all day, seemed like the right thing to do. Shaking his head to ward off these penetrating thoughts, a knock at the door came to his rescue.

"Yeah."

"It's room service, Mr. Hawthorne."

Maggie moved into the bathroom out of sight as he silently applauded what an intelligent move that was as the attendant wheeled in a stainless-steel cart.

"Where would you like me to set this up, sir?"

"No bother, I will take it from here." Doug handed him a ten-pound note then held open the door for his exit.

The smell of freshly cooked food brought her out reaching for a linen napkin and tucking it into the subtly exposed lace of her sexy bra. It sure did not hurt his eyes to view the exposing hint of creamy breasts. He wheeled the cart over to the small table and held out her chair. "Mademoiselle?"

She grinned and sat as he pushed it in slightly.

"Tea?"

"Yes, and hurry. I am not a morning person, Hawthorne."

"Ah, so we've gone from Doug to Douglas to Hawthorne already? Any other names you want to disclose this morning?"

"Oh, I can assure you I have plenty but want to keep the delusion I am a lady, so don't push your luck." He handed her the porcelain china teacup brimming with hot dark tea as she added the cream.

Hawk couldn't resist adding a comment. "I can assure you, Maggie, you are every inch the lady. I'd welcome a repeat another time of your parading around in front of me in that skimpy silk piece of material you'd call a nightgown. Or, skip it entirely. It would all be your choice."

Blushing over the first sip she had no reply for that, yet managed to stutter out a few seconds later, "this is the elixir of the gods, I swear. Now, will you please feed me?"

Her blush increased as he eyed her warmly.

"Absolutely."

The large Wedgewood blue plate was filled with scrambled eggs, sautéed tomatoes, and mushrooms in a hot butter sauce with sausage links on the side. Although she was starved, Maggie ate slowly enjoying the time with him. He had finished several minutes before, but sat and kept her company regardless.

"Will I be okay to use my room tonight?"

"I'll advise you once I confirm with Zamir and the team. I'll send a text by late morning. Maggie," he stopped in mid-sentence, eyes boring into hers. "I have to know. Is there anything else you are not advising?"

She removed the napkin from her lap and placed it on the table. "Nope. Zilch. Nothing else."

But Hawk housed no doubt she was lying. Just then his cellphone vibrated and the message he was awaiting finally arrived. He handed it over. She read it then handed it back.

"You've been in touch with my father?" Her tone was deadpan serious.

"That's pretty apparent in the response. Collect your things and pack. When we have the all clear, I will bring them to your room. I recommend on your way to work to find a secure area and call the general."

She stood and marched over placing stocking feet into her shoes, put on a blazer then reached for her crossbody bag. Eyeing it quickly to make sure it housed everything required for the day. Lifting her other bag with her netbook tucked inside, she moved over toward the door never uttering a sound.

She saw the puzzled look on his face and wanted to scream out at him, *what do you expect? A pat on the back, LC, for overstepping boundaries?* Instead, she remained silent.

Hand on the door latch she opened it then turned partially, "You know what, Hawthorne, you are a pain in the ass. I don't need your permission to talk to my own father. Nor do I need you to watch over me like I'm some damn fool."

Her chest heaved as he watched the movement intently.

"I'm sure your dossier related I stick my nose where it doesn't belong and yeah, sure, my father has helped me out of a few legal jams. But I don't need your advice and don't want it. So, how about you return my bag to my room and if it's not secure enough to your liking, leave it at the desk. When I return this afternoon, I will stop there first. If it's there, I will either get another room or hotel. I hope I'm making myself perfectly clear here."

He stood, but long before he could get to her she had closed the door. When he opened it she was nowhere to be seen? Fuck. He had not intended to sound so bossy. But didn't she understand underneath that stubbornness? He never wanted any civilian to get hurt. Especially this civilian. The daughter of a former general. He had no choice but to let this ride. But could imagine, as a grin appeared on his face, how pissed off she really was right about now.

\*\*\*

Maggie was stewing when she bumped right into Zamir in the lobby knowing it was intentional. "Ouch, oh it's you. How about stepping aside to let me pass." She weaved around him and out into the overcast day not looking back.

Zamir arrived at Hawk's room and didn't bother to knock, the door was slightly ajar. "What the hell did you do to her? She's in a real bitchy mood this morning."

"Hell, if you can figure that woman out. Advise me where the fuck I've gone wrong."

Zamir grinned slapping his associate on the back. "Shit, no man on this planet could do that. Give it up."

"Yeah, well that's not so easy. Killing is easy, Zamir. But that woman is not easy to just walk away from. Let alone forget."

Zamir would not offer any relief and hell, why should he? It was time Hawk got snared. The point of the matter was Zamir was enjoying Hawk's discomfort. This was a rare first.

"Hawk, her room was secure. I just was waiting for her in the lobby to advise the team found no signs of identifiable sources that had entered and rummaged her room. Nor did I have any issues during the night. Whoever it is must be satisfied she is no threat. But I never got that message relayed. I appeared to be in her way. In an attempt to exit quickly."

"Good. I need to leave her bag in there. Now let's get the hell out of here. Are you set on your location?"

"Yes. I have the access I need and extraction when it's complete. I fathom they are going to split into two groups to throw off who they believe will be monitoring them. I'm positive they have no bloody clue it's us. If they even had the scent Mossad was on their sad asses, they'd quit now. Or, do us all a favor and take their own sorry lives."

"I see you still put yourself above all the rest of us, Zamir. What a pompous arrogant jerk."

"I could kill you and disappear before any discovery is made of your lifeless corpse."

Hawk grinned. "Need caffeine, do you? It appears you both would make a dynamic couple. She's pretty to look at but a bit less than grand first thing in the morning."

"We don't all wake the same, friend. If you are going to ever win her, you'd better figure out another way. Or, give it up."

Zamir stopped his verbal opinion long enough by swigging two cups of tea. "Let's do this."

Hawk maneuvered around Zamir and used a small electronic device to gain access to her room and left the bag. Finished, they both glanced down the hallway. "Stairway. Best option. Go ahead of me and check it out. I'll follow in a minute and meet you outside and we can head toward St. George Square.

The old stone alley they walked through reeked of piss from some vagrant that occupied its whereabouts the night prior. Between the buildings, they moved in through an old wooden door, up several rickety flights of steps to the rooftop high above. Hawk glanced out over the ancient city of Edinburgh.

"Your gear is already here, right?"

"Affirmative. Well under protection beneath several old wooden crates. The bells from the tower will ring at twenty-hundred hours. That's when it will happen so my shots will not be heard."

"Your belief is that it will be there and not at the library." Hawk never doubted a man's gut instinct especially Zamir's. "Okay, I will take your lead and move opposite and assist."

They both went about securing Zamir's location when Hawk nodded silently, slipping back down the way they came up to move ahead with his own plans across from this building.

***

Maggie stopped across the street from the main entrance to the library glancing around. It all seemed secure enough, so she rang her father and hardly got a word in the moment he answered her call. Yes, it was clear. He was livid.

"No Pop, this time I did not get involved. Trouble found me. I mean it."

"Listen, Margaret," she hated it at her age when he or her mother used her full first name. It immediately made her shrivel to six years old. "I want you to cooperate fully and do exactly as he or anyone else with his team requests, understand?"

"Affirmative, Pop, I will. I know they'll snitch on me if I do differently."

Her father detected resentment of his well-meant interference knowing when someone of his stature exited the military, they never leave it behind completely. Especially with a daughter like Maggie.

"Your mother is shopping. I will not mention this to her. I am off golfing. If you need me you had better text or call me, young lady. Am I making myself crystal clear?"

She could not resist knowing it always made him smile. "Affirmative, General!"

Maggie signaled off and nearly pitched the cellphone into a sewer drain when she glanced up and saw one of the 'members' walking her direction. Damn! This was indeed a stark reminder she had to be careful with her phone calls, location, and tone of voice.

He stopped next to her while she waited for the pedestrian signal to flash green not acknowledging him in the least.

"Excuse me, you are Miss Cohen from the University of Bristol. Or, perhaps I'm mistaken?"

She glanced up at him for a moment, deep in thought. "Yes, have we met?"

"No, but I saw you when I attended a meeting at one of your conference rooms. Are you working with the Edinburgh Library on tonight's special events?"

"Actually no. I'm training staff members on a new software package for the library. But I may for the unveiling. It could be fun."

That seemed to her all he needed to hear. "Yes, I and friends will be here as well. If we see you again, I shall say hello. I am Erez Horowitz." The signal beeped as they hastily crossed together. He to the right, Maggie left up onto the curb.

"Shalom, Miss Cohen."

"Have a good day, Erez."

At her temporary desk in the learning center of the main library, she toyed with her cellphone flipping it over and around. Should she let him know? Typing both names, she transmitted it to Zamir and Hawk.

Zamir responded right away – *confirmed*. But she heard zilch from Doug.

One of her new trainees approached. "Miss Cohen, I am not Sharon. She rang in unwell this morning and I moved our one o'clock to now if you are okay with that. I will train her after you depart if that works."

"Absolutely. Go ahead and log on to your computer. I will walk you through the manual and passcode procedures to enter the new system."

Two hours later Maggie was finished. "If you are comfortable and do not have any questions, then we are all set."

"I'll review the manual tonight and help Sharon tomorrow. I think I grasp this and feel ready to begin on Monday."

"Great," Maggie was suddenly distracted. She swore that Doug had just passed by the central entrance. But, upon closer evaluation, she thought she must have been mistaken. Gathering up all the paperwork and bags, she headed out checking in every direction but could not find him. She shook her head to clear the cobwebs. It must have been a coincidence.

She wrapped on the closed door of Professor Winslet's office and waited. His deep, Scottish accent worked through the thick wood. "Enter. Ah, Maggie, how's it going? I've been using the program and we are extremely pleased."

"Wonderful, Malcolm. I'm finished. You had one lady phone in sick, so we moved my last appointment up. I'm heading back to the hotel to work a bit there and then I'll return for the cocktail party at seven."

She stood in the doorway, one foot in and one out. "I'm going to try and hop on the last flight tonight to see if I can make it back to London. Should I disappear later, I wanted to thank you for bringing me here and the lovely hotel accommodations."

He stood, then walked around his large mahogany desk and extended a hand to her. "Pass along my compliments and greetings to Seth."

"It will be my pleasure." She released his hand and exited the library walking the short distance to The George.

"Yes, Miss Cohen?" The front desk clerk had her attention. "Did anyone leave a bag for me here at the front desk?" He looked perplexed. "No, and I've been here all day. Would you like me to ring the bellhop and inquire with him?"

"No, that'll be fine. Thank you."

Her room looked very thoroughly cleaned as her bag sat on the bed. Good. She logged onto her netbook and looked at availability for the eleven o'clock flight and calculated if she left the event by nine, she could be at the airport by ten and have enough time for check-in. Accessing her British Airways itinerary on their website, she changed the return flight and had the exchange electronically processed. This would save them a hotel night and the fee was minimal.

Closing the computer then unzipping her bag she removed a dark red mid-knee length cocktail dress, black hosiery, and high heels. She'd have time at the airport to change. Finishing her shower and dressed she blew her hair dry and pinned it up then used a curling iron to frame soft curls around her face. Placing small ruby and diamond earrings into her lobes, Maggie closed her bags and took the elevator down to the lobby just as her cellphone rang.

She stopped at the front desk sliding her room cards toward the reservation agent when she noticed it was from Hawk. She had no desire to speak with him right now as mixed emotions coiled throughout her body. If it was urgent he'd be persistent.

"Would you mind securing my bags here until I return later tonight? I'm going to an event at the library. But will be back to claim them for a late flight back to London."

"Absolutely, Miss Cohen, please check back in when you return, and we will load them into your cab. Do you need me to call you one now?"

"No, I have one waiting just outside. Thank you for everything. I really enjoyed staying here." Maggie smiled up at him as she signed off on the invoice.

It took less than fifteen minutes to arrive at the event by cab. If the foyer was beautifully decorated the grand exhibit room was over-the-top as she was quickly swept up into the festivities. Middle-Eastern music played softly in the background.

A waiter approached with goblets of sparkling champagne poised gingerly side-by-side on a highly polished silver tray. Reaching for one, she carefully eyed the room filled with well-dressed attendees. She could not see Doug anywhere. But spotted Malcolm. Weaving her way through clustered groups of people, she suddenly felt a chill run up her spine. Stopped, turned in a full circle then shrugged it off and kept moving. But it persisted, nagging so.

"Ah, you look lovely, Maggie. Come, let me introduce you to a few of our benefactors. I've spent the better part of the afternoon with them and they were impressed by our new software." She smiled looking at the high-profile diplomats that she instantly recognized from London. But the noise kept rattling around in her brain as she kept thinking, *where is this warning being directed from*? But nothing was apparent. Damn, this was not good. Maybe it was just the overall atmosphere of what was to come. Something dreadful.

"Miss Cohen, we've received high praise and regards for your program. If you permit, I'd like to give you my card. We may be interested in obtaining these rights and contracting your services in Tel-Aviv."

"Mr. Shakaki, it is a pleasure to meet you." She slid the business card into her purse. "I've read many of your papers and find them fascinating. If you are interested, I'd be happy to liaise between our offices." They shook hands while he smiled warmly down at her. She could tell straight away he had an eye for the ladies especially when he was away from home. Maggie had heard all the rumors. Dislodging her hand, she moved toward the next introduction.

Hardly hearing what Malcolm was saying, Maggie looked over his shoulder and caught a glimpse of Zafir, Davide, and Horowitz along with two other men. This reinforced the belief that this was indeed the whole group of five now together in one place.

If they were here, then this was not their target and that explained why Doug was no place to be found as he and Zamir must have figured that out already. She finished sipping the drink and placed it on the table behind her group. "Gentleman, if you would excuse me, I will move now to the exhibit. Malcolm, thank you again and you know how to reach me."

Through each area Maggie looked with interest at all the artifacts nonchalantly monitoring her party of five. Exiting the hall, she weaved a path between those standing outside smoking cigarettes to hail a cab.

"Yes, to The George Hotel please." She spoke to the cab driver while pulling out her cellphone and ringing the St. George's front desk. "Hello, Margaret Cohen. I left two bags at the desk this afternoon. Could you have them brought out to the front entrance now? I am on my way in a cab than on to the airport to catch my flight home."

"Yes, Miss Cohen, I will have the bellman ready for you, curbside."

"Thank you."

They averted through St. George Square and halted as dozens of people were milling about seemingly unable to get out of the way. When she saw the police and coroner's vehicles. There had been something of an extreme nature that took place to bring so much law-enforcement to this location.

"Any news on your radio we can tune into?" She was sitting forward talking with the cab driver. "Don't know, miss, it looks like it just happened." He turned on the BBC2 and listened. It sounded like they were catching the last bit of a new flash.

"*It is unclear where the two shots came from. But one source said it was a rooftop of one of the buildings. There are two suspected terrorists lying dead and the area has been cleared while the bomb squad dismantles them. Accounts are coming in that they were wired with explosives to disrupt, and we suspect kill, as many attendees to this outside concert tied in with the new Israeli-American exhibit at the library. More to follow. We now return you to the station.*"

The cab driver shut off the radio. "This is bad. The misses will be calling me any time now on the cellphone to make sure I'm not in the thick of it. Don't you worry none, miss, with all these coppers around we are as safe as can be. Wonder who shot them? Must have been deadly aims, don't you think?"

She had to suppress a grin at his heavy Scottish accent somehow managing to understand most of what he had said. *Who had shot them?* Then the light bulb went off. She knew exactly who. Zamir and Doug. But wondered what the hell was going on. Bristol first and now here? What was next? That meeting tomorrow night was going to prove very important. Now it became crystal clear. A trip to Stonefield House was in order.

It would normally be handled by one of their clerks to collect books and fees. But, Maggie felt it should befall her. Not deliberately putting another in any danger.

At her gate, she looked around at those gathering for the late-night return to London and stopped, barely containing a soft gasp. Two were sitting and three standing. It was Zafir and his group. Her stomach lurched, heart, pounding uncomfortably. If they made it through security, then they were not transporting any explosives. She silently hoped and prayed.

Should she just leave and spend the night at an airport hotel and fly back in the morning? Subconsciously, Maggie felt the need to run. So intense were the feelings she nearly had a panic attack. Then managed to get it under control by breathing deeply. *Yes*, she thought silently, *I just need to take it one breath at a time.*

It worked as an announcement was made.

"We will now begin boarding in five minutes. Flight fourteen sixty-four from Edinburgh to London-Heathrow at gate six. Please have your boarding cards ready."

Maggie barely heard what was said as several seconds passed. Finally, it penetrated when the gate attendant spoke a second time. "May I have your attention. We are now boarding British Airways flight number fourteen sixty-four from Edinburgh to London-Heathrow. If you are traveling with small children or need assistance, please proceed now. All business class passengers may board at any time."

That was Maggie. It was now or abort.

She rose and held her card out for the agent to scan and boarded the aircraft walking down the ramp deep in a mental fog. Under the seat in front, she stowed a bag. Then sat glancing out the small window at the well-lit airport and up toward the dark sky. It was at that moment when she felt her lower lip quiver and nearly broke down and cried. Biting that lip hard enough to taste a bit of blood, composure finally returned.

"Miss, please buckle. We will depart shortly."

Maggie realized the entire aircraft had boarded and she had not heard a sound. No one was sitting beside her much to her relief. Glancing down and pulling out the cellphone, she turned it off. Securing it, she leaned glancing through the seats but was unable to see beyond the third row in her cabin. She surmised they were back there in coach. Or, had not boarded at all. She had no clue.

"Ladies and gentlemen, welcome on board this British Airways flight bound for London-Heathrow. It's a clear night and with these winds we expect our arrival to be on time." The pilot's voice was deep and soothing as they taxied down the runway and were soon up in the sky at altitude. She had never prayed for so long or so hard in all her life as she did during the entire flight.

When the wheels skidded down on the tarmac, Maggie's breath finally returned to normal. Had she even taken one during the entire flight? Hailing a cab as soon as she was outside of arrivals, it was a sorely welcoming sight when the cabbie pulled up curbside to her apartment building. The temptation was nearly overpowering to drop her bags and raise both arms high into the night sky and thank the heavens she had made it home.

Throwing the keys down on the kitchen table, she set her bags in her bedroom, went into the bath and washed up then climbed into bed stark naked not caring about clothes. She was wiped out. Completely feeling leagues beyond her own comfort zone. It was not like anything she had ever been through before. "And," she whispered out into the dark room, "I never want to ever again."

Tucked neatly in her crossbody bag hanging off the back of one kitchen chair, her cellphone was vibrating like crazy. She heard it. But, chose to ignore it.

\*\*\*

Doug's frustration and deep concern mounted from not reaching Maggie. It increased when he went back to the hotel and found she had checked out and instantly assumed she had returned on the last flight back to London.

What the hell? How did this woman think? She had passed right through St. George and must have seen the activity. Damn chit. Furthermore, they were on the same flight together. Her and the Zafir group. He rang INTEL.

"Hawk here, I need a confirmed manifest for British Airways fourteen sixty-four just landed at Heathrow, STAT. I'm standing by."

The information relayed brought both relief and irritation. She was on it and the craft had landed without any issues. He leaned up against one of the thick-paned hotel room windows and pressed his face against the glass. For a split second feeling the coolness penetrate through his forehead and into his thoughts. She was okay. He knew. Taking a deep breath, his body calmed, mind re-engaged.

But why was she not responding to him? He glanced down at his watch. It was now zero one-thirty that's why. Sure, she was home now and probably sound asleep. He'd have to wait until later in the morning then catch up with her at Barney's Pub. "Okay little woman, the chase is officially back on." Turning, he walked out of his room and headed straight for the bar. Ordered up and threw back two damn good glasses of scotch before heading back up for the night.

***

Waking from a very restful sleep and knowing she could saunter in anytime today since she was not expected back until Monday, Maggie stretched. Then sat up placing her well-pedicured toes onto the carpet. Reaching for her silk robe, she wrapped it around securing it tightly and headed to the kitchen for a much-needed pot of tea.

Faintly in the background, she could hear a persistent buzzing. Removing her cellphone from the crossbody bag, she checked the messages. It was Doug. All of them. He had texted her four times. The last one apparent he was clearly agitated.

She decided to respond with just an "*I am home now*" and sent it off. She showered and dressed for a regular work day. A soft moss green suit with a crisp chocolate brown silk blouse and put a dab of perfume on. Then grabbed her work gear and headed out. *Oh, what a gorgeous morning*, she thought. The sun warm on her face. Leaves bursting with bright hues of golden red, yellow and orange gently wafting down to the still green grass. How she loved fall weather!

It felt like a brand-new day, a new lease on life. But she had managed to work through such dark fears. Upon rising this day, Maggie felt ready to conquer the world. "Thank you, God." She blared out loud as a passer-by paid her no mind.

Truly displaying an engaging grin, she stepped through the stairwell toward her office as Caren was up and out of her chair in two shakes. "Hey. What are you doing in here? I thought your flight was for mid-morning?"

"I caught one late last night. I needed to get back to handle a few things. How's it going? Anything I need to attend to straight away?" Caren towed along following Maggie into the large office.

"No, Seth has been in and out already. Pleased to no-end by the emails Malcolm sent and it looks like you or he may be traveling to Israel soon."

"Wow, that didn't take long. I just met them last night. Anyway, we'll see. I imagine he and I will wrestle over who takes this one. He may win just because he's the boss."

Maggie gazed warmly down at her desktop. "Ah, yes, my flowers look just as pretty as when I left. Thanks for taking care of them."

"Sure, I bet it's not the last time we see something from him."

Maggie glared at her. "Now I remember. I need to call human resources and get you replaced immediately." They both broke out in laughter. "Get out. I have things to do."

Caren had her hand on the doorknob to pull it shut, "Paul has things all set for you."

"What time is the meeting?"

"Six-thirty, for one hour."

"Ok, I'm going to work on some files. Thanks as always for keeping the hatches battened while I was away. I know I tease you. But it's much appreciated."

Caren nodded shutting the door mumbling just loud enough for Maggie to catch most of it. "*What the hell has gotten into her. Is she going soft? She must be up to something else.*"

As Maggie's line buzzed she maneuvered sideways in her chair and glanced out toward her assistant's office. "How the hell did she get in there, answer a call and buzz me with it in ten seconds?" Shaking her head, she picked up the line.

"I have Sean for you."

"Put him through."

"Hey there, when did you get back?"

"Late last night. I thought I'd pop in and clean things up before I call it quits for the weekend. What's up?"

"Want to meet us tonight at Barney's, say eight-thirty?" She toyed with that. If she left here later and went home for a late lunch she could stay and watch the live stream of the meeting and still catch up with them.

"Mags, are you still there?"

"Sorry, yes, can't blame it on jet lag since the flight was just over one hour. I'll be there. I'll take a cab over and meet up with you."

"Are you sure? We can get you."

"Yup, I have work to finish up here and then things to take care of at the apartment before I head out. Barney's in Portishead?"

"Yeah, it's just opened, and Sasha heard it's a great spot. See you. Got to run."

Maggie had no time to say goodbye before the line went dead. Upon opening all the emails, she quickly got things out of the way. It was so nice to travel with a netbook. Her pocketbook started to vibrate again. She laughed while reaching behind and inside of it nearly toppling backward. She grabbed the corner of the desk just in time. The message was from her mother.

Maggie burst out laughing unable to contain it as she read the message. "Your father said to text you and say be a good daughter and not get into any more trouble. But neglected to mention what the hell he was talking about. Anything I need to be worried about?"

Maggie bit her sore bottom lip and replied, "No, just Pops being Pops. Remind him I am nearly thirty. Sorry,

Mum, I've got to run. Catch up with you both soon. Love you..."

She'd feel much better working this all out from home. But wondered if a stop to Stonefield House would be a good idea. Hmm, she thought about that for a few minutes then buzzed Caren. "Do you have that chaps name at Stonefield House that owes a large sum of money carried over from the summer program?"

"Yes, I'll send it now."

She waited for the email file and attachment then printed it along with the list of books, other details, and final bill then tucked it all into an envelope. Maggie wrote his name on the front and placed it in her purse. Grabbing her netbook and bag, she engaged the out of office for her email changing it to Monday and stopped at Caren's door.

"I have some errands to run. Then I'll be working from home this afternoon. If you need anything, call me on the house phone, okay?"

"Does, Pop know what's going on? Should you leave a trail just in case you are missing come Monday?"

Maggie's grin expanded with each word uttered. "Maybe I'll keep you around to watch my back. Thanks, and yes, Pops knows a little bit. But don't worry. I know you've heard this more times than anyone. I plan to keep my nose clean. I mean it. But I have one small thing to take care of. That's it. Why don't you head out? Let the intern handle the rest. Our load is light until tonight's meeting."

"Thanks, I'll do that. Maggie, please be careful."

"Righto. See you Monday."

Shortly, Maggie was back at the flat circling the inside of it like a caged lion. For some reason, this didn't feel right and before she went to Stonefield, she'd need to figure it out. "Damn." She mouthed out. "I can't go today. This will completely raise suspicion since I saw them in Edinburgh."

Making a sandwich and tea she sat down outside on the balcony and finally allowed her mind to wander to Doug. What was his case? He said he'd go back to Wales. What the heck did he want with her beside information? Just to use her, she was sure. Just like that first night when he knew Zafir's meeting was taking place under her professional roof. Yeah, it was clear. She was just another informant. Another piece needed in the puzzle.

Good excuse as any she surmised. Pops would advise his crew to use *any measure to complete the mission*. Did that include her? But what was his mission? Then there is Zamir. A mystery all on his own. A true badass from a true badass organization; Mossad, The Institute for Intelligence and Special Operations to perform deeply-dark covert operations beyond its borders. With or without other countries knowledge or assistance.

INTEL missions, weapons confiscation, preventing terrorist acts... "Ah, yes. That's it. HAMAS is here developing sleeper cells against Israeli's. Zamir was here to wipe them out." Maggie stopped to glance around knowing no one could have heard her down below. Then continued a silent evaluation. Doug must be his contact along with Perkins covering the Ministry of Defense, aka MoD, and MI5.

"Shit. I really do need to be very careful now."

Her cellphone chimed at six twenty-five with a reminder the live stream was about to begin. Flipping open the computer, a sly grin appeared at her own usage of modern spy techniques her own Pop had shown her. In secrecy of course. She chuckled placing feet up on the corner of the desk and tilted the swivel chair back a bit.

Simultaneously both the front and back cameras scanned the room continuously as the two side cameras remained immobile. Zafir was standing up at the front of the room as more people came. Maggie focused more closely taking in the clear outline of Perkins sitting in the rear neatly tucked on a chair. Then Zafir began as the hairs on Maggie's arms raised.

"Radical Islamism has brought you here for the first time or back again to learn more and assist our cause. For thousands of years, our society and culture have been mistreated and misunderstood. I, along with others, will engage you in who we are, why we are here and how you can help us. I am Michaez Zafir, or just Zafir if you want to address me. Since we are in Great Britain, I will leave the formalities of our culture at home."

"There are those in high government posts, military venues and society figures that deem us, terrorists and extremists." There was a pause as Maggie moved a bit closer to the screen.

"But I am here to tell you we are a friend of England, of Great Britain and of the world. We pray in peace, live in peace and speak with peace in our hearts. Join us in spreading our message of Allah's love, God's love to everyone."

"But, there are those that will hate us because of the color of our skin. The accent in our voice. They consider us cold-blooded murderers. Journalists say they report the news. But it is all fake. They report what they are paid to say by high-ranking officials. Companies that line their pockets with gold and their tongue's with lies."

"We know the truth." Rumbled out from a few strategically placed people in the room. Maggie had a chance to see Davide, Horowitz, and others. "We must be heard. There are those in our own country, our own countrymen that damage our reputation. They take our lands. Kill our brothers, sisters, mothers, and fathers. Even our children are not spared all in the name of good government. Israel should be ruled by those that love the country and would see it prosper. It is time for our growth to exceed our pain and house a Palestinian Islamic State."

He turned away slightly and engaged a remote that activated a slideshow displaying the horrors and destruction to homes, businesses, and residents of the West Bank and Gaza Strip.

Groans surfaced around the room.

For forty-five minutes he pounded it home and she could hear anger while voices rose at what they believed to be injustices. He had them, at least more of them. He was good, potent, powerful and very deadly. No wonder Mossad and the British Army had teamed up with MI5 on this one.

"We have positions that need filling and your assistance will be key to our success. If you want to be that person," he halted while his four brothers in arms stood up beside him. "Then look at us closely and find us. Tell us how *you* want to help. Come back to other meetings. Bring friends with you. There is so much you can do for this cause. For us all. Now, are there any questions?"

One brave soul, Maggie thought, spoke up. It was a woman who gravitated toward Horowitz and spoke directly to him. Although it was Zafir that replied. "Is there any intentional harm done toward others?"

Maggie sat up straight. That *was* a very bold statement by the woman.

"Yes, if necessary we will strike back if struck first. No different than you would defend yourself from a stranger's attack, correct?"

"Yes,"

"More?"

"If there is a need to reach you and we do not find you on campus, how do we do that?"

"If it is a private meeting you are interested in, leave word for me at Stonefield House. I will find you. Around the back we have a slot in the old wooden door. Drop a note in there. It is a very secure location. It will reach me. Anyone else?"

The Room grew quiet.

"If there are no further questions we will adjourn and meet again here next week. Same time. Keep watch for postings on the boards."

The meeting broke up as the room cleared except the notorious five and Perkins. Maggie was about to log off and get ready to go out then hesitated. That damn curiosity that killed the cat kept her watching.

"I'm monitoring the site to see if anyone else was transmitting. It may take some time before I have a location if there is one."

Maggie gasped out loud. It was Perkins!

"The account has been transferred and you will need to lay low for forty-eight hours minimum before you begin the next phase. You are well supplied at Stonefield so I do not anticipate any issues. I have advised my HQ that I've monitored this gathering and after I finish editing the tape, I will send it to them. I'll erase anything incriminating and enhance a bit of the dialogue. By all accounts, it will appear like a well-structured and legal meeting." She nodded to the group of men as they left the room.

Maggie's mind reeled.

Shit! She was cozy with Doug and Zami, but also Zafir. What the hell! Did Doug know? Did they both know? Judas Priest, if ever she needed her father it was now. He'd be so pissed at what she'd done but she had to make sure no one found her IP and transmission. Grabbing the cellphone from the desk corner she pressed the speed dial button.

"Maggie, is that you? What's wrong?"

"Nothing, Pops. Well, actually something is a bit off."

"For cripes sake, girl, tell me now."

She filled him in hardly surprised by his angry tone.

"Pops, what if Doug and Zamir already know she's the double agent and is playing her? What should I do?"

"First you find that student right now and make sure he wipes his hands from everything. Second, you need to lay low, Maggie, I mean it this time. This is *bad stuff* and you are nearly up to your chin in it. If you want to go on living you'd better stop. You get on the horn with that kid now and call me back. Then we'll talk some more."

He hung up abruptly as Maggie looked down at the phone, hesitant, as the adrenaline kicked in.

"Paul, is that you?"

"Yes, it is, who are you?"

"Miss Cohen, I need a *big* favor and now. It cannot wait."

"Okay," his voice was a bit shaky. "What do you need me to do?"

"Erase anything you have that could link that live stream to you or me and make sure no one can dig deep and find it. Can you do that?"

"Well, I can, Miss Cohen. But that's illegal." She nearly chuckled realizing what they had done was just that.

"I promise you I will take the heat for anything if it happens. Can you do it right now? I'll hold while you take care of this."

She could hear his fingers striking the keyboard at rapid speed and after about four minutes of tapping her own pen on the desktop, she finally heard the news she wanted to hear.

"Done. It is all set. No one will find out, Miss Cohen."

"Paul, you are a lifesaver. If I ask, can you set this up again next week on short notice? I won't lie. It's dangerous. But I swear to you on all that's holy, I will cover you completely. One more thing. No one can know of this. Period. Not family, not friends, not teachers, okay?"

"Wow, it's a hot one?"

"Smoking."

"Okay," his tone very serious. "I promise. Can I get hurt by this?"

Her reply was short and clipped. "Nope. Not on my watch. I'll make sure, and Paul, thank you. If you need to reach me do so only by my cellphone. Don't leave any messages. If you can't reach me that way, send a text then delete it. Good?"

"Yes, I got it."

"Okay, I'll see you soon." She hung up and shut off everything making sure all connections were severed. Glancing at the wall clock it was now seven forty-five. A call to her Pops was in order then a quick change of clothes and a dash to Barney's. *I'll make it by hell or high water*, she thought. *I need that damn drink!*

"Pops, we are all set."

He asked nothing further. "Okay, daughter, we will be in touch." He hung up on her abruptly this time as she stared at the cellphone for a second before calling up a cab for eight-fifteen. Hurrying, she changed into soft, tight-fitting gray bootleg jeans, black granny boots and a pink cashmere sweater with a skinny black leather belt around her waist. Touching her makeup and dabbing on some perfume, she was outside just as the cab approached.

"Barney's in Portishead, please."

As the driver pulled up to the curb, she paid him in a hurry, slammed the door shut and dashed inside. The place was lively as hell when she arrived just after eight thirty-five and immediately was harassed.

"You are late!"

"All by five minutes. Can't you cut a girl a break? I've been busy."

"Oh, shut up and sit your bony ass down. We've ordered you a blue drink. One of those damn martini's you like so much to help improve your disposition.

"Oh, I forgive you for being such an ass," Maggie chimed. "But looking at your drink glasses nearly empty and refills already here, what time did you guys arrive?"

"I told you I should give you a ride. Eight or so."

"For crying sakes, you are a sorry bunch of lushes. Damn the lot of you have a leg up on me."

"Yup, that's why we ordered you something strong. Oh, and that brooding, good looking chap you had that half date with is over at the bar. He seemed to know you'd be here tonight."

Turning sharply, Maggie gazed at his backside and knew it was him. One tall, long line of blue jeans that fit tight over his damn hunky butt. She picked up her drink as if in a daze and headed in a straight-line right toward him.

Ready to do battle.

He turned just before she arrived. His eyes nearly blazing the clothes off her back by the intense look in them. She took a big swig of the martini, placed a boot up on the foot rail and prepared to lock horns with him.

# Chapter Eight

"I hear you've been looking for me? I'm assuming the General contacted you."

He stared at her for way too long. Something was different about him tonight. His arrogant cockiness was still there, but his eyes looked wistful, almost withdrawn, as she drew in her eyebrows and removed the foot dispersing with the distance between them.

But still, he remained silent. While his eyes commanded her total attention, and had it. She was mesmerized. Sucked right into the swirling vortex where she nearly felt like dislodging her heart and just handing it over to him.

"There's a discussion we need to have. But it can't happen here. Nor can it wait. Finish your drink. I'm taking you out of this place."

This was not a pleasant question. It was an angry demand. For once she could not fight him and had to know what was going on. "Okay, let me say goodnight to my friends and I'll meet you outside." She swigged the rest of her drink down feeling the strong spirits warm her insides, setting the empty martini glass on the bar top.

Standing at their table noticing how their voices were growing louder by the minute, Maggie finally had their attention. "Guys, I'm heading out. Sorry about this. But I've something to do and can't explain it now."

"You are not in any trouble are you, Maggie?" Sasha looked more than concerned having watched Hawthorne leave the bar already. "Nope, just got to go. I'll catch up with you over the weekend." She turned placing her crossbody on her middle section and walked outside into the now cooler fall air.

He was leaning up against the side of the building and looked reckless as hell. But more than that he looked damn good.

"You are scaring me a bit, Doug, can we talk now?"

"No, let's go back to my place. I'll bring you home when we are through. The Rover is just over there."

*Of course,* she thought, *he'd drive one of those or a jeep.* That made perfect sense. It was the personal vehicle of choice for most guys in the military.

He opened the passenger side door as she got in. "Where did you say you live?"

"I have a flat near campus. That's temporary. But, my house is in Chepstow."

"Is it in the military zone?"

"No. Dammit. This is just not convenient for me that your father is a general. I have to be very careful with everything I do and say."

"You should have no worries there. He sings your praises."

"That's what you hear. I may hear something entirely different."

They both grinned.

"How long are you going to keep me? Should I have packed a bag?" *There, that's better*, she thought. *Sarcasm will keep us distanced.*

She realized quick enough he would have none of her antics. "Stop the shit. We have a lot going on and I must square things away with you or tuck you out of sight. Those are your father's orders."

"Tuck me away?"

"Quiet, I have to think. It's a bit difficult right now. I have mixed feelings about this."

What did that mean? Had he been using her as she thought before? Had the tides shifted because her father called him? Forced his rank? Would her Pops do that? Maggie shook her head letting out a sigh. Yes, she knew he would.

It was a short fifteen-minute ride then Doug was pushing the garage door button. It opened as he drove in and closed it behind the rig. She was out in a flash and headed toward the entry.

"Go ahead in it's unlocked. I need to grab my bag. I'll be in shortly." She quickly realized that was a partial truth. Knew he was going to advise her father she was in his custody. Quite sure he was dawdling behind to send him a text or something.

Setting her crossbody down on the marble kitchen countertop, Maggie eyed the home and was amazed at how neat it was. Too neat. But not shabby awful as far as decorations. She scrutinized more closely not seeing any tell-tale signs of a female living here. Then again, she had never asked him if he was involved with someone. Leaning over, she unzipped the boots ready to leave them on the mat next to the door.

"I wish you'd stop presenting your backside. I have enough on my mind already."

She stepped out of them standing up straight and moved to a series of framed pictures, black and white, above a handsomely carved Italian marble mantel.

"Are these of your family?"

"Yes, both military and civilian."

"Are they nearby?"

"No, my parents actually live in Edinburgh, my brothers," he stopped and pointed toward to other pictures, "live on bases in the U.K. with their wives and kids."

She turned seeing he was no longer there as she looked at all the other pictures and smiled. It brought back her own family memories of being a young girl with her sister, Elizabeth, and brother, Kevin. Both now married themselves with kids. Full-fledged Army brats.

Over a shoulder a wine glass appeared as she sipped on the Pinot Grigio wondering if he kept alcoholic beverages available for his other guests as she moved on. "You have a nice place. I'm a bit surprised. I expected it to be neat but not like this."

"Women always want to see the inside of a man's place. Can you tell me why?"

Her grin was seductive.

"Yes, we are born snoopers and like to see what hidden treasure we can uncover about the man we are interested in." She had not realized how that sounded.

Two large chunky footrests were side-by-side in front of the gas fireplace as he hit the ignition button and it started up. "Sit." He sat opposite. A whiskey or scotch with ice in his left hand and sat resting arms on thighs.

Maggie sat, crossed her legs and just simply waited.

"The General," he paused, collecting his words cautiously, "because he is your father and very worried about you, asked me to have this talk. Are you tampering again when I thought we agreed you wouldn't?"

"You asked me specifically if I had anything else I could tell you and at that time I wasn't lying."

"So, I should have been specific and asked you what you were not telling me? It's all a play on words, Maggie."

"Okay, I did have something else in the works. I told my Pop because I wasn't sure what to do. I never expected to find this out."

"Neither did we. You did us a tremendous service. This all could've come to us when it was too late."

"So, you didn't know? How about Zamir, does he?"

"Neither. She has been a trustworthy ally for several years."

Maggie felt his anger knowing who it was directed toward. "You can't bring her in yet, I know it. What can I do? I have a way into Stonefield that will work and won't lend suspicion to anyone. You're all going to have to face this. You need me."

His eyes bore into her blue ones holding them hostage. "Did you tell your father about this idea of yours?"

She set the empty wine goblet down on the stone hearth and started to stand. But he held her down, hands gripping tightly. She did not flinch.

"Stop running from me. You will get nowhere here, and I assure you I will locate you."

Was this the time she told him she had wrestled with feelings for him long enough? Idiot, of course it was not. But deep inside her mind she could hear the words. Yes, she would take a one-night stand. Then let it go. This deep, searing need to be close to him. With him, had her nearly mumbling the words out loud.

"I'm not running from you." She let his hands stay where they were without voicing how hard his grip was. "I didn't mention it. I had actually forgotten about it when I was watching the live stream."

"Well, we are going to use you for the next several meetings if we need to. Whoever that young assistant is that rigged this up for you, well, he did a hell of a good job. Even MI5 and the MoD techs can't locate the IP source of transmission. You've got yourself a true genius. I don't want his name mentioned ever to assure he is safe. Do you have it all arranged for the next meeting?"

Maggie grimaced not sure how much he'd appreciate her response. Then it would be obvious she planned on tapping into this further. "I do. Don't you want to hear my idea of getting into Stonefield?"

"Shoot."

"I had a list running of students that have been on campus for the last year that have overdue accounts in the library. Chump change most of them, but I did find one that has racked up quite an amount. I'll go and pay him a visit on behalf of finance. Since I do oversee that department in an off-street way."

"Who is it?"

"Daniel Levy. I can access his student ID if you want to bring up your computer. I can remote in and you can send it to your people and see what turns up. But I know he's part of their cell."

"Why are you so sure, and how do you know it's a cell?"

"Because when you unexpectedly joined me for dinner in the Tempus that night up in Edinburgh, I had watched the five of them cross the road together and knew I had a match. Confirmed when I looked up his name in our admissions files. But that's not all. I saw them cloistered together two more times. Once at the library event and then on board my return flight from Edinburgh to London last night. Too coincidental that picture I showed you matched one of them with the cell shot I took. They must be a sleeper cell. I know about them from my Pop."

"Why didn't your father ever enlist you for military intelligence?" His tone was clipped but his eyes were sending a different message now.

"He never tried. I think he believed I'd be under his boots too much and he'd tire getting me out of trouble."

"He'd rethink that now since it seems to be a constant factor."

Shrugging one shoulder, she grinned softly. "Yeah, Pops loves me."

"I've got that confirmed. He told me to treat you with kid gloves and watch you like a hawk. Which I'm sure he didn't realize how that sounded. Went so far as to advise me you have at times even outfoxed him."

Her smile grew.

"Are you hungry? I can whip us up something while we have another drink." He released his steely grip and stood to take her glass along with his own and headed back toward the kitchen.

She followed.

"How often do you actually stay here?"

"Not much now. I'm going to put it up for sale as soon as this is all over."

"Where are you going? Some remote exotic retirement location like Cyprus or Turkey?"

He grinned realizing she knew of the Rapid Deployment Bases on both. "No idea."

Well, that was as noncommittal as one can be, so she backed off. Internally embarrassed she had toyed with hoping to stay the night. *Idiot*, she thought, *I need to let this all go.*

He had been speaking but she was deep in thought. He neared leaning up against the counter while she sat on a bar stool.

"You didn't hear a word I just said, did you?"

"Ah, no, I am sorry. I got lost for a minute. Please repeat it?"

"Would you like an omelet?"

"Love one, put in anything you like." She hopped down and poured another glass of wine motioning over to his empty glass. "Want me to get you another scotch?"

"Don't worry about it. I'll get it in a minute. What is this plan of yours? Were you going to just walk on into Stonefield unannounced, someone with your rank and stature at the college, and think you'd go snooping and fly under their radar? Do you have any idea how well-trained these guys are?"

"I'm going to ignore that for now. Have you seen the feed from Perkins? If you have, you need to know she's doctoring it. I have proof."

"Did you delete the file?"

"Yes, but I saved it to a flash drive."

"Is that back at your apartment?"

"Nope, I have it with me."

He stopped with his back to her flipping the oversized omelet, that she hoped they were sharing, and slid it on to a large plate moving it between them taking out two forks. To her, this now seemed a bit too intimate.

"You just keep surprising me, Maggie."

She blushed slightly. The heightened pink on her cheeks increased by the warmth of his gaze. "We can load it after we finish eating. I'll let you view it and I'll do the dishes. This omelet is delicious, thank you." She reached over into her bag and pulled out the flash drive. "Here it is my only copy."

He flipped it in his hand and got up from the opposite stool. "You'll find what you need to do the dishes under the sink including the drying rack. I'll be in my office down the hall from the living area. Second door to the right."

She looked under the sink and removed the washing liquid, sponge and drying rack and set about washing the dishes and pan. When it was done she wiped them dry and put them away cleaning up the stove and counter. Shutting off the light, she grabbed her bag and checked her cellphone then logged onto the net and checked emails.

Her friends were very concerned. Sasha had emailed her a couple of times from the bar after a few shots and drinks, Maggie was sure. She should've been using word check before sending it. As the last message barely made sense. She emailed her back. "I am fine, won't be staying home tonight and it's not what you think. But, I'm safe. Don't worry. I'll catch up with you by Sunday sometime or Monday at the latest."

Stopping at the entrance to his office she glanced to her left then straight ahead. Indeed, there were two bedrooms. Great. She would have her own room tonight. Safe and sound under his roof. If indeed she had no choice but to stay. Walking in, she rolled another chair over beside him and sat down. Silently picking up on the exact time of the meeting by the closing speech Zafir was making. Driving his passionately spoken point's home.

He safely removed the flash drive but kept it in his hand. "For your safety, you need to leave the room while I secure this. Only a precaution just in case you are ever taken against your will, that you are not aware of where I have placed it."

"Oh," she said, rising, then sliding the chair back. "That sure sounds promising." Then left the room.

Back out in the living area she began to pace. Not emotionally prepared to sleep over. Especially with no warning, overnight clothing, and necessities. He caught her by the window the shades already pulled. "You're antsy."

"Yes, I don't have to stay, do I? Can you take me home now? I wasn't prepared for a sleepover if it comes down to it. I don't have anything I need."

"Sorry, we can't chance it tonight just in case. This is only a precaution. Perkins is the one I'm most concerned about. INTEL could not link her to you or your student assistant. But this is just in the event she gains information that would pose a threat to you."

"I know."

"Do you want to sit and talk, have a drink, tea, anything?"

"No, if you don't mind I'd like to settle in. Which room is mine for the night?"

"Mine."

Her heart did stop beating just at that second.

"Doug, you have two rooms and probably an arsenal at your disposal within arm's reach in each of them. I bet if I lift the cover off that bench I'll find a gun. Inside that desk draw a large knife. How am I doing?"

He was grinning, slowing her progress and cornering her over toward one wall. "Are you on the prowl,

Lieutenant Colonel? For it sure seems like you are. Voice your intentions."

He smiled openly now neither letting her pass nor touching her. But there was no available space for her to move in.

"My home is secure, absolutely. But, every place has a weak spot. I don't believe we will encounter any unwanted guests. Just to be sure I want you right beside me, and Maggie, that was your father's orders. I was not to let you out of my sight for forty-eight hours."

"What?" She questioned softly, now not wanting him to move further away, but closer. "I'm to stay two nights?"

"Yes, possibly longer. We may be commuting to and from our offices together."

"If they're going to come and get me here, they could come and get me at my flat, and I'd be more comfortable there." Her voice was barely above a whisper, breathing shallow. "Surely you have a thousand more important things to do than play sitter for me?" The quiver in her voice was apparent to them both.

"Are you nervous by my closeness?"

She licked her lips. "I am."

"Tell me why."

"That night you left me so abruptly, I…"

"Felt our connection?"

"Yes, but more than that and it bothered me."

He paused lifting her chin with one strong, tanned finger. "Then?"

"Then I saw you with that woman and I was pissed."

"I asked you in that card to not pass judgment."

Right now, Maggie wanted nothing more than to kick his shins. The tone he was using way too sexy, tinged with a bit of arrogance. She didn't have an answer readily available to his question and didn't want to give one.

He smiled crookedly.

She moved under his arm and around with lightning swiftness and headed toward her bag as he caught up in two strides.

"Are you going to keep fighting me? This? Because I can assure you I will outlast you and win. I take no prisoners, Maggie."

That did it. She was pushed to the edge wanting this man. Damnit, he knew it. Using every weapon short of taking her in his arms to drive his meaning home.

*And why*, an internal voice hollered, *didn't he do that?*

Did he want her to ask? Like hell, she would. She'd not take this bait one stinking bit. But he did have one last round to fire and shot it point blank direct into her heart.

Grabbing her by the wrists he secured them behind her back pulling her tight against the full length of his strong body. "Let me make this perfectly clear. Then there will be no misunderstanding between us."

He leaned down and claimed her lips in a soft kiss. Lightly touching them again as they both felt her knees buckle. His hands quickly released her. Grasping both hips tightly and pulled her close as her hands wound up and locked behind his neck.

What began as his only way to prove he wanted her had now backfired on him by her open response. He lifted her legs up as she wrapped them around his waist. He released her lips, retreating just inches, breath warm against her cheeks. "We are going to make love now, Maggie. If you truly don't want this, you'd better say so now."

His room had just one light on in the corner as it sprayed a soft glow about the room. He placed her on top of the covers then rested down beside her. *Oh God*, she thought, *he's going to torture me to beg by taking this so slowly. While all I want is to feel him inside of me right now.*

His finger glided effortlessly up her cheek as he leaned in and possessed her lips. Maggie's deep sigh brought his tongue to her own. Her right hand found his belt buckle releasing it. He grinned. "You set the pace, sweet, and I will be happy to follow along."

*Good*, she thought, *perhaps he would become her hostage. Her hostage of love.* With that in mind, she set about taking from him exactly what she wanted, and she wanted it all. Acting just like she'd never see him again. Extracting every ounce possible.

Two pillows were propped behind him as he sat up partially and watched every move she made. Shirt off, hands roaming over his chest encouraged to bolder discoveries as his breathing changed. She felt his breath on her face, the heat from where her fingers explored then leaned closer and kissed his stomach.

"Ah, Maggie," his voice was deep and raspy, "What will be left of me when you are through?"

She had no reply. Rising on knees she unsnapped his waistband and unzipped his jeans. Her eyes glazed over, lids closing slightly at the sight of his swollen manhood pressed tightly against his boxers. Brazenly she moved further down his legs, stopping to kiss him there, before removing his pants completely.

His whole facial expression was one she'd never seen before. But then again, she'd not been this bold with any man, ever. Her long delicate fingers rested on the outside of his boxers as she watched him intently.

She moved her fingers to the inside of the waistband and down letting one hand encompass all of him. He blinked slowly, eyes never left her face. Ever so slowly she began to move her hand causing a friction that brought out a deep moan from deep inside his throat. Quickly she moved discarding her clothing. Above him now, his boxers off, she whispered softly. "Open your eyes."

Just as she took every bit of him inside of her.

The heat enveloped them right away as she started swerving her hips. Rapidly he swung her back and moved in and out at such a speed, she clutched him so tightly, nails digging into his back clinging for sweet survival. Sweat broke out on them both, bodies glistening as he seared upon her body and mind his potent passion. As they shook, bodies locked tightly together, he glided one hand gingerly across a cheek and leaned down and kissed her until her toes curled.

# Chapter Nine

Wrapped tightly and tucked against his side, head resting on his shoulder, Maggie finally started to breathe. The room was awash with light from the full moon in the sky. He dislodged and got up from the bed and went over and closed one of the two large floor length drapes. Returning, she was immediately brought back into his arms.

Her mind got busy. *When* she silently contemplated, would he say, "*we should not have done that?*"

As usual, she fully expected the other shoe to drop.

"Maggie, this should have waited until the mission is over." She didn't retreat as he half expected. Prepared to grab and hold on if she did. Instead, her hand began to roam through the hair on his chest, circling slowly down toward his navel. He placed a hand over hers to halt further progress.

"I know," she softly whispered. "But what's done is done. I'm sure you can lay it to rest for now. Don't we have until morning before we have to return to other things?"

"Yes, it can wait a few hours more." He pulled her up on top of him. Hardly toe to toe, but lips to lips while grabbing a heap of her silky long hair.

"You knew this was going to happen."

"Yes. I won't lie, I wanted it too."

"I can make no promises."

Her heart sank a little, but her reply was honest. "Neither can I." As she moved off him seeking to gain her own pillow. But his steely grip brought her right back up against the warmth of his body. She sighed giving in as sleep started to claim them both. At some point she felt him bring the covers up over them. Once more she tried to put some physical distance between them. Once more he wouldn't have any of it.

Zero six-thirty finally shook him awake and to Hawk it was late, but to Maggie it was damn early. "Why do you do that? You clearly were not retired long enough to allow your body clock to adjust to civilized sleeping patterns."

He laughed slapping her on the rump. "It will take me years, if ever. You're just going to have to adjust and that's that."

"I don't take orders, soldier, so forget about it." He rolled her onto her back pressing his body full length over hers.

"This seems like the best maneuver. Butt naked and beneath me. Then I can truly keep an eye on you." He leaned down and kissed her, nipping her neck until she started to squirm. "Dammit, what was your father thinking when he directed me this order? We may never leave this bed."

"I can't always read my Pops mind, but don't you go and start thinking you can control me by all this great sex. Just forget about it, LC."

Rapidly his mood changed. She knew why. It was the reference to his rank. Bringing his mind right back to the position they were in. Not the intimacy they were sharing. But the one she wished was not upon them due to her meddling.

"Let's shower. Then we can discuss the day's events." He rose and walked from the room to the bathroom. She heard the water start and got up from the rumpled sheets smiling, bare ass naked, and joined him in there. *Why not*, she thought. *There is still some time to take advantage of him.*

Maggie could feel his intense stare, eyes raking her head to toe as she walked into the steam ahead of him.

Biting her lower lip trying to keep it all in perspective, his words penetrated bringing her back to reality.

"I thought you may resist, woman thing and all, for not having your personal stuff with you."

She licked a drop off one of his nipples. "Oh, you mean shampoo and curling iron stuff, right?" She could feel how he responded to her touch.

"Shit. You are trouble. A lot more than your Pops will ever know."

She giggled. "Right now, I think you and I need to finish this meeting."

Toweling off, she slid back into her previous night's clothes feeling like a brand-new woman. A bit conscious of little make-up she roused around in her crossbody bag and discovered few things still in there that would help her to feel better. *Hard to face a handsome man like this in the morning*, she thought, *without looking a bit more polished.*

He was in his office when she passed by, halted, stepped slightly backward and leaned inside the doorframe. "What is your preference? Coffee or tea? Black, cream, sugar?"

"Coffee in the morning. Put in an extra scoop in the brew. I like the java jolt. Cream will do."

He seemed engrossed as another thought took hold. "Why don't you let me snoop around the kitchen. I'll rustle up breakfast while I make your coffee."

"Have at it."

Rummaging, Maggie found enough food to make an egg and bread strata. Then wondered if she had enough time to allow it to bake. She called out to him. "Can you hear me from there?"

"Yes."

She softly laughed believing he could hear a pin drop in the garage. "How much time before we leave?"

"Unclear. I'm working the better part of an hour at least."

Forty minutes into the bake she checked it and it looked nearly done. It just needed five or ten minutes more. Maggie had just finished viewing and responding to the last of her emails on her cellphone when she felt his arms come around her, cheek pressed against hers. "Smells damn good. Enough to get me up from working and come and find out what you've concocted." He left her and went over and opened the oven door then glanced up at her.

"Okay, you may turn out to surprise me again. I didn't figure you for any kind of a cook." His grin was devilishly handsome as she raised both brows.

She hopped off the stool and grabbed the hand towel removing the hot dish from the oven and set it up on the burners to rest for a few minutes before they delved in. "I'm going to ignore that. It's a Spanish Strata. You may need to restock. I used a few items from the fridge."

"You carry this recipe around in your head?"

"It's not that difficult I can assure you. A few leftovers and that's it."

Two plates were sitting next to the spatula. "Do you want another cup of coffee? I made enough." He looked behind and poured it into his mug, adding cream.

"I see you have tea. Good. How much longer before we eat that?"

"It really is piping hot and needs to cool down. Why don't you go and make the bed, reload all your stored weapons and run a 5K? Then come back. Shouldn't take you more than fifteen minutes."

He took the hand towel swirling it up as she bolted from the kitchen down the hall. She knew the sting of that especially if the tip of the towel was wet. Her brother, sister and her use to do it all the time to each other. When they had dish duty and were still all under their parent's roof.

He was hot on her heels, grabbing and missing, as she bolted up and over his king-sized bed keeping it between them.

"You planned this!

"No, you brought it on yourself with that sharp tongue. But since we are here, and you said we need to kill ten minutes," he walked over the top of the bed so fast she had no time to run the other way, "we can stay in here until it's ready."

In a split second she was pinned beneath him.

Her face flushed, eyes glowing, Doug rolled her on top of him. "You seem to like me on top, soldier, any particular reason for that?" Her boldness caught him by surprise. But that was not all. He knew this was dangerous. Allowing her penetration into his heart. *Fuck*, he internally yelled at himself. *This is my fault. I should not have suggested this to the General. She's going to be darn right angry if she ever finds out it was my idea.*

Having no clue what her next move may be, he kept her legs pinned beneath his own. "I've got to tell you something. When I said your father had ordered me to keep you under my wing, I stretched it a bit."

She stared at him not uttering a word.

"I offered to keep you here and he readily agreed it was the right decision for now."

"Are you telling me for selfish reasons of your own you did that?"

That damn grin of his was nearly Maggie's undoing.

"Yeah, call it man lust if it must be labeled."

"A hostage." She smiled up at him lifting her head and bringing their lips closer. "But Pops agreed?"

"He sure did."

"He'd be pissed as hell, LC. I didn't pull the fast one. You did."

"Somehow, I think your old man pulled one over on me."

Her grin grew. "You were not sure of my reaction that's why you have my legs pinned down. Well now... that's interesting."

"To prevent unruly ideas. Of which you seem to be overflowing in. Do you think we can eat now?"

"I rather enjoy the pillow talk. But yes. I'm sure it's cooled down enough. Besides, I'm starved."

He had two heaping platefuls as Maggie's own stomach was filling up watching him begin to consume a third. "This is amazing. You've got to make it again."

"Hmm. Comment to be released another time, LC. But it is good. I'm glad you had those jalapenos and spicy cheese. Added a true hot Spanish flair to it if you like it kicked up a notch."

"Believe me, woman, the hotter the better when it comes to you."

Removing the dishes Maggie could feel the heat on her cheeks. She was blushing again wondering what this man did to make her feel so different?

"Let's finish up and head to your place and look things over."

"Do you think I can stay there tonight?"

"Absolutely not. But we can pick up what you need for another night or two as a precaution. That I was dead serious on and so is the General."

"Can we stop at the package store on the way back?"

"Actually, I have something else in mind. A diversion. How about a ride?"

"What, on your motorcycle?"

"Yes, thought we could meander down to Cornwall. Seems like a good day. Are you game?"

"What's the motive? You trying to get me out of town?"

He stopped reaching for his Rover keys and eyed her cautiously. "You got to stop doing that. It's like you're invading my thoughts. Someplace I'd like you to stay out of."

"Nice diversion, but it won't work. Answer the question." She was following him out of the kitchen to the breezeway and into the garage where he opened her door. "Smart ass, the General advised as much. Clearly, I didn't believe him. I figured it was an overly loving father. I see I'm wrong again."

"Ah, don't let it linger." She was enjoying the back and forth."

"Your dossier said you went to Oxford. That didn't surprise me. But seriously, you should have been grabbed by MI5 at least. Are you aware they recruit the brainier types from both schools?"

Appreciating the compliment, she toyed with telling him. "MI5 and 6 tried to recruit me against the wishes of my Pop since I had, well, you know, run-ins with them every so often. Ok, stop looking at me with that sadistic smile. I got into places I shouldn't have been and didn't leave well enough alone when I should've. So there. A once in a lifetime omission of guilt. But I did manage to gain contacts and information they couldn't. Seems I still can, eh? But don't you dare tell my father I made this statement. I will vehemently deny every word of it."

He roared with laughter. "You can hold a conversation with no one in the room, Maggie. I don't know quite what to do with you outside the bedroom."

She reached over as he grabbed her hand giving it a squeeze. "I'm not at a loss for what you need there."

She grinned. "You got that right."

"Is your car out back?"

"Yes, pull around through this alley and we can enter from a different access. It's more secluded and would be better for us. Lower visibility, less lighting."

He stopped the Rover and parked it. "I take it you've had situations before where you needed to get into your flat in a more cautious way?" He continued, "This seems like a prime location. Let's head in through the back. Let me go ahead of you. Hand over your keys."

He took them as they reached the door. A strong arm came up blocking her as he removed a penlight and shined it into the lock then swept it entirely around the frame. That's when things really got interesting. He inserted the key and waved her along as he diligently went from room to room with something that was on his watch. "Wow." She breathed out. "This is just like James freaking Bond shit."

"Shut up. I heard that. I need silence." She knew without looking he was smiling.

***

She had to admit to being completely engrossed and amazed at his training. He was the real thing. Pointing to a specific spot just inside the living room, Maggie stood still realizing Doug wanted her to remain there until he signaled or spoke.

Minutes ticked by and she wished he would hurry. The tea had kicked in and she had to use the bathroom. But he had to be sure checking everything that she would touch, press, push, grab, secure, sit on. But she was growing impatient. Then her curiosity turned to anxiety. He walked back in from the kitchen and halted at her writing desk. Jotting something hastily down, he returned and handed it to her.

She read the note. "Have Sasha or one of your lady friends call you on the house phone. This is what you will say." She handed him back the note and removed her cellphone putting it in silence mode and text Sasha.

The home phone rang blaring through the rooms as she nearly jumped out of her skin and hurried to answer.

"Maggie, here."

"Hey, Sasha, what's up?" She listened on as her friend continued the preplanned dialogue to perfection. "I rang you last night and sent you a text. What's going on? Where'd you go after Barney's?"

"I met up with my sister, Roger, and the kids. We headed to the coast. They wanted me to see their new weekend retreat. I guess my cellphone must not come in well there. But in all honesty, I didn't check. I was having a blast with the kids."

"Do you want to meet up tonight?"

"Can't. I have some work to do. Then I'm meeting my parents and will probably hang out with them in York for a day or so. I may take Monday off. I'm not sure yet."

"If things change ring me."

"Okay, will do." Maggie put the receiver back in the cradle and looked around. He had left the apartment. She walked into her bedroom taking out of a closet a small duffle roller, set it up on the bed and began grabbing clothes.

Out of the bathroom with all her essentials, she left the roller in the living room while taking out a recyclable cloth grocery sack and filled it with things from the refrigerator. Slinging that over her shoulder, Maggie just knew he had taken her keys. So rolled her duffle out taking the rear stairs and exited outside.

She slid onto the soft leather driver's seat of her BMW placing her bags on the seat next to her noticing the keys were in the ignition. Shifting into first, she left the way they had come. Then noticed his rig was vacant from the parking spot. Driving slowly through the alley and out onto the main road heading to Chepstow, she pushed the radio button on and relaxed while sounds of Mozart filled the inside of the car.

The ride took less than twenty minutes as she turned into his driveway and one of the empty garage bays. He pulled in right beside as they shut off vehicles and got out.

Walking around, Maggie grabbed bags as he reached in and put his hands on hers. "I'll get them, you did great."

"Wow, that was really eerie. The hairs all over my body are still standing straight." She walked in ahead of him hardly able to wait for him to divulge what he had uncovered back at her apartment.

He set the sack full of kitchen stuff down on the counter letting her take care of that. Then headed with her bag down the hall leaving it on a corner chair in his bedroom.

"Did you bring enough supplies?" A small smile toyed on those lips of his.

"Never mind that, what did you discover?"

"Bugs. Loads of them. Not the type an exterminator can come in and get rid of. Your place has been accessed by a pro. It's apparent you are under suspicion and it's by the dirty hands of MI5. I recognized the listening devices and house no doubt they are theirs. It's clear who was in there, Maggie, it was Perkins. There are no explosives. But I want you to pay close attention to me now. When you go anyplace at all, you need to be aware of your surroundings. Always. People, events, gatherings, everything. Especially your cellphone and laptop. Don't, and I repeat, don't let them leave your side. Not even for a split-second. No one uses them but you. Period."

She shook. Arms crossing over her chest as if to hold her body together. Doug's initial reaction was to take her in his and lend comfort. But he held his ground. She needed to work through this. Understand it was serious shit. *She did bring this on herself,* he thought *and would require every bit of strength to get through it.* Toughening her up more was going to be imperative.

"Okay. What else?"

"I will be part of a team that will sweep your office Monday morning to make sure it is clear. Zamir will monitor Perkins. He's shrewd and I trust his judgment completely. If you want to finish putting your things away go ahead. Then come into the office. We can discuss more detail there." He turned abruptly, almost absently, Maggie thought, watching him walk down the hall. As her body went into shock and mind went well into overdrive. She felt so alone.

"Does this mean our field trip is canceled?"

"Yup."

 "That's all right."

He knew it wasn't and offered no words of comfort.

# Chapter Ten

Standing just inside the doorframe of his office, Maggie didn't enter. Oddly enough feeling a bit strange now. It was just a touch of some kind of déjà vu. When putting things away in the kitchen, it had felt like she'd been doing that for twenty years in this man's home. Yet the idea of unpacking the duffle rattled her.

He glanced up. "I'm almost finished. Come in and take a seat."

Instead, she strolled along one wall looking at pictures of him and his men. It was apparent he had spent much of his adult life serving in the British Army. He was a proud man. Could see it clearly. Staring at them, she knew he had done tours in Northern Ireland, Sierra Leone, and the Gulf. Other areas could not be identified.

Finally, she reached his desk and vacant chair on the side of it and plopped down. Something was different with him too. She could tell by the look in his eyes.

"What is it now, do you have questions?

"Nope but you sure are sly one. Rather a bit of a cheeky monkey."

"Ah, your first term of endearment for me. Pops used to call me that when I was little. Did he tell you that? Surely it was not in my dossier."

"Nope, it just seemed to roll off the tongue."

She giggled, relaxing a bit.

"Bring back memories?"

"It sure does. He was a ruthless, focused, hard-ass military man and still is. But would often cut the three of us slack when Mum would bear down on us with one of her own brand of attacks. They make a helluva-good team."

He lifted his boots off the top of the desk and swerved his chair close to hers grabbing both hands. "I think you will stay longer than a few days. If you need more stuff, we'll just go buy it."

"It's bad?" She chewed on her bottom lip.

"Yes."

"What can you disclose from INTEL?"

He ran his left hand up through his hair and kept the right messaging both of her palms. She glanced down marveling how both fit into one of his. But there was more. His hand was strong, warm and very comforting. It was hard for her to digest these hands had probably killed others. Many times.

"I'll know more when Zamir finishes his assessment of Perkins. He's meeting up with her tonight. As a matter of fact, so will I."

"I don't mind you leaving me here alone, but can you secure me a pistol? I can shoot quite well."

He had toyed with this idea already and stood to take her by the hand clutching it within his own. Then walked them out of the office stopping at a hallway door. Punching in a series of codes the door sprang open with lights illuminating the stairway down.

"You are not going to trick me into going down there then lock me up, are you?" His laugh bordered on evil as she hesitated, holding back as he tugged her along down several steps.

Then Maggie's eyes opened wider. "Holy shit. This is amazing."

"I've never in my day seen holy shit, Maggie, have you?"

"Cut it out. What in the world is this place beside your arsenal? Oh my God, it is a bloody command center. Are you sure you are only a Lieutenant Colonel? Do you have people working for you here hidden away someplace? Where's James Bond? Can he keep me company while you are gone?"

That teasing didn't go unnoticed. But for them both time was not a luxury right now. He chose to ignore her questions. "You said you wanted a weapon, right?"

"No, LC, I said I wanted a pistol. I should have watched the code you entered. I think I could retry it by the tone I heard."

He stopped dead in his tracks as she landed hard up against him. "You'd better not. That keypad is more than tone sensitive. It is also sensitive to my prints only. You could cause a *very* large issue here."

"For crying out loud I'm glad you told me. I might have been a bit too curious later when you were gone, and I was bored…." Her tone deadpan serious.

He shook his head. "You could turn out to be a royal pain in the ass. Now come along," as he pulled her further into another room. Her jaw dropped. It just kept going on until they arrived at a final one.

She stepped in behind him, eyes truly bulging. "LC, this is a fucking firing range."

Opening two heavy wooden cabinet doors he stepped aside. "Pick your pleasure."

She immediately reached for the Sig Sauer P238 Tactical Laser with custom aluminum grips. Turning it sideways in her hand, Maggie smiled inwardly loving this gun. If indeed one could place passion on an object of death. She had fired one many time with Pop at the range outside of the base in York. It was snug and powerful. Exactly her type of weapon.

"Used this once before I see. why am I not surprised?"

Ignoring him, deep in concentration, she took out a pair of safety glasses and placed them on. Checked the safety was engaged, secured a six-round mag then turned, standing in front of him. Removing the safety, she engaged the slide serration and pointed the red tactical laser at the furthest target and shot. Her aim was dead on.

Stepping back, she fired at the closest. Bullseye. Clicking the safety, she didn't hand it back. Just removed the mag and placed it in her pocket, set the glasses on the shelf then grinned, shaking her head slightly.

He was grinning back.

"I'd like a few extra mags. Can I keep this outside the home in case I need it? Would you have a low-profile holster in the event I want to secure it in a private area of my body?"

"You do your father proud, Maggie. Yes, you can take it with you. I assume you already have a permit?"

"My father is a General. I am all set, LC."

He took two extra mags from the slotted draw beneath the presentation of handguns and a holster off the hook. Then handed it all to her. "I have to leave soon so let's head up. I want to brief you on my home security system and exit routes."

At the top of the steps, he shut the door as a beep sounded confirmed the door was locked tight. "I'm beginning to feel like a prisoner, Doug, I may need to get outside. Is that possible?"

"Sure, this way." He led her back toward the living room, opened another door into the dining area then out to a large backyard. She was completely surprised. It had trees, shrubs and even a bird feeder with actual seed in it.

"You've got to be kidding me. Do you mow a lawn and feed birds? You better not be using them for target practice."

Not awaiting his response, Maggie was like a kid at the seashore, sand so inviting She kicked off her shoes, nearly tumbled over removing socks then walked in the soft grass. "Ah, this is just what I needed. Now, how about saying I can go further afield and take a short stroll. Better yet a bike ride?"

"No can do. This is a secure area. But beyond our perimeter you are off limits. Don't horse shit around with me and say you won't try anything. Just don't do it."

His tart and angry words hit home. "What about when I'm at the office. Can I use the exercise room at least? Honestly, I can't remain immobile. I'm used to the activity. I'll go nuts. You can't expect me to just lie dormant."

She stared at him waiting for a reply. Anything. But it appeared to Maggie that he was deep in contemplation about her and what to do. He seemed a bit off his edge to her.

"You are not liking this, don't try and fool me. Regardless of whose decision this was, you are feeling my presence here as more than an intrusion. I get it."

He started to speak but she moved back slightly and held up both hands toward him. "Let's leave it at that. So, can I do anything I just asked?"

"I don't know. Hell, Maggie, I'll see. This may not be long at all. We're just taking precautions for your own good. You understand that don't you?"

*Yes*, she thought. *Now, Doug, we are getting to the crux of it. You too are feeling trapped.* Before she could begin a defensive argument, his next words really struck home.

"Would you prefer to take an LOA and head home to your parents for a few days? I'm sure the Professor would understand, and you could still work from there."

She pursed her lips while glancing down at bare feet.

"No, that's running, and it would look suspicious. Let me get this prioritized. To allow it all to sink in."

"Right. Fine. Now the only one that may suspect you know more is Perkins. But, she cannot be removed until the full degree of her cover is known. Zamir is monitoring her when you are with me. So, what's the old rule of warfare?"

Walking back inside together, they spoke in unison. "Keep your friends close and your enemies closer."

But Maggie had another idea. "Right, so let me bump into her Monday and engage her in conversation. I can pull it off. She will walk away believing I'm no threat at all. You can assist greatly here by suggesting she locate me. Sending her my way. I need her trust and so do you and Zamir. Their group's curiosity needs to be halted dead in its tracks. Don't you agree?"

His cellphone vibrated just as he was about to launch his opinion. Stopping, he read the message from Zamir; "*nineteen-thirty, waterfront.*"

"Was that from him?"

"Yes, we are all meeting at a public location to review the latest intelligence information."

"Does she know that you and Zamir prevented the bombing in Edinburgh at St. George's Square?"

The look on his face said it all. She had guessed right. "You know what? You have to stop taking it one move further and just back down." His tone was angry as he stood straight. All at once Maggie felt like a wounded creature and wanted nothing more than to hide. Get out. To get out quickly and right now.

She backed away one step as he grabbed her by the arm. "I was there, Doug," she whispered. Refusing to flinch even with his steel grip hurting like hell. "I saw the coroner's car and all the special police. I listened to that live broadcast on BBC2, and nowhere at my event could you be seen. You didn't find that location an issue at all. It doesn't take a rocket scientist to figure out what you and Zamir did. He is a trained killer. You both are."

He released her then, grabbed a small gear bag and stormed out of the house. She let him go. It was too early for his meeting and he'd not reviewed evacuation procedures. Sitting down in a comfy chair near the window, she looked out over the large acreage he held and wondered who took care of the grounds. Surely, he must hire out being away from home so often plus spending time at that temporary flat near his teaching assignment. She wondered if he even had a teaching degree at all. Probably not.

She found the remote and hit the button as the walled panels slid apart and into their slots presenting a large screen television. Miss Marple was on Mystery Theatre as she sat back and realized her shoes and socks were still outside. Walking out, she could hear his voice, angry and deep. Unable to refrain, Maggie quietly inched closer.

"She's a bit high-strung, bitchy and quite spoiled. Shit, this is not what I signed up for, babysitting the General's daughter. But I've been given orders. This is not what should have brought me out of retirement. I'm needed elsewhere."

There was a pause in the conversation as a bug of some kind kept buzzing by her ear. She swatted at it until it finally flew off. Listening on, anger rose until it peaked with intense hurt. "Yeah, Zamir, the *perks* are great. But, I have no plans on pursuing this further when it's said and done."

*Fuck you*, she nearly spewed out. *Did you think I am that stupid? That spoiled to not have a pinch of common sense?* She was not spoiled rotten. Not used her family name to gain things. Had paid for her own schooling and still paid for all her own needs. Apartment. Other shit and proud of that. Damn, why did his words dig so deeply? Resting palms over her heaving chest, a plan formed in her head that was born out of two choices. Fight or flight. A firm decision was made. It was time for flight.

Reaching into her pocket while quickly moving to the further part of the yard, she rang her sister. "Beth, I need your help."

"Maggie? What the hell is it now? I know that tone."

"Here's what I want you to do."

Back inside, Maggie sat down setting her shoes beside her and put on socks. Miss Marple was still sleuthing so she watched and waited. Her leg was swinging over the other leg as tears formed in her eyes. What did he mean by '*perks*?' Had he been fluffing overusing the word 'sex?' Oh, Lord, it was all just shit! He had used her because he was stuck here. What an idiot she was falling for him. There was no connection between them. Just her deep desire for it. *Fool*, she chastised herself silently. *Damn stupid fool.*

The sound of the breezeway door slamming shut caused her to momentarily hold a breath.

"Your father has contacted me. Apparently, your sister needs you. When you didn't answer your cellphone, she rang him concerned you may be in trouble. Seems she's aware of all your past antics as well, huh, Maggie? Anyway, you are free to leave here and go to your sister's place. You can head out right now. Unfortunately, I can't bring you. He is aware of my meeting."

The words running rampant in her head right now were not fit to be heard by anyone. Clutching, no digging her nails into the chair arms, Maggie internally demanded a halt to unnecessary internal thoughts. Then felt a glimmer of happiness at besting him. Finally, raging blood pressure settled as she looked up into his perplexed face.

"What?"

He scrutinized her closely. A trained eye. She had to be very, very careful until she got clear of him and this house. As if an angel above knew she needed immediate assistance, her cellphone vibrated.

"Maggie, here. Oh, hi, Beth. Yeah sorry, I didn't see your text earlier. I was wrapped up in something, but… what? Yes, I can come right away if you'd like. I'm free. Is everyone all right?" There was a pause while she looked up at him and remained in tight eye contact not wavering one iota. Tone changing from casual to concerned.

"If you are sure, okay then. I will pack up some things and be on my way shortly." She stood, ready to kick him in the balls but refrained and stepped around and headed toward the bedroom to claim her bag. Then stopped and turned slightly avoiding direct eye contact.

"Do you mind if I retain the pistol for a while?"

"Listen, I have a feeling you just pulled one on me." She nearly laughed as he pointed a finger at her. Instead, she looked at him, perplexed.

"If I find out you did, there will be no stone left unturned until I locate you. Mark my words. Understood?"

"I really am not following you, Doug. It's my sister. She needs me. Period. I never unpacked my bag. Would you mind grabbing that and I'll gather up a few things from the kitchen? I'd appreciate it."

Anger was written all over his face as she moved on toward the kitchen feeling damn smug. As they met in the garage and she put in the BMW the small bag of groceries, it then occurred to her something else needed to be said to seal this.

"If you need to reach me I'll keep my cellphone handy. I'm not sure what's going on down there, but I may stay until Monday then drive up from Cornwall."

Touching his arm, Maggie wanted to draw blood. Instead, she softly smiled. "Take care." Then climbed into the car, started it up and drove off observing him walk outside the large garage, hands on hips. A large smile appeared on her face. He'd never hunt her down. Would not dare. She would then use her father as a powerful barrier.

All this success was short lived when suddenly she felt her skin prickle, stomach tighten up. "Oh, fuck, what now? Was I wrong in doing this?" An eerie silence permeated the inside of the car as she continued to drive along. But her stupid, stubborn and unrelenting pride had driven her to it and never was she one to back down. Two points her father had driven home to them all; never be in a position where you have to say sorry, and never back down. Onward she drove taking the entrance onto the motorway toward Clevendon.

Her cellphone was on the dash as she hit the phone app. "Call Sasha." The ring seemed loud on speakerphone as it echoed around the inside of the BMW.

"Hey, are you going to tell me now why all the drama?" There was an uncomfortable pause. "Where are you?"

"On my way, I'll be there in less than fifteen minutes and will explain what I can then."

\*\*\*

Doors could not be slammed any harder than Hawk was right now when he reentered the house. "Bitch," he growled out. Then sauntered through noticing the door from the dining room to the backyard was ajar. Remembering how she had followed him in and he had shut and latched it. Walking out he looked around, it must have been when she retrieved her socks and shoes.

Then over by the corner of the garage, a few feet from the window where he was talking with Zamir, he spotted an earring. Her shoes had not been in this area, nor anywhere in this vicinity. He was sure of it.

The earring sat in the palm of his hand as anger, such as he had not known in years, sprang forth. She had done this. Duped him. Had called her sister with some cockney story who then rang their father and the girls plan hatched. Oh, how pissed the General would be when he realized Maggie had done it to him again. This time using her own sister as bait.

Latching the back door, Hawk entered his study and hit the key on his laptop entering Interpol's website. Elizabeth and Roger Summers names were accessed as their complete financial records were opened for his review. He cared little for the goodly amount in there. All he wanted was to see if they had indeed purchased a second home in Cornwall. He slammed his fist on the desk causing several items to fly off onto the floor.

"Wench!" She had probably gone out to get her shoes and socks and heard his voice and went over and eavesdropped. Oh, Fuck. He had been pissing nails, spitting bullets and angry as hell when he was talking with Zamir.

He glared back at the computer screen. They had just purchased a second home all right, but it was on the Isle of Wight. He shut it off, got up, then locked the room. Gear loaded in the Rover already, he turned the key in the ignition and shifted into reverse and drove away toward Bristol. He lifted the cellphone off the dash and made a quick call, glad the General's wife picked up. Somehow her soft tone reminded him instantly of Maggie's.

"Anne, Douglas Hawthorne here. I'm looking for Beth and Roger's new number."

"Sure, Hawk, are things ok? My husband said if you rang to provide help in any way I can."

"Yes, it's all good, no worries. I just wanted to talk with Beth for a quick moment."

Thanking her, he punched in the number as Beth quickly picked up. Her voice shaky, she answered. Instantly Hawk knew why.

"Beth, Douglas Hawthorne, is Maggie there yet?" There was a giant pause on the other end while he was sure she collected her thoughts or was texting her sister with maddening speed.

"No, but she's on her way. I'm not sure when she will arrive. I don't think she left your place with enough time to get here."

"Really, I was thinking it wouldn't take her that long to get to the Isle."

She gasped out loud totally taken by surprise. "What?"

"Yeah, don't bother to contact her. I'll do that myself. Shortly. Have a good night."

He hung up and made one more call. "General, you and I have both been played for a fool. We need to talk. I hope you have a few minutes."

# Chapter Eleven

"Damn that daughter of mine! Both! I know this is about them. Go ahead, Hawk, report."

"General, I left her inside my home and went out to the garage to ward off a bit of anger at her attitude. I received a call from Zamir and we exchanged a few words about her. I had no knowledge she had moved to the backyard area near the garage and overheard the conversation. I believe I was venting trying to remove the thorn she put on my side and she overheard. I admit her reaction was quick, resourceful and swift. She played me for a fool. Using you."

"Damn, chit. She always was a handful. I surmise she used Beth and Roger? That does not surprise me. Her sister would do anything for Maggie. Where did she say she was headed?"

"To their new vacation home, Sir, in Cornwall."

"Hell, and be gone. They did buy a second joint but it's on the Isle of Wight."

"I know that now, General, the real question is where the hell is Maggie? I am meeting Perkins and Zamir shortly and have no time to go looking. But clearly, she's up to something and crap, General, I'm sure it will land her in hot water. Prepare yourself, again. I'll contact INTEL and have them run down her cellphone location."

"Negative. She's too smart for that. Probably has already disengaged the GPS or shut the damn thing off. I believe she's in the clear if she's out of our hair and headed south away from Bristol. Let her have her jaunt and think about what she'll do next. I will place an agent near her apartment and monitor for activity. If she is with any of those friends she hangs around with, Lord knows where the hell she may be. You go about your business now, Hawk."

"Roger that, I'll report back later."

Hawk teetered between laughter and anger comfortable that Maggie was now in the hands of the General. Pulling off the main road and into the parking garage, he flashed the Rover's lights once to signal then locked the vehicle up. Leaning against the cold metal railing, he glanced toward the Radisson. Knowing she would not be stupid enough to go home. All the same, he'd check it out after the meeting.

Zamir and Perkins approached. *This is more like it*, Hawk thought, *not that shit she was putting him through before.*

Hawk nodded to them both. "Perkins, Zamir, what's up?"

Zamir stared at him briefly as Perkins moved closer to them. "I have a copy of the meeting." She handed them a flash drive. "We are not getting closer to having enough to bring them in. This video will show you their meetings are peaceful enough with no real harm going on there. I couldn't detect any hidden messages being transferred. You review it and see what you find. We need more time. I need more time."

"That's not going to work, Perkins, we need to evaluate this now and escalate the process." Hawk glanced at Zamir seeing a flicker of something come across his face before it was quickly masked as he spoke.

"This needs to be expedited. Command wants this taken care of yesterday. I have other places to be."

"Put them off longer. It's just too soon."

Hawk just listened having deposited the bogus flash drive into his inside jacket pocket. Looking forward to comparing it with the one Maggie provided later when he arrived back at his house in Chepstow. He spoke up now putting an end to the speculation about her.

"I've finished the report on Cohen, she's clean, Perkins. But I want you to engage her more often. Watch what she does. But HQ has finalized their reports. She's not an issue and has been removed from the suspect manifest. This is just a precaution."

She nodded.

"How much time are you requesting?"

"Hawk, maybe two weeks. Do we have leads on their next hit?"

"Negative. Use your time wisely. What about Zafir's location?"

"Nothing. The background from student affairs doesn't match at all. It has him listed as residing in a building that has been closed for renovations. It appears someone has not entered the correct data. I'm on that. I've been in touch with campus housing and they're researching it for me."

"Damn, Perkins, the fucking body count is piling up. Who knows where their next strike may be. You need to move faster, get this done."

***

Nodding, feeling somewhat relieved and smug, Perkins left confident she had pulled it off. When they viewed the flash drive of the meeting, she was positive the extra time needed would be given. Pulling into her parking spot and locking the car, she rang Zafir on a newly purchased cellphone.

"It went well. No, they didn't ask many questions. The maximum we can bank on is two weeks. Then they will increase manpower on us." She paused glancing around. "I'll see you soon." Hung up and went into her apartment.

***

Zamir had removed his iPad and inserted the flash drive as they monitored it briefly, "What do you think?"

"She's crap. If Maggie hadn't seen that real video, then we'd be two steps behind. Perkins is shit."

"She could conveniently disappear now."

"Perkins? No. She's got to fry. A strong message will be delivered out into the field."

"What are your ideas on the next location?"

"Nada, waiting for INTEL to '*run their data*' and see what they come up with. You and I could both be eighty before that happens. We need to break in further. I'm half toying with using Maggie. She's a knack for cutting through the crap and getting the job done when it's essential."

"What's your plan? Or *who* is your plan? Do you think she's got what it takes?"

He had to grin visualizing her in the basement selecting the handgun as if it was a long-lost lover. "You should have seen her using the SIG. That damn female has managed to escape me using all the means at her disposal and using them very well. She basically fucked us all including her own father."

"Oh, I'm sure that went over really well."

"He's used to this. I am damn well not. Feels like I need to throw the towel in. I don't want any part of her bull-shit. Not that I've got the patience to bother much more with her beyond gaining our end."

"Ah, that I doubt. I'm sure you're just pissed she's backed you up to the wall against your will. Don't you think?"

"Kiss my ass."

"So, sleeping with her didn't alter anything?"

"Nope."

"Liar."

"Fuck off."

Zamir slapped his long-time contact on the back with a resounding thud, placed the iPad inside its case and walked off, spewing over a shoulder, "You'll eat your words. I'd stick my neck out on it. You'll be chasing her again before long. She's a lot more than fluff and you know it."

Turning on his heels and briskly walking away from the waterfront, Hawk entered the Radisson and wrapped on the hotel room door loud and clear.

One of the team agents monitoring Maggie's apartment opened it up. "Hawk, didn't expect a personal visit."

"You got anything?"

"Nope, no lights, the blinds are up as you left them earlier and we've seen no activity at all. The surveillance cameras around the perimeter have not picked her or any of her friend's vehicles. We ran cellphone usage and it's bizarre. Almost like she's vanished."

Hardly the news Hawk wanted so he didn't even stick around. Nodding on his way out and slamming the door shut, he took the back stairwell down to the lot.

Walking back along the waterfront to the parking garage he stopped, leaning up against his Rover with keys in hand but did not unlock the doors. All the addresses had been run on all four of her friends. HQ did not feel teams should be utilized to put them under surveillance due to funding. Instead, they had to be resourced to Perkins comings and goings and Zafir's cell group. He did not have the time now to drive to each location. Three were in the circumference of Bristol and one in Clevendon. "Oh yeah," he muttered into the night air. "That has to be it – Sasha is in Clevendon."

He rang up HQ. "Hawk here, I need the phone number and confirm the address of Sasha Lewis, Clevendon. STAT." He waited for the transmission to his cellphone while unlocking the door and starting the vehicle.

Leaning his head back against the neck cushion, emotions he didn't want to recognize tried their damnedest to rise. Hell, he knew she was pissed. Staged this thing with Beth and ran off. That was her MO. But one thing was perfectly clear. He had a job to do and she kept getting in the way.

His cellphone vibrated as he viewed the address provided by INTEL. Sasha's home was fifteen to twenty minutes away. But right now, he was beat. Done with it all. So, he drove off and headed home and was in bed in thirty minutes.

But sleep did not come quick enough. He could detect that lovely scent she wore all around the sheets. Rolling to one side an internal struggle began. One that he was not used too and glanced at the digital clock knowing a message to her now would probably not be answered. *The hell with it*, he thought. *She is just not worth it.*

***

"Maggie, why are you roaming at this hour? Are you ready to tell me what happened? Or, do I hit you with a sledgehammer, so you can sleep? Do you want a valium? Shot of something strong? What the hell is it?"

"Sasha, you and I have known each other since we were seven. I've always gotten myself into one scrape or another. This time is different. I don't know what to do."

"Can Pops help you?"

"He's already stuck his neck out for me and now I have to go at it alone. I don't want him compromised again."

"What about Hawthorne, can he step in?"

"No." She was not going to tell her she'd been with him. Had committed the cardinal sin and slept with him. How he had used her. But she honestly admitted to herself she allowed it to all happen. Screw him. She was done being nice, practical or predictable, done. It was time for a bit of growing up. Face facts and to stop getting into these messes. After this one, she was through, period. That quiet country house further south and cat sounded wonderful right about now.

"Can't you tell me why you made that crazy request to have me call you at your flat, on your home phone? What's up with that planned script? Did it work?"

"I'm not sure, I think so. But I can't explain it all right now."

"Mags, you are scary at times. Something tells me your shackles are up for a good reason."

"Yeah, there you are spot on."

"Okay, no more questions. Your room is ready. We are locked up tight for the night and the security system is engaged. Your car is in the garage with mine, so no one can gain access to it. Go on. Go to bed and try to rest. You know you can stay as long as you like." They hugged at her door.

"You are a saint, Sash, you have no idea. If I'm gone when you get up in the morning don't be pissed, okay? I have a lot to take care of."

"Where will you be?"

"Don't know yet. I'll sleep on it. But I'm quite sure it's better you don't know."

She hugged her again and stepped in leaving the door ajar. That damn deep voice played over in her head until she buried her nose in the pillow begging the saints and angels to make it stop. Just before sleep finally claimed her, she heard him again. As if he was talking while laying his head on the pillow next to hers. *"You got to stop doing that. Invading my thoughts…"* What had he meant by that? Just as shit stunk, Maggie knew it was too late to ask.

Finally, exhaustion claimed her as she managed to sleep until the sun started to lighten up the sky. As her eyes opened, she swung her legs out of bed, walked into the bathroom to clean up and then dressed. "I've got to get out of here," she whispered softly into the otherwise empty room.

\*\*\*

A persistent knocking sounded at Sasha's door as she climbed out of the shower, put on a robe and with caution, proceeded to the front. Peering out she saw a familiar face and opened it.

"Doug, what are you doing here, looking for Maggie? Come in. She must have slept through your knocking while I was showering." She moved aside and let him pass before closing the door. "Wait here, I'll go get her."

"No, I'll go. Otherwise, she may opt to climb out a back window. Which room is it?"

"Second door on the right, ah, yeah, go ahead down." Sasha went into the kitchen to start a pot of coffee and saw the note on the counter.

"Sash, thanks again, I had to bug out early. I'll be in touch soon, M."

Turning around she jumped, startled. He was standing right there, hands on hips with an angry look on his face.

"She's not in there," as he glanced at the paper in her hand. "Is that a note from her?" He didn't await a response taking it and reading it. He set it back on the counter, opened the door out to the garage and saw a slot vacant, door still closed.

"You have a security system and code, right?"

"She has the code. Come to think of it you are right. It should have toned a warning when I opened the front door. She must have shut it off when she departed." Hawk nodded, turned, then strode right out the front door. Sasha waited, believing he would slam it shut. But all she heard was the faint sound of a click.

She stood there totally perplexed. Immobile for a few seconds. Had this been a lover's spat and Maggie was holding out on her? What had happened to them? She shook her head totally not understanding any part of it. Picking up her cellphone she sent Maggie a message. "He was here."

The immediate response back was brief, "Thanks."

\*\*\*

Maggie parked her car three blocks from her apartment. Using the storage room access in the basement, she came up through the stairwell to her fourth-floor apartment and entered it without being seen. She assumed someone was monitoring the place. Crouching, she maneuvered around getting everything she needed and stuffed it all in a recycled shopping sack then exited the building. She figured no one heard her because no one showed up even when she reached her vehicle.

Back in the car, she headed toward a familiar place that was safe. Hawkhill House would do even if part of the name contained part of his. A slight smile creased her lips for a moment then disappeared. Hawkhill was a small bed and breakfast within twenty minutes commute from the office and a place she did not need to present ID. The clerk had said cash would work fine when she rang earlier and reserved under a bogus name. She pulled in and parked in the rear.

"Miss Wellington, welcome, we have a nice suite ready for you. How long will you be our guest?"

"A couple of nights. Perhaps longer. I'm not totally sure. How does your availability look for the rest of the week?"

He reviewed the flat screen computer monitor before him. "Excellent if you need to extend your stay. That will be one hundred pounds. We serve a full breakfast between seven and eight-thirty. If you need any supplies for your room; tea, cream, please ring or pop down and I or the Misses will help you."

"Thank you."

"Do you need help with your bags?"

"Yes, I have three and that would be lovely." He was such a gent helping her up the two flights of steps to her large two-room suite. Then waved off a tip as she removed some pound notes. "No, it is my pleasure."

Maggie smiled and locked the door behind him.

Hawkhill was just far enough away from Bristol and offered the country feel Maggie craved right about now. Just enough space between her, her family and Hawk to provide some semblance of peace. Taking out her netbook she quickly replied to several emails. Including Beth to advise she was settled and fine. Then finished with one to her father.

"Pops, I'm sorry I got you involved this time. I'm a bit ticked you and Hawthorne were going behind my back. But, I'm going to take a day away from you all and go to work tomorrow and resume my life. I'll talk to you and Mum soon." She hit send and shut the computer off. Any replies could wait for another time to be viewed. Setting it aside, key in hand, Maggie left the room and stopped at reception.

"Hello again, Miss Wellington, how can I help you?"

"I was thinking about going horseback riding. Is there anything local?"

"Well, yes. My brother and his wife have a riding establishment just a short walk through our back fields." He moved from the desk and pointed out beyond the patio. "Just over there. Their stable serves all levels of experience. Would you like me to give them a ring and let them know you are coming?"

"That would be wonderful."

He eyed her attire. "I see you are ready. Excellent. Just give me a minute."

"David, Peter here. Do you have a slot for one of our guests? He glanced at his watch, "excellent, I'll send her right along."

"Go ahead, Miss Wellington, they are expecting you shortly and have a slot open for ten-thirty on their one-hour and two-hour rides."

"Thank you very much." She meandered out through the fields enjoying the warm fall sun on her face. It was a gorgeous day to horseback ride along the coastal trails overlooking Bristol Harbor and Wales. When she returned she'd amble down to town and rent a bike and get a true day of exercise. Cellphone shut off and officially being ignored. At least until tomorrow. Today it was her day and she'd be damned if her Pops, friends or anyone would step into her world. She needed a reprieve and was taking it.

# Chapter Twelve

"What's your level of experience, Miss?"

"Average. I can post, trot and gallop."

"Follow me, we have a nice filly saddled up and the group is about to venture in approximately ten minutes. Would you prefer the two-hour tour?"

She handed over forty pounds. "Yes, and thank you for taking me on such short notice."

"It is our pleasure. Now if you would follow me?"

It felt wonderful to be back in the saddle as Maggie just listened to the chit-chat amongst the other riders as they rode the outer border of Clevendon Court. The brilliance of the leaves was magical. A kaleidoscope of colors off into the distance over the hills toward the bay. Weaving along the coastal path up to Weston, Maggie released a long sigh of contentment into the warming air feeling so refreshed at being right here, right now.

One of the young ladies ahead turned slightly in the saddle and engaged her for a moment. "I'd love a grand gallop down on the sand. Do you think they will do that for us?" Maggie grinned guessing she was all of thirteen. Charmed by her exuberance recalling such a time in her life when she felt like grabbing life by the horns and never letting go. She and Beth were always gulping down every moment with total unabashed excitement. Ah, to be so young and carefree again.

"Don't think so, look," she pointed just around the trails dusty bend. "Our starting point." The girl turned forward as Maggie pictured keen disappointment upon her face.

Dismounting, she thanked them again and strolled at a snail's pace back through the fields. Bending down along the way to pick a few late fall wildflowers for her room. Then stopped to gaze up at the cloudless blue sky, watching birds swoop overhead. This was one of her few 'ah' moments of late and Maggie felt wonderful to just be here.

"How was it?"

She smiled up into the owner's face.

"Just what I needed. I'm grateful you arranged that so quickly. Now I'm wondering if you can pull another rabbit out of your hat. Can I can pester you again?"

He smiled. "What would you like?"

"A bike. I'd like to cycle if I can with quite a few hours left before dark. Is there a local bike shop around?"

"Well, how about right here? We have a few bikes we keep in storage. Helmets included and sure the wife would be pleased to pack you a lunch."

*What a perfect place this is*, she thought. "Can I look at them? I'd love to take you up on your offer."

Following him around the back to a large garage, he opened another door and there they were. Three very appealing bikes as Maggie eyed one thinking it must be his wife's. The frame seemed right for her as well.

"I'd be very happy to pay you for as long as I use it," she paused knowing he was going to refuse. "Please, I insist. You've been so kind to me already."

His contemplation was short lived. "If you insist as it seems to be important to you. I'll just pop in to see the Mrs. and bring a lunch out to the desk for you to pick up. When you return the bike, just bring it in here and put the lock back in place."

"I sure will."

He left her while she wheeled the bike out of the storage unit, helmet dangling off a handlebar, and leaned it up against the side of a barn. Returning a few minutes later,

Maggie had changed clothes and went back to the desk. A smile grew on her face to see a paper bag lunch and water bottle right next to it.

Peddling while shifting to harder gears, Maggie knew the '*Mrs.*' Had quite a nice trail bike. Climbing up a bumpy path, the coastal route loomed straight up ahead.

The wind was crisp and at times quite strong along the route as her hands felt the biting cold. But she didn't care. The crowning glory of the day was that she had forgotten about Doug and all the issues happening. On the return the pull was too great. Stopping, Maggie set the bike against a rock, climbed to the top, took out her lunch bag and ate. Watching the ocean swells tumble in then sway out along the shore. She sighed.

*Fool.* She silently said. *I do hurt. Those words he said sting like bloody hell and I can't shake them. Damn him.* Drawing strength from deep within, she was glad just this one time she'd left her cellphone back in the room. For her resolve was weakening with every bite she chewed on the cucumber and mayo sandwich.

But even if she did ring him what would she say? Something like; *hey asshole, I'm not some spoiled brat. But, yeah, the sex was good, so thanks for that.*

She burst out laughing. The sound evaporating against the roar of the waves crashing against the rocky shoreline. Finishing up the half sandwich she reached inside and found a small baggie with two chocolate coconut drop cookies and smiled in earnest. "My favorite cookies. How the heck would she know that?"

Then her mood changed. Suddenly her hands came up as simultaneously tears started to flow down her cheeks. Leaving a nasty streak in its wake. She didn't care while touching cold fingertips to her face. She wondered if any cry could be considered good. Then shook her head several times trying to get a grip on these fraught emotions.

This was not love. It was hurt. Hard, hateful hurt and she wanted it to go away because the void left not being with him was nearly too much to bear. She had indeed run away again. As he had said before. Already knowing it was her trait. But in doing so had run smack dab into the hard wall of her emotional truth and had nowhere to go but backward. Backward into a past ridden with these same situations. To realize if things were ever going to change, *she* had to change.

Securing the bag on the bike rack with the Velcro straps, Maggie began the tougher ride up the trail back to the bed and breakfast. Securing the bike and helmet and locking the shed door, she felt the grime on her face and went in through the side noticing the owner was not at the desk. *Thank heavens*, she thought, *I must look a mess.*

Standing in front of the mirror she was mesmerized by the waif that looked back. Tear streaks, a haunted look of sadness stared and blue eyes pooling with tears. Again. Stripping naked right then and there, Maggie climbed into the shower and turned on the water allowing it to beat down as hot as she could stand. Glancing down, she watched the dirt empty into the drain and hoped along with it, some of her sorrows.

When she climbed into bed it was clear a longer stay was in order. That night her mind was blank. Tired from rigorous outdoor activities and the release of pent-up emotions. Finally, she slept.

Tom Petty's "*You Don't Know How I Feel*," woke her at seven in the morning as she sauntered into the shower and stood there for several minutes like a zombie. The piping hot water sprayed every inch of her that ached from riding yesterday. Although her body was tight and complaining, to Maggie, a little bit of pain felt good.

She'd take her time this morning and have that long leisurely breakfast in the wonderful dining room. What the hell, she deserved it. Now downstairs sitting comfortably in a chocolate silk suit with a red blouse, she kicked off her pumps and sipped a piping hot cup of strong Irish tea. In the background, softly playing, was a classical piece by Haydn. One she'd heard on the night they went to the symphony.

She was alone in the small, very well decorated breakfast lounge as outside the double-wide French doors to the patio hung several bird feeders. Recalling in his backyard how surprised she'd been he had those.

Just sitting there feeling like this was the calm before the storm, Maggie's mind drifted to that first night when he and Zamir had joined their party. Was that just a week ago? How do you feel like you know someone so deeply, yet, feel like you can't do without them in your life? Does it take thirty years to realize you love someone? Or, just thirty minutes? Was it all crazy and she along with it?

It seemed always easy to say thank you and move on. Or in Doug's case to lie and bug out. The reality was stark. It smacked her squarely in the face these days. It was true she had never really been in love. But something had happened in their short span together, and she knew it would do her no good to deny its existence.

After pushing the breakfast plate back and setting the napkin on top of the table, she rose, picked up her things, placed them in the car and headed out for the short ride to work. But something was different. She was different. The air inside the BMW was different. It felt like this was the longest ride of her life and it all felt terribly wrong.

Her solar plexus wrenched up into a tight ball and never settled.

\*\*\*

Caren pulled into the garage and parked on the second level. A good mood, even for a Monday, turned abruptly as she sat down at her desk. The frame of that witch, Perkins, was filling the door frame. Caren placed a hand up covering her nose. The scent of that woman's perfume filled the office nearly causing her to choke.

"Hi, Caren, is Maggie due in this morning?"

"Did you have an appointment with her, Susan?"

"No, but I wanted to discuss something with her of urgency."

"Is there anything I can help you with? If not, I can let her know to contact you as soon as she arrives."

Caren never liked Perkins. Recognizing from the get-go that she was extremely snobby, overbearing and not at all likable as Maggie. But she had other reasons as well.

"Would you happen to know why the meeting room for this past Friday night's group was changed at the last minute? I attended to represent the paper and went to the wrong area."

"Yes, in fact, I do. Maggie didn't do that. I did. She was out of town in Edinburgh on library business. I noticed the group's numbers grew. I had no choice but to move the room. Why? Was there an issue besides that?"

"So, Maggie had no idea?"

"No, as I said. Not at all."

Caren's grin grew as Perkins abruptly turned and walked off. She rose and glanced out toward the parking garage just in time to see Maggie's BMW coming down the drive.

***

Maggie pulled in at the parking garage across the road from the library and noticed immediately it was full. Normally she walked or cycled and came in a whole lot earlier than this. But today was different. She was in no rush. Grabbing her case, she locked her car and walked toward the ramp following the exit sign. Pausing, Maggie noticed Caren's vehicle in the first parking slot. Good, she was in already. Continuing in and across the street, she entered the library. Smiling at the receptionist, she took the stairs up toward her office.

"Good Morning. You look refreshed and must have had a great weekend. Get settled. I had a visit from Perkins and she had her panties in a snare again."

Maggie grinned. "So, when are you going to tell me how you really feel about her? You must have been in early. You have the first slot near the exit. I'm vehicles from you."

"Well, considering you are never late, I'd say this is a first. Do you want tea?"

"Nope, all set." Recalling the delay in departing for the Inn's sumptuous breakfast was delicious. "But thanks. When you have a chance pop in and give me the ditties on Susan."

It was near three when Caren did. "Sorry, I've been transcribing the Professor's notes and he must have had a busy weekend. Because nothing made much sense. Good thing I understand him so well, or it would all be a mess."

Maggie laughed knowing about his cellphone messages and how he left notes. His email etiquette was deplorable for a man of his stature. Thank heavens he used spell check on everything when he remembered.

"Sit, so tell me."

"Well, she stood in the doorway and gave me her sweet, wonderful, pain in the ass attitude."

"Those are not the details I was aiming for. Aim higher."

Caren smirked. "She wanted to know why you changed the room location for Zafir's group last Friday. I told her you had no knowledge. That I did it because of the group's size."

Maggie thought for a moment, pen tapping on her desktop. "But how would you know that the numbers increased? You may have let a cat out of the bag."

"Shit."

"Yeah, that word works. What else?"

"She wanted my total assurance that you had no knowledge and then walked off with not so much as a thank you, as normal. Maggie, I really detest that woman."

She had stopped listening to Caren, now deep in thought. "How many do you have for this week?"

"None, they have canceled. Zafir sent me a message saying he'll not be requiring the space any longer. They had secured a new location."

"How did Paul know where to set up cameras?"

"I advised him with the change."

Maggie didn't want to alarm Caren but had to put one final question out there. "Did she ask about my 'assistant'?"

"Nope, not a word." They could both hear Caren's phone ringing across the distance. "I have to get that so let me know if you need more?"

Maggie nodded as Caren rose and left while reaching into her bag and removed her cellphone. There were messages from her friends, so she replied she was fine, at work and would reach out soon. Then logged on to her personal email and read one from Pops.

"Your Mum and I are expecting to hear from you soon, Maggie. Contact when you can. Love, Pops."

She picked up the phone and rang them. "Hi, Mum, it's me. How's it going?"

"Maggie, are you at work? Are you, all right? As usual, your father gave me splintered details."

"I'm fine, Mum. Don't worry. Yes, I am working. It is all good. You can stop fretting now."

"Well, why the drama? You used your sister. Douglas Hawthorne called here as well looking for her phone number. Just what the dickens are you up to now?"

Maggie paused deciding how to answer. Clearly puzzled why he would have called her Mum. "No, I did not use her. I asked for help. She could have said no. She's done that before. No harm no foul. Is Pops out golfing?"

"Yes, with three cronies from the Army and will probably be home for dinner. I'm leaving with your Aunt Sofie for pea knuckle and will ring him and leave a voicemail I heard from you. Can we call you at home tonight?"

"Sure, but not on the home phone. I'm having trouble with the port not charging. I will go shopping soon and purchase new ones. Ring me on my cellphone, okay?"

'Okay, dear, love you."

"Love you both, Mum."

Maggie placed the cellphone down glancing at email. No messages from him as her spirits dampened. But had that been expected? *No, not really*, she thought. He was tougher at this game than even she was. Oh well, the sex had been fantastic. She'd leave it at that. Looking at the wilting flowers she picked them up off the desk and emptied them into the receptacle. Then placed the pretty crystal vase on the floor. She'd take that home sometime, clean it out and properly store it. Maybe by letting it slip out a back window to the pavement below. She smiled.

Grabbing the headset and placing it over her ear, she hit the speed dial for her sister. "Beth, Mag, what did he say to you?"

"Cripes, Maggie, I felt like I was on a damn witness stand. He has quite a manner about him, doesn't he?"

"I'm sorry you were on the other end of that. So, what did he want?" Maggie's voice came out testy and knew it would not hit Beth the right way.

"Listen, I tried as always to cover your ass. But he had it all figured out before he rang to see if you had arrived. He knows, Mags, you were not headed to Cornwall because we were on the Isle. Your little ploy didn't work on him." There was a long pause as Maggie inhaled sharply almost forgetting her sister was on the other end.

"Are you there?"

"Yeah, sorry Sis. I'll keep you out of this from here on. I'm at work and have a ton of things to do. I need to bug off. But I'll email you soon. Promise. Beth, I'm truly sorry. Love to you all."

\*\*\*

In the distance, outside, Maggie heard the tower clock chime six. As her stomach grumbled, she realized the day had gotten away from her and she had not eaten lunch. *Oh well*, she thought, *I'll grab a bite on the way back to the Inn.* Glancing out of her opened door, she realized how quiet the floor was. Everyone had left for the night except Caren. Across the hall her light was still on. Rising, she shut everything down and locked her door walking over there.

"You're still here. Do you need any help? I can stick around."

"No, I'm done. Hold on and I'll walk out with you."

On the way up the parking ramp, Maggie looked over at Caren who was on her right side. The air seemed charged around them as she spoke up. "Caren, what's wrong?"

"I don't know, really. It's this awful feeling I have in the pit of my stomach. Honestly, I've not had this since Steven blindsided me with news of his mistress and wanted a divorce."

"Five years and you've never had it since?"

She smiled faintly, shakily, at Maggie. "Yes, and it's creeping me out that I can't shake it."

"That's kind of odd, Caren. I've felt like that myself off and on all day since breakfast."

"I don't know. I hope it goes away soon. Who knows? Maybe the M is backed up and it will take me three hours to go three miles. Anyway, see you tomorrow." She had arrived at her car first.

"Bye, have a good night and if you need to talk call me on my cellphone, okay? I'll be around all night." Her voice drifted off as she moved further along into the parking garage.

Maggie arrived at her car, opened the passenger door and put her things in then moved around and pulled open the driver's side. Her gut wrenched tighter. She started toward Caren's car then stopped. Dead in the middle of the parking garage. Faintly, she could see what she was doing and watched. Unable to move and did not know why.

Caren stopped and set her briefcase down to remove her car keys and looked over her shoulder. Inserting the key in her red and white Mini-Cooper, she opened the door and placed the bags on the opposite seat and sat there for a moment. Then immediately locked all the doors.

Relief spread across Maggie's features as turning, she walked back and sat inside her own car preparing to close the door just as an explosion rocked the entire level of the parking garage. Igniting several vehicles parked between hers and Caren's. She launched out of her car, keys clutched tightly, as something solid smashed into her knocking her right down to the ground as debris flew all around.

Off in the distance, the sound of sirens growing closer filled her ears along with heavy ringing. As if in a trance, she picked herself up off the pavement not even aware of the blood dripping from oozing cuts. Her hosiery, skirt, and blouse nearly ripped to shreds with sections beginning to absorb the blood. The flames were so intensely hot she was forced to stop and watch in total horror.

Viewing through watering eyes, all that was left of Caren and her little car, was a burning frame and body inside. That horrible picture would stay embedded in her mind for the rest of her life.

Vehicles halted, surrounding her. But she did not see them. Tears were streaming down her dirty face. Keys still clutched in her hand. A voice came out of nowhere.

"Miss?"

No response.

He shook her slightly getting in front of her face.

"Miss?"

She looked up then at the police officer. Dazed and shaky, muttering out, "Oh my God." Then fainted.

He caught her in his arms and lifted her, moving them away from the chaos as the fire department, bomb squad and others took control. Someone approached him as he rested her down and covered her with his heavy jacket. "Keep her warm, the medical team is on the way. I've dispatched a message to Hawthorne. He should be here shortly. Stay with her."

Hawk and Zamir were in opposite parts of the city when their pagers engaged simultaneously. The message on the small screen read, CAR EXPLOSION AT MAIN PARKING GARAGE, U OF B.

Hawk immediately responded. "On it."

He was fifteen minutes away and it felt like it was the longest of his life. He grounded the car to a halt and parked as close as was allowed. Getting out, he pulled up the yellow strips as they were being taped in place by armed uniformed local police officers. The investigation well underway.

Flashing his top clearance credentials, Hawk proceeded further up from the first level to the second. Several investigating units were on the scene. Some he recognized from MI5, others were local. Evaluating the surrounds, he knew right away it was an act of terrorism.

Perkins was up ahead as he moved toward her, scrutinizing closely as a black body bag was being placed in the back of a coroner's car.

"Who is it?"

"Unconfirmed. I just arrived and have not found the lead agent on the investigation. I'm awaiting information.

"Any witnesses you are aware of?"

"No, I was in my office on campus when I heard the explosion. It took me nearly thirty minutes to get to the scene and gain access up here.

Hawk nodded.

"Where were you and Zamir? Is he on his way?"

"Unclear on his location." Hawk did not respond to her first question while leaving her and moving through debris. Then he saw it. Maggie's car. Spinning around he looked amongst the throngs of investigators and could not see her anywhere. But noticed the driver's door ajar. Inside he found her purse and netbook and grabbed them both, leaving the car keys sitting there on the seat.

"You can't remove those, Sir, that would be tampering with evidence." Hawk flashed his credentials. "Do you know where the woman is that was in this vehicle?"

"No, but Major Blain is up there closer to the wreckage and may be able to assist. It seems too coincidental the car blew as this passenger was departing. The first officer on the scene had to pry the car keys out of her hand. She was in shock. I put them on the seat and was told to keep watch on the contents inside."

"I'll take these, you keep the keys." His tone brooch no further argument as the officer stepped aside. Hawk moved on toward the medical vehicle. "Major Blain, Lieutenant Colonel Hawthorne, British Army. Here under special orders of the MoD. Do you know who was in the vehicle that exploded and where the passenger is that was trying to leave in that BMW?"

"We have an ID on the deceased. Caren Abbott, employed in the main library under a Miss Margaret Cohen. Who is right over there being attended to by the medics if you want to speak with her. She's very shaky and banged up, Sir."

"Which unit is it?"

"It's the second one around the back." He nodded to Blain and headed in that direction.

He glanced over and saw Perkins engaged on her cellphone and under closer scrutiny realized it was not a unit issued one. He pulled his own cellphone out and rang HQ. "Hawk here. I need you to page Perkins to another location away from this investigation right away. Yes, right now."

He hung up and watched her pull the other phone out of her side holder, glance at it and walk down the parking area to an alternate exit. Once the door closed behind her he reached the second medical unit.

He could hear her voice now. It was very weak.

"I don't need the clinic. I'll be fine. I know my blouse is torn to shreds. Don't you have anything you can lend me? No, I don't want any meds. Just do what you have too. I'm pretty tolerant of pain."

The minute Maggie saw Doug she tried to get up. But the medic held her steady while he continued to remove large shards of glass from her upper arm and shoulder. She was bleeding in several areas of her body. But thank God, with closer scrutiny, no further signs of injury were visible. She had just a very tattered black lacy bra on exposing her even more, abraded skin. *Damn*, he thought.

"Hawthorne."

"Maggie."

His heart stopped beating as he sat down curving an arm around her bare and cold skin. Sitting just inside the back of the unit, he reviewed that her skirt was badly ripped, her hosiery tattered, but otherwise, she looked okay.

"I'm so sorry, Maggie."

She leaned her head against his shoulder as the remains of a long braid shifted softly against his cheek. He squeezed her. She winced as he made eye contact with the medic. "Assessment."

"A few deep wounds along with cuts and scrapes. If she had been fifteen feet closer, she'd be in a body bag. Damn fortunate."

That part he could have left out as Maggie started to whimper. Hawk stood, removing his jacket then sat back down. When she was fully applied with ointments and bandages, he held it out. With unsteady movement, she put her arms in. Coming around the front he zipped it up all the way and grabbed her hands into his.

"Will you come home with me?"

No fight remained in her. He could tell.

"Yes. But my things are in Clevendon."

"Are they at Sasha's?"

"No, at the Inn. Can we go there now, please?"

Not once had she ever used that word. He was without a doubt having difficulty suppressing the need to strike out at anyone seeing her like this. Then he thought of her associate. "Have they notified her next to relation?"

"No, I have. They are on the way to the coroner's office now to ID her."

"Can you walk? I'm a level down."

"If you help me I can. You took my bags out. What about the keys? I'm going to need my office set."

"I pulled your office ones off. Your car is damaged beyond repair. It will be towed to HQ for a full sweep. Forensic will need to go through it with a fine-tooth comb. When they are through, I will receive the report. Maggie, you'll be getting a new car."

"Oh."

"Come-on, let's get your things and get you home."

She limped slightly, her right side all banged up from hitting the unforgiving paved ground so hard due to the force of the explosion. He stopped at the top of the second level ramp where there were fewer people. "Let me merge your bags, hang on." The strength in her grip minuscule as he hurried, slinging the bag over his shoulder. Then swept her up into his arms and carried her the rest of the way down. Continuing under and beyond the yellow tape and balanced her while he opened the Rover's passenger side door.

"Will I need to go to HQ tonight and make any further reports? I don't think I have it in me, Doug."

"No, if they need you they go through me."

She felt relief for the first time in many hours.

"Now, where is this place?"

"Clevendon. Off the M, not more than fifteen minutes. I am so glad to see you." She said it so softly he could barely hear it over the Rover's running engine. He glanced over as her head rested back, eyes closing. He watched her closely now noticing her shallow breathing.

God, he was upset.

He tapped on then spoke softly into his earpiece. "I've got her, General. She's pretty banged up but doesn't need hospitalization. At least not at this juncture. The unit patched her up very well.

"Give her a good night's rest. But if you have the chance, Hawk, see what she can tell you. There is a missing link here and we need it."

"Roger that, Sir, I'll be in touch. I'm taking her back to my house where she will stay and recuperate. I'm sure she's going to go to the funeral. But I or someone from my unit will be with her."

"You're a good man, Hawk, and a damn good soldier. See fit to do what you need and keep me posted."

He disconnected the piece and went into the Inn. He explained what he could to the owner's wife as she hastily took him up to her rooms to help aid him with collecting Maggie's things. Doug paid the rest of her bill, grabbed everything and walked out putting it all in the back of the Rover, closing the back hatch as quietly as possible.

He pulled into the garage as the automatic door closed behind. She never woke. Not even when he reached in and took her out of the passenger's side, inside the house, and unzipped and removed his jacket. Followed by her tattered clothes then settled one of his white tee shirts over her. Not a sound. She was lights out and he was worried. Worried as bloody hell and hoped shock had not set in.

# Chapter Thirteen

It was nearly zero two-hundred when he shut off his computer and was reaching for his light when he looked and saw her leaning against the door frame. She looked so beautiful. Interesting he had not heard her approach. She must have walked so softly with all her injuries and wondered how long she had been standing there watching him.

"I would have come if you called me."

"I needed to get up and move around. I am so stiff. Can we talk?" In a moment that was so quick, Hawk reached her taking hold of her waist, drawing her close to his side, and walked them both to the sofa. Gingerly he sat her down and pulled over the hassock and sat in front of her, waiting.

She shook her head to clear the clutter then found her voice at last. "She told me something this morning when I got in. I was later than normal and that is usually my spot where she parked, Doug. But today the lot had filled up and I was several vehicles away."

"What did she tell you?"

"Susan came in looking for me saying it was urgent. Caren offered to help her not knowing exactly when I'd arrive. She asked her why I had changed Zafir's last meeting location to a larger room. Told her that without my knowledge she moved it because the number of attendees had outgrown the previously assigned one."

She stopped, momentarily moving slightly on the seat then briefly shut her eyes, wincing from the pain. "Do you think I could have a glass of very cold water?" He rose and went to the kitchen reappearing shortly and handed it to her. He sat back down, hands taking hold of hers.

"I guess Susan did not believe her and asked a second time if I had any knowledge of this change. Caren denied it. Doug, Caren knew I had our student rig the cameras for the live stream but protected me. She contacted him to let him know she'd changed the location. But never advised me. She said Susan left without another word. I think they were going to do that to me, today, but believed Caren was behind it not I."

"Possible, Maggie. It could be a warning as well. If they were not one hundred percent sure they'd have taken you both out."

She shuddered, moving forward onto his lap, her toes dangling just above the soft, thick carpet. His arms came around holding protectively, with a strength that brought Maggie some semblance of relief. Right now, it was clear to them both she needed him. Tears fell as her body went limp.

Never in all his years had such a woman affected him so deeply. When she hurt, he hurt, and right now she hurt like bloody hell and would for a while. He caressed her hair, let her tears be absorbed by his shirt then realized she had cried herself back to sleep.

With such care he lifted her up and set her in the middle of his large king bed. Then took off his clothes setting them on the closest chair and climbed in. She moaned and moved to his warmth right away. While he held her feeling the bandages beneath the cotton shirt. Fuck. He hated her like this. His anger lay barely suppressed below the surface as he swore in silence that these irrational and inhumane actions had to be stopped. Zarif and his cowardly group would all be stopped even if it was the last breath he took.

Finally, Hawk fell into a very troubled sleep. If she twitched, he woke. At zero eight-thirty he rose and tucked the blankets around her and took a shower, made coffee and breakfast and went to work in his office. He texted Zamir the details of their conversation last night. It was only minutes before he received a reply. "Comrade, she will have her revenge through me." It was at that very moment when Hawk realized she had touched Zamir's life as well.

Maggie slept through most of the day as her eyelids fluttered open and squinting, she rose on sore elbows feeling every bit beaten up. Glancing around the room she slid her legs over the side of the bed and waited a while for her head to steady. Her bags sat in on top of his dressing table. Wincing, she walked over and opened it and changed into a soft pair of dusty rose velvet sweats and was trying without crying, to put on the hoodie and zip it up when her cellphone rang. Reaching for it, Hawk was suddenly there removing it quickly and looked at the incoming number before handing it to her before it went to voicemail.

"Maggie." She spoke softly answering the call. He reached over while she was listening to the caller talk and pulled her back against his chest. He felt her body melt into his.

"Yes, hello, Mrs. Abbott. I am so very sorry. My words cannot possibly express..." There was a lengthy pause, "Yes, I will be there. If there is anything at all I can do, please ring me." Another pause ensued as Maggie concluded the call with, "Your welcome. I am thinking about you all."

She placed the phone inside her right hoodie pocket and sat beside him on the bed. "The funeral is the day after tomorrow in Minehead. Can you take me into the city, so I can get a rental car? Oh, I need to call the Professor."

She was rambling as he took the cellphone from the pocket and placed it on the bedside stand. "The Professor knows. The library and the adjacent parking area is on lockdown for at least the next forty-eight hours while the investigation continues. Classes are canceled today in memorial of Caren."

She stood and paced then began to feel weak and leaned against the wall. Truly not sure her legs would hold the weight much longer. He did not hesitate and picked her up. "Do you want to come into my office and rest on the sofa while I work? Or the living room?"

"No, I really need to go home, Doug. I have a black dress there I keep for funerals. Isn't that morbid? I need to get it."

"Give me your keys and I'll go. I can't have you out and about for a few days until you gain strength." He set her back down on the bed and covered her up.

"They are in my bag over there. Rummage around. I don't care." She yawned, turned to one side and dozed right off. He found them in an inside pouch and left engaging the security system on the way out.

At her place, he signaled over to the unit and they signaled back acknowledging of his presence. He found what appeared to be the correct dress. Fishing around, he took out black hosiery, change of undergarments, bra, and black pumps. On insight that few men would have, even after being with a woman for many years, he reached into her closet and grabbed a black trench coat and umbrella in case it got chilly or rained.

He met Zamir out in the back alley where he parked.

"She is well enough?"

"Yes, weak. No real fighting spirit right now."

"It will return, Hawk, after the funeral. She will wake with vengeance in her heart and you will need to watch her more closely than ever before."

"You've seen this happen."

"Yes, many times."

Hawk set the items in the back seat. "What's the status on Perkins?"

"She has requested an LOA from her post at the campus citing personal difficulties. I just received a transmitted copy of her request before I arrived."

"Was it approved?"

"Yes, to begin right away."

"Shit, that's not good. She's going to go into hiding. Dammit, Zamir, we have to get access to the cell's housing."

"Agreed. Timing is crucial. Word around is that they are preparing to extract."

"Where?"

"Not clear. Possibly London or out of the country to Spain."

"Fuck, we have to find out. I think I can leave her for a while. She was resting when I left and appeared to be down for the count." Hawk shut the door and engaged the security locks. "Let's go in your vehicle. Who is accessible that we can take down? It's time for action."

"I'm with you on that. Let the bastards know 'we' are here."

"What's the plan?"

"Kohein. Earlier I monitored his movements to the docks. He boarded a large cargo ship. I say we start there."

"We need to stop at my house. I've got the right gear ready for this."

"Why don't you take your vehicle back, then."

"No, better I leave it here for now."

Zamir started up his vehicle and they left the parking area and were at Hawk's house in twenty minutes. Maggie never heard them enter nor depart with four large gear bags. He jotted down a note and left it folded so she'd see it by the bedside stand when she woke.

"You always wear that much black paint?"

"You just don't need as much, Zamir, so shut the fuck up."

"Do you have the guns, ammo, and explosives?"

"Not my first day of playing in the park, dude. Explosives we won't need. I'm thinking more along the lines of a natural charger. Let's use those fuel tanks and have some fun." They both looked at each other and grinned. When they arrived on base at the private docks, silently they left the vehicle and slid all the gear down into the boat. Maneuvering the small fishing vessel out of Bristol Harbor, Hawk skippered while Zamir focused on the map.

"Once we cross international waters I will inflate the RIB. Our target the Federah is close. He glanced at his cellphone as a message was coming in. "INTEL advises hostiles."

"Good. I need to relieve the world of a few more assholes."

Both men laughed.

Sixteen miles beyond international waters Hawk killed the engine and weighed anchor. Zamir slid night vision specs on scanning the deck of the Federah. "Four posted with weapons. Two forward, two aft. No nets on either side so grab the webs. I'll monitor while you inflate the RIB."

"Just like old times. Barking orders like I'm your damn bitch." Protected with a slim wetsuit, Hawk slid into the dark waters as the RIB quietly opened and expanded.

Zamir handed down the customized motor and extra cans of fuel. The final gear bag was loaded as Zamir climbed over the side using the buoy netting while throwing out a jabbing retort. "You're getting soft, old man. Time to retire, eh?"

"Shit on you. I was retired."

"Yeah, and *who* needed to be called back to wipe *your* ass."

They grinned as Hawk started the motor. At a low hum, barely detectable if one was not listening for it, they approached the Federah. No wake followed behind.

Large black rubber suction cups were attached to the RIB and the metal side of the ship simultaneously. Which kept it from drifting off from the massive waves the ship was generating. They used webbed gloves that temporarily adhered to any surface allowing them to climb up the high sides of the ship. Special weapons were slung over their shoulders and harnessed to legs and around each of their waists.

This was black six. A discreet covert op that few would ever know of other than HQ and the General. Two men following their own orders. Both from different countries, but working as a tandem for this mission. To sink the Federah. But before that occurred, they would delve deep into the hold and see what they could find to pass along to INTEL.

Using hand signals only, they crept silently along the expansive deck averting men smoking, talking and drinking. Maneuvering down inside to the hull, they located crates of illegal weapons. Two SAMs and a large heavy metal box. This instantly became a major focus.

Zamir pried it open as both men stopped for a second looking at each other, amazed. It was jammed full of illegal, previously confiscated, CIA counterfeit money. Hawk spoke into his mic breaking silence. "How the hell did this get into their hands. This is U.S. goods. What the fuck."

Zamir nodded opening a smaller box. It held several bogus passports with pictures of faces they recognized from all the photos generated by MI6 and INTERPOL. This was the good shit they were looking for.

Hawk shoved them into an inside vest pocket and Zamir the paperwork as they disarmed the two SAMs and sabotaged the reactors placing them gingerly back inside the crate.

Zamir signaled Hawk he was ready as they moved further down and back to the aft to locate the massive fuel tanks. They mentally marked the location and began their silent ascent. Back on the deck, they simultaneously spotted Kohein who swigged on a bottled beer completely engrossed in a card game going on with other crew members. Hawk sneered. Hand ready to draw his Beretta, silencer attached, and place one shot right between this dude's wildly looking unibrow. A flash of Zamir's smile brought Hawk back to the situation at hand, following him over the side.

Silently they climbed down into the RIB, shoved back and moved the craft around to the rear and secured three cellphones encased in waterproof cases and activated them. Hawk launched the RIB as they drifted backward by the powerful wake of the Federah. When they were at a safe distance, he engaged the motor.

As the RIB bounced against their anchored fishing vessel, Zamir jumped on board then threw out a line to Hawk. Grabbing the rope, he secured it to the RIB's bow then closed the distance and got on board. Releasing the line, the RIB drifted behind the boat.

The two men stood side by side as Zamir started up the engine and shifted the gear lever as Hawk laughed. "This never gets old. I have no fucking idea why I'm retiring."

"Yeah, you do. She's waiting in your bed."

This somber realization brought him back to reality in a flash. "Thanks."

"Yeah, don't worry about it. But I'm with you there. Don't mind shooting my rifle, blowing things up and removing crud from the earth."

"I'll take the helm. You go ahead and change then I will."

With both the boat and RIB secured back alongside the Navy's floating dock, they climbed up the metal ladder with gear bags and out onto the busy street filled with other military members. None of which paid them any attention at all. At Zamir's vehicle, they stored the gear as he locked it up once again.

"Did you like fireworks as a young lad?

"Shit, yeah."

"Shall we?" Zamir had his cellphone out turning it on as Hawk did the same.

"Indeed, it's a lot more enjoyable when it's shared with a comrade."

Standing side-by-side on the pier overlooking Bristol Harbor, it looked just like a regular, ordinary Monday night. They simultaneously punched in a sequence and sent it to the units attached to the hull of the Federah. In unison, they lifted long distance night vision binoculars and scanned in the same direction.

"Ah, my friend. As promised. Fireworks."

Wide grins spread across both faces as Hawk slapped Zamir on the back. Both of their cellphones buzzed. The message was the same. *Mission complete.*

They headed back to Zamir's vehicle, got in and left with him dropping Hawk back off at his Rover. As he got out, Zamir's comment momentarily halted him. "Head home to her. Keep a good eye on her. She's going to try and get out from under your watch soon, my friend."

Hawk walked around the side and got into his vehicle knowing there were fewer assholes in the world now. Putting the Rover in gear, he drove the short distance back to Chepstow.

\*\*\*

Maggie had read his note climbing from bed desperately needing a shower and something warm to drink. Tea. She found though, that his loose tee shirts were much kinder to her abrasions and cuts than anything she had in her bag right now.

Showered and toweled dry, she was trying to apply antibiotic gel the medic had given her, twisting sideways when a cry of pain sprang forth from her mouth. She saw his reflection in the bathroom mirror. Then bit the inside of her cheek not wanting to show weakness in front of him any longer.

"Here, let me do it." His voice was soft but as she stared at him she noticed the traces of black upon his face. She knew. He had been out on a covert mission someplace.

Handing him the ointment, her eyes watered heavily even though he was trying to apply it gently. Then new bandages were added. Reaching over he grabbed the clean shirt she had found not caring it came from his draws. "Lift your arms." She did as the shirt slid overhead and down her body resting just on mid-thigh.

He pulled her up against him. "What can I do for you. Something to eat? A cup of tea?"

"Tea would be nice."

Leaving the bathroom, Hawk, headed toward the kitchen. Shutting off the bathroom light Maggie saw her dress, shoes and the other items she had not even thought of and smiled. He'd make a great companion to someone, someday.

In the kitchen, she moved slowly up to the stool and sat on top as he handed her a piping cup of Irish tea. "So, soldier, tell me truthfully where have you been all this while. My best guess is blowing things up."

He turned abruptly and stood with hands on hips staring at her then suddenly broke into laughter.

She joined him with a smile.

"Maggie…."

"Come on I need to get my head out of the funk it's in. Help me out here. Tell me something real."

He leaned over the countertop toward her, arms rested on top. "We took care of one of them tonight and collected some items of value along the way. I'm positive we pissed off those that are left. Zafir, I have no doubt, will be seeking some type of revenge because of it. But who gives a shit. What's done is done."

"Really, give me more."

"We never may find out who did that to Caren, which of them or one of their recruits. But it seems more than suspicious that Kohein was on the ship. Furthermore, we discovered illegal weapons and cash. The Helo that monitored above confirmed our mission was successful."

"You sank a cargo ship?"

"Indeed, we did and took one more asshole from the equation."

"One down, four to go?"

"Affirmative."

"What's going on with Perkins?"

"She's filed an LOA with the university."

"Was it approved? If you can't find out I can."

"Yes, it was approved. Maggie, I should not need to tell you this. You must stand-down."

"Shit, that's going to make it hard to find her. She'll go dark. When does the library open back up?"

She was apparently not listening to him – oh what a surprise. "Don't even think about it."

"Yes, we have to contemplate this for a moment. Hang on. Just give me a chance to explain my thoughts."

He leaned close to her catching that wonderful whiff of seductive perfume that heats up when their bodies are close. It left an indelible mark upon his senses.

"Okay, go on." He figured he'd better hear her out. Knowledge is power where she is concerned.

"If I make myself approachable it will give a false impression that I don't know anything. If I stay in hiding what kind of message will that send to them all? If she's on LOA she will be looking for me. I am sure. If for nothing, just to confirm if Caren ever did talk to me before the incident."

*Her reasoning is good*, he silently admitted to himself. "Okay, you go to work the day after the funeral and remain in the building all day. You stay away from the bistro, parking garage and all other areas of campus. I will bring you in and out."

"Negative, if you do that she can ID you."

He frowned.

"Let me return to my apartment keeping the team across the street monitoring me. You wire me if you want and bug their bugs with your own. But let me go home."

"You are really not strong enough, Maggie." He smiled inwardly listening to her confirm that she had been in her apartment already, and was fully aware of the team posted nearby and had used the word '*dark*' for Perkins. *Damn*, he thought. *She would make one hell of a great agent.*

"Yes," she reached over and rested her hands on his as he turned them around and held them tight. "But I will gain strength, Doug, and I have to help. Caren and I were close. This must be done for her and her family. Now work with me so I do it right for once."

She made sense now. Hardly irrational and spontaneous as she had been of late. "Okay, I'll hire a cab to take you to the funeral Thursday and assign a few plainclothes officers to monitor you. Your driver will be one. He will wait and take you to Caren's parents after for the gathering. Then bring you back to your flat. I will take a team and sweep your place during the funeral leaving detailed instructions on a note. The best place to put that is in the refrigerator in the egg box. Then burn or flush it."

"Thank you. This means a lot to me. I'd much rather work with you than against you and my father. Will you let him know what we are doing?" She broke into a soft laugh then stopped as it hurt inside.

He did not laugh at all.

"I don't like this, Maggie, but I have to admit I agree with your line of thinking. Do you still have your weapon and mags? I'm going to want you wired the minute you leave here and keep it on until I take it off."

She smiled shyly. "Just where will this wire be hidden, LC?"

He came around the counter and lifted her off the bar stool. "Can we talk about this in bed?"

Leaning her head against his shoulder she had wanted to say, "when I am stronger, Doug...," but stopped with memories of his hurtful words still fresh in her head.

He placed her down in the middle, got in and turned on his side as they faced each other. But did not touch.

"If Susan doesn't come in to see me, what will happen?"

"That bridge will be crossed as this is all worked out. My guess is she will come to the funeral and do it. But not after."

"She's the mole, I know."

"Yes. I can't lie to you now."

She lifted a hand momentarily then retracted it before it touched his chest. "You said you'd do anything for me."

"I did."

"Does that mean I can ask you a question and your reply will be totally honest?"

"Yes."

"I heard you outside talking with someone and you really were right about me. Spoiled. Basically, a bitch. No arguments there from me. But was it truly because my father ordered you that you tolerated me? I understand you helped me because it was *his* order. After seeing what happened to Caren, I'm beginning to understand that much of what has happened is completely out of your control."

Shifting her back he leaned on his side and massaged her cheek, his hand weaving into her hair as it spilled around the pillow close to his.

"When I reached the scene, and saw your vehicle door open and could not readily locate you, but saw the body bag being removed to the coroner's car, I hit a place inside I'd never been. I've watched men get hit and die. But reaching you at the unit and watching the Medic attend you, well, that was something I don't ever want to witness again."

He paused but Maggie was impatient. "I don't understand. What are you really saying here?"

"It's no longer a promise to your Pop, Maggie, it's a promise to you. I'd give my life for you and when this is finished I'm going to retire again. Hopefully for good and try to settle down. So, we can start this in a better place. The right way. But until then, we still have something major to take care of."

Tears formed, one slowly slipped from her watery blue eyes as he leaned down and kissed it tasting the saltiness.

His voice was deep, filled with raw emotion that nearly caused her to break down in a full cry. But something somewhere deep inside was holding it back.

"Okay, soldier, I agree."

He leaned over and kissed her. As their minds and hearts blended, so too did their bodies. His passion for her was clear. But more healing needed to be done. He wrapped arms around her as she rested her head on his shoulder. "Maggie, tonight you're safe. I'm right here. Nothing will harm you."

She sighed into the dark bedroom and drifted off asleep.

# Chapter Fourteen

She stood before him dressed only in a black, silky, lace trimmed slip with hosiery on her legs. "So where is this wire going to go?" In the palm of his hand was the tiniest dot of a wireless microphone that she had ever seen. "Wow. That's it?"

"Yup, indeed it is. Perhaps now you wished you had taken that post with MI5 after all. Welcome to the world of espionage, Maggie."

"Damn, maybe I should reconsider."

"Oh, no you won't." His knuckles brushed against the top curve of one breast bringing a flush to her cheeks. His grin roguish. "Nice to see some color back in them, love. You're set and ready to go. Watch what you say from here on - if you understand my meaning."

She did. Others were now listening. That meant no suggestive comments to the LC. Although she figured whoever was on the other end had heard plenty over the years.

The horn honked outside causing Maggie to jump. "Shit. Can you run out and tell him I'll be right there?" Then they both broke out into laughter realizing what she had just said. That was one of Doug's men waiting for her in the cab. Grabbing her dress off the bed she unzipped it and lifted it putting her arms in through the three-quarter length sleeves. He zipped it as Maggie slid her feet into the black pumps. Removing the pearls from the dresser, she put her earrings in while he attached the necklace. Taking the umbrella but leaving the trench coat, Maggie walked beside him to the front door.

"Talk to you soon." He leaned down and pressed his hand to the mic then kissed her. She walked down the stone path to the waiting cab and smiled. Her bodyguard/driver was big, bulky and handsome. As he opened her door and as she got in, they smiled at one another. She saw him nod to Hawk over her shoulder.

Inside, Hawk took all her packed bags and loaded them into the back seat of the Rover then paged the other team to meet him at her apartment.

*** 

"Here you go, Miss Cohen. I'll be right here waiting for you outside the gate when you're ready."

"Thank you." She did not bother to ask him his name.

Stepping out of the cab she walked up the path toward the large group of people beginning to gather coming in from several directions in the cemetery. There were so many here to pay final homage to Caren as strong emotions caused Maggie's eyes to mist. She spotted Seth walking over and touched his arm when he arrived.

"Hi, do you know where the Abbott's are?"

Seth was looking her over carefully. "Hi Maggie, yes, over there." She left him with not so much as a bye but did nod as she weaved her way through the large mass. Susan was between her and them. Which worked out perfectly as Maggie kept on a path directly toward her, forcing a meeting.

"How are you doing, Maggie, are you holding up okay?"

"Thanks, Sue, how are you doing?"

"Well enough. I was hoping to catch up with you after, would that be possible?"

"Sure, I'm heading to the hall. Are you going?"

"No, I have things to attend too."

"All right. Why don't we meet back here?"

"Good, I'll wait and see you then."

Walking along, she finally reached Mr. and Mrs. Abbott as the three of them clustered close. Heads bowed in toward each other. "Mr. and Mrs. Abbott, I am so very sorry," Maggie whispered. "If can do anything, please let me know?" Caren's mom blew her nose and smiled shakily to Maggie. "Dear, I've been hoping to say this now while I can still think. Would you please go to the office and box up Caren's things? If so, would you drop it off to us sometime?"

"Of course, I can."

"Maggie, there is no rush. I just had to do this now as my husband and I just don't have the strength to go and take care of this ourselves."

"I understand completely.

The Bishop of Wells, a very close and personal family friend, moved over to the casket with two altar boys to assist. One holding the Good Book and the other holding the woven brass chain attached to a large open weaved lantern. Inside the ever so familiar scent of burning incense. Which was now permeating the air all around them at the burial location.

Why did such a strong, yet stimulating scent need to be used for only funerals? Caren's family clustered close as Maggie stepped back glancing at those that gathered while the Bishop spoke. "We are here to celebrate the life of Caren Abbott. Taken by our Lord at this young age. Join me in prayer as we begin this special service." All heads bowed. "Our Father, Who Art in Heaven…"

Maggie finished voicing the Lord's prayer softly then added another silently. "Dear Lord, please help me to make peace with this and help Caren so her death was not in vain." Seconds later she felt it. The adrenalin up her spine knowing what she would do. The letter. Someplace it was tucked in one of the pocketbooks left at her flat. If it hadn't already been located and confiscated by the team members who had been there or going in today with Doug. She would take it to Stonefield. Lying to gain entry.

A solid plan formed. Maggie admitted to herself that it was a long shot. But could work. She folded her hands in front of her coat, head and eyes lowered and spoke softly so those monitoring her would not hear.

"Caren, I promise you on my life I will see those punished that did this to you and help you have the peace you deserve. I swear it."

A dark chill followed as the plan in her mind was sealed in concrete. Convinced this was not about acting irrational. No. She'd have revenge after all. She knew darn well the Good Book says, *An Eye for An Eye*." Glancing up, she saw the disinterested look on Susan Perkin's face and felt for the first time that raw, cold anger that those who kill without thought, fear or justification must acknowledge. Certainly, Perkins and Zafir's group never felt it. How could they? *Bastards that kill innocents did not have emotions at all*, she thought. *Cowards. They were all nothing more than cowards.*

Controlling it now was difficult for Maggie while glaring at Susan, watching her closely. She seemed to be looking for someone. But whom? Maggie searched all the faces as the voice of an angel suddenly brought much-needed distraction just at the right time.

"Dear, are you coming to the hall now?"

"I am, Mrs. Abbott. But first I must speak with someone. Then I will be along. I have a cab waiting to take me, so I should not be too late." She patted her arm as they both blew their noses on hankies. Mrs. Abbott was quickly gathered up by loved ones and taken away. Then Maggie felt a grip on her arm. It was Susan. Who held tight the entire walk toward Maggie's cab.

"Are you staying at home tonight?"

"Yes, I'll be there. What did you want to talk with me about?"

"I am sorry to bring this up now. But I'm going to be away for a spell."

Maggie waited silently looking at her with open concern trying to mask the inner turmoil boiling inside.

"Caren, did she mention I was in there Monday morning looking for you?"

Maggie stopped and looked at her confused. "No, but she did say she wanted to talk with me. I recall her phone rang as I walked out, that she'd be back later. Come to think of it she never did. When I left at six her light was on and we exited together. But, she didn't bring up anything of importance. I'm sorry. Did you need something? I can do it tomorrow. I plan on going in for a while."

"No, no worries, Maggie. Are you sure you are up to it, going in so soon?"

"Yes, I told her Mum I'd pack up her office and bring things around to them sometime. They don't have the strength to do it and it's something I need to take care of." They had reached the gate. "Do you want a lift anyplace? This is my cab."

"No, my car is just around the bend. If you need anything ring me, okay? Are you getting a new vehicle?"

"Not sure. The insurance company is working it out. For now, its cab services until I know what's coming next."

Maggie could discern clearly that the concern in Susan's voice did not equal the coldness in her eyes. Maggie felt like stabbing her right there and her handsome cab driver could throw Susan's lifeless body in the trunk and dispose of her in a proper manner. In Bristol Harbor.

Disengaging from Susan's grasp, calmness slowly returned to Maggie.

"Thanks, Susan, if you do need anything it would be best to send me an email." She opened the cab door and shut it with a resounding thud. "You okay, Miss Cohen?"

"Not really. I feel like doing someone true physical harm. But thank you for asking. Oh shit, I forgot people are listening. So, will you all just forget I said it?" She was mumbling and knew it.

"Miss Cohen, where to?"

"St. Richards Hall please, it is," he interrupted her, "I know Miss. Hawk gave me your full itinerary. I just needed to confirm."

Just the mention of his name stirred warmth in her heart. Temporarily helping to ease her anger and the will deep inside to really kick someone's ass. "Thank you."

Just before she got out of the cab he halted her turning toward the back seat. "I will be around the parking area when you are ready." Handing her a card with just a phone number on it. Otherwise, it was stark white and blank.

"Just text and give me two minutes and I'll pull around front." She understood. "Okay unknown soldier, I understand." Her humor was not lost on him.

Inside she weaved her way through the crowded hall. It was brimming near capacity making it difficult to reach those she knew without being bumped or bumping someone. "Maggie, hold up," it was Professor Lichens. "You're not planning on going in tomorrow, are you?"

"I have too, Seth. I promised Caren's Mum I'd pack up her things and bring them by sometime. It would be proper sooner than later. Don't you agree?"

He nodded. "Okay, but then I want you to take a few days off. You have stores of hours you never utilize. Take them now. I mean it."

"Can we meet in the middle? I have a few reasons to be on campus. Is it okay if I use up a week? You let me do what I need too? It's very important or I'd not mention it." She silently hoped those listening in were not reading more into this than she intended. At some point, she fully planned on ditching the damn listening device.

"Maggie…"

"Seth," she interrupted. "Truly, this is important. I can't stress it enough." He grabbed her by the hand. "I've got a bad feeling about this."

"Ignore it. This time, Seth, I have my head screwed on right."

"Okay, but if you need me you had better text."

"You've got a deal." She squeezed both his hands then moved on to locate Caren's immediate family amongst the throng of people gathered.

"Maggie, you were the last person to see her. We don't understand. Did she say anything at all about someone wanting to do this, hurt her like this?" Her sister Anne was eleven months her senior and they were close like Irish twins. Vaguely recalling snapshots of them in Caren's bedroom when she had been there once or twice.

"No, not at all. Even a hint. But I assure you the special police and investigators are working very hard to find out. They've shut down the library and the garage for a few days while they work."

"It makes no sense." As Anne's lower lip quivered and tears began to fall. Maggie's welled up as well as she reached over and pulled Anne into an embrace. "I agree. Come on. Let's get you something to eat. Or, at least drink."

"No, that's so sweet of you. I know why Caren adored you. Loved working with the library and thought so highly of everyone there."

Maggie just could not listen to this any longer. The command of her own emotions too raw to continue. As suddenly they were both engulfed by others and Maggie was able to slip away, off to a somewhat vacant corner. Pulling out her cellphone, she texted her driver right away to come and pick her up and was deeply relieved when he replied right back he was already outside. Across the large room, she caught sight of Mrs. Abbott and waved, then took the closest exit.

"Can we make a stop on the way to my flat?"

"No. Strict orders."

She had forgotten. "Shit, I knew that soldier, sorry." As their eyes met in the rearview mirror. "Okay, straight home it is." All she really wanted was to get there and place her hands on that envelope then take a very hot bath. He stopped the cab out front and waited for her to shut the door and walk through the front entrance. She hesitated just inside the lobby and glanced back. He was still there, and could see he was texting. She assumed it was to Doug to let him know she was now home

Maggie immediately went to the refrigerator and opened it up noticing it had been restocked with a few items. Quite sure it was done to prevent her from leaving the apartment. Inside the egg crate was a note. Unfolding it she read his writing; *"phones are bugged, rooms are otherwise clear. The team will continue to monitor. Text if you need anything. Will be in touch. Stay safe and be smart."*

Disposing of the note properly, she walked through to the bedroom and stopped, smiling slightly. For there, on one fluffy pillow was a lovely, long-stemmed yellow rose. Picking it up, she inhaled the delicate scent. Then set it back and lied down, head on the same pillow and soon was fast asleep.

It was dark when she rose and turned on a few lights. Slowly, she removed clothing along with bra and listening device and rested them on a high-back chair in the corner of the bedroom. Naked, she walked into the bathroom and turned on both water spouts and drew a hot bath. Dropping a mesh filled with luxurious herbs and oils in, she pulled her pink silk robe off the back of the door, slid it on slowly cringing from the pain, then tied it securely.

In the kitchen she placed the kettle filled with water on the stove. Then took out the metal canister filling an infuser with tea and set it on the countertop. Back in the bathroom, she tested the water temperature with her hand then turned the handles off stopping the flow. The kettle was chiming when she returned. Filling a separate ceramic pot with the steaming hot water, then dropped the infuser in. Placing it on a small tray she carried everything into the bathroom setting them next to the tub.

Disrobing, she climbed in and stretched out. Toes not quite reaching the end and relaxed sighing into the emptiness of the room. Her hurt, cut and bruised body felt like it immediately started to heal. Twenty minutes passed as she reached for the teacup and poured cream and dropped sugar in as the rich tea followed. Sipping, Maggie felt strange. Encased in a cloud feeling little but anger and wished the day would end and the next begin so she could get moving. After all, what could she do in the middle of the night? Staying in this apartment was not her plan. Tomorrow she'd begin her own agenda by first going into the office.

Setting the china cup back down on the tray, Maggie stood removing the rubber stopper as the sound of water gurgling down the drain brought thoughts of how quickly things can change in one's life. Just like that and something wonderful and spirited like Caren was no longer a part of this world. Sliding back into the silk robe, she reached down and removed the tray taking it with her to the living room setting it down on the coffee table. Then leaned over and switched on a light.

Suddenly, she sat straight up. Remembering the bag and envelope. Quickly she went into the bedroom locating it at the bottom of the armoire. Digging deep, her hand located the envelope and upon close evaluation discovered it hadn't been tampered with at all.

Oh, thank you, counter-intelligence people! She wanted to scream out.

Placing it on the dresser, Maggie unzipped the top pouch of her netbook and tucked it beneath the cables used for charging. It covered it completely hidden from view.

Setting her cellphone on the bedside stand, she pulled back the coverlet, blanket, and sheets. Taking out a tee shirt from the dresser and sliding it over her healing body, she climbed in and shut off the light holding the rose in her hand and fell into a deep, troubling sleep.

***

"I need an update."

"Hawk, not much sound at all just the tub running and the tea kettle, she's very quiet."

"Thanks."

The cellphone was in his hand as he sent the message. "Rest well."

Maggie woke slightly hearing something. Then rolled over and lifted it off the stand and read the message. Her reply back was a bit different, Hawk thought when he read it. "Nice touch on the flower, soldier."

He could almost feel her sadness from across the miles that separated them. *Damn*, he thought while running fingers along the side of his office desk. He wanted to head over. Hold her. He knew, though, he could not. Not tonight.

***

She was in a large abandoned warehouse. Rafters exposed with old leaded windows high above. Some of the panes of glass were broken as Zafir and his gutless band of killers was torturing Caren. Maggie could only watch on in utter horror. "*Hey, assholes, over here. Can't you see me?*" She kept yelling. But none of them even glanced her way as

Caren's upper body was covered in explosives. Legs suspended off the cement floor as she sat strapped in a large wooden chair.

One of the men was across the room and all the others opposite. Laughing and drinking shots of some clear liquid while Zafir moved a long pole toward the chair. Then, slowly started to wiggle it away from beneath Caren as Maggie watched on unable to do a damn thing. Legs immobile.

"Bitch, as soon as that chair moves far enough your feet will touch the ground and your body will disintegrate. There will be nothing left to ID. If they scrape all your remains and try to piece them together, it won't fill a pill box. How does it feel waiting for your world to end and no one will ever know what happened?"

The air curdled with sick laughter as the pole inched the chair further and further until...

Maggie tried in vain to get in between them as the chair moved enough and the explosion rocked the warehouse. Blood, clothing, bones, flew around the room splatting against her face. She reached up and touched the gross substance. It was wet and still warm. She pulled it off, scratching her skin as her piercing scream filled the bedroom.

Caren's blood continued in a never-ending flow dripping down as Maggie bolted upright, chest heaving, sweat on her upper lip. Hands touching cheeks, she realized it was not blood, but her own tears. "Oh, my fucking word," she softly mouthed out. "What the hell was that all about." Wiggling over she grabbed a tissue, then took the whole box and rested it on a hip. It was going to be a long night, she just knew. Oh, how she wished he somehow could feel what she was feeling right now and come over.

As she laid back and fluffed up the pillow, Maggie was afraid to even close her eyes. Afraid of what she would see next. But sleep finally did claim her as exhaustion helped her rest more soundly through the rest of the night.

# Chapter Fifteen

"Maggie, when you are through ring maintenance they're waiting for your call to bring the items wherever you wish. The van is ready."

"Okay, Seth, thank you. Caren didn't have much except some family photos and a few knick-knacks."

"I've Edna coming in with a pot of tea for you. Would you please look through all her files and computer programs and copy what you think I should review?" He set a flash drive down on the desktop. "Anything in paperwork not needed, pile on this side of the desk and I'll have Edna shred it later."

"I'm glad you let me use her. She is like my own Mum but somewhat less nosey." They shared a small grin between them. To Maggie, it felt good to be engaged with Seth or any normal human after last night's terrorizing dream. *Good lord*, she thought, *if this continues to haunt me, I may have to turn to Prince Valium after all.*

He patted her on the back. "You have ample vacation and personal time. At least take next week off. Will you give it some thought?"

"I've done just that, Seth, and I will. Don't forget our conversation. It's important."

"Can you give me more detail now?"

"No, and I won't unless it's essential. Should it turn in the wrong direction, then this will not be a good situation for me. Let's pray that we don't need to go down that road at all. Regardless, you may see me here a few times while I'm on leave."

He shrugged not liking this at all. "Be careful."

"I will." Then looked up and he was already heading out walking by Edna who was coming in.

"Dear, here's your tea. I will set it behind on the table. If you need me for anything, the Professor has cleared most of my day for you. Just give me a buzz."

"Thank you, Edna, for everything. I'll have some things for you soon. How do you want it sorted, in one lump stack or as it accumulates so it's not so much to shred at once?"

"Any way you decide is fine."

She was so sweet. Maggie felt the weeping creeping back again. If Edna had not been there looking at her like a little-lost-girl, she'd have banged her hand to her head to knock some sense into it.

While deleting files, she came across a stored document with a title she could not readily recall. Opening and scrutinizing it, she quickly realized Caren had known more than Maggie realized! Fourteen months of data had been collected on Stonefield House. Including a deep well of information on all their prime targets, off-campus activities, various backgrounds, classes, passport details and more. The spreadsheet went on to include when they entered the country, if they were on a study or work visa, and who their sponsorship was with. This was extremely strange. Was this something Doug could use? Why did she have this and who the hell was she working for?

Interesting enough, Susan Perkins name was listed as AOD-Adult on Duty for contact. The last five boarders who arrived were listed by last names only. But Maggie knew who they were. The latest members of the HAMAS sleeper cell; Zafir, Davide, Kohein, Levy, and Horowitz. But, it was the spreadsheet very well hidden behind this attachment that stunned Maggie and sent her straight into the twilight zone.

These names were directly connected to Susan Perkins only. Although Maggie did not recognize them, they linked contact locations in London, Edinburgh, Madrid, Paris, and Palestine. She voiced rather loudly, "Holy shit, what does all this mean?" Then anxiously glanced up to see if anyone was passing by.

She inserted the flash drive from her pocket. It was not the one Seth had left for her and proceeded to copy all the information. Then recycled all the files so they couldn't be retrieved by anyone if they should get their hand on Caren's computer.

As an extra precaution, she wiped the hard drive, closed all programs and rebooted the system and double checked they were indeed removed.

While tucking the drive into a pocket that was when it dawned on her. That bomb was not meant for Maggie. Someone, someplace, knew without any doubt what Caren was doing and they meant to kill her. *Oh my God*, her brain silently screamed. *Do you get it yet? You did not get her killed! Caren was a secret agent.* All this time and right under Maggie's own nose. Shit. Her Pops would lie down and die when he found out about this. Or, perhaps he knew? Was it Caren who may have reported directly to her father? Was that how he discovered what she had been up to way before she called him for help?

Fuck! How many people around her were tied into this web of espionage? Sitting back, Maggie's body went numb, but her mind accelerated to warp speed. She sifted through all the events, information and people she'd been with or around since this began and started to wonder about Hawthorne and Zamir as well.

Shaking her head violently, mentally chastising herself for possibly being played for a bigger fool than previously imagined, her mind truly ran wild. Doug had seemed truly concerned. But was he? Why was that team monitoring her? *No*, she thought. *Don't go there. Doug is real. The something happening to us is real, isn't it? Oh, god, I need to stop, or I will go mad.*

Gasping air, Maggie tried to calm down as the magnitude of this discovery rested heavily on her shoulders. Shoulders still hurting from all they carried up till now. Right hand back on the mouse, she continued reviewing all the documents relieved it was the only one.

All the files relevant to Seth's department were copied on his flash and left on the corner of the desk. She swiveled her chair around and opened the small horizontal filing cabinet and sifted through each folder and formed two piles. Those to be read on the right side and shredded on the left. Completed, she moved the flash on top of the right and stood stretching.

Walking out and into her own office, she removed her netbook and when it was up and running, inserted the flash and watched the attachments open. Good, it was all there. She copied it to her hard drive and inserted a separate flash and created a backup.

Suddenly glancing up, Maggie startled. For in the doorway studying her closely, was Susan. A cold shiver ran up Maggie's spine.

"How are you doing? Cleaning things up so you can take time off?"

Maggie was acutely aware of how important her next sentence would be.

"I'm okay. Just going through some files and getting things in order. Yes, I'm taking time off next week and then will reevaluate everything. How about you?"

"I've taken a short LOA for personal reasons. I'm here today to finish things up just like you."

Maggie's suspicions rose.

"Do you need any help taking Caren's things out? I have my car outside. I can give you a lift."

Maggie twisted in her seat smiling, knowing she had her SIG right in the bag and at this range, she'd never miss. "No, but thank you. I have to finish up then meet with Edna and Seth before I leave."

"Do you have Caren's things all packed up? I can take them with me and drop them off someplace if you want."

"You know what, yes. Then I won't have to haul it in a cab. Can you drop it off at my flat? Then I can continue working. Would that impose too much?"

"Not at all. Is that the box and her laptop?"

"Yes, I can call maintenance to help you down, but it's not very heavy. She really didn't have much beyond some personal items. I was quite surprised."

Susan lifted the mid-sized, cardboard box. "I can deal with this. Will leaving it outside your flat be safe?"

Maggie contemplated the question. Then remembered the listening device attached inside her bra. Assuming once Susan left a team would be called in. Reaching into her purse she produced her extra keys. "Good idea. We shouldn't take that chance. When you leave, set them on the counter and thanks again, Susan, I owe you one. This is a big help."

"Least I can do."

"Here," Maggie wrote down details. "This is my address just behind the Radisson Blu. It's best to park out back there are more slots and if you are very fortunate the elevator in the front will work. If not, I'm sorry. Rarely it does."

Perkins took the paper with the address and set it on top of the things inside the box. "No worries." Turning she left the office as Maggie suppressed the strong urge to take out the SIG and shoot the bitch straight in the back.

***

Hawk's cellphone vibrated while he was with Zamir at his house in Chepstow.

"Hawk here." He listened intently then replied, his voice loud. "She what? Affirmative, have a team assembled and await my orders. Keep them back until I advise to proceed."

"What's happened?"

"Maggie. Our can't-leave-things-alone sleuth. She lured Susan into bringing Abbott's remains back to her flat along with her laptop. That woman is really beginning to scare the shit out of me. You know, Zamir, she told me MI5 tried to recruit her and she declined the offer.

"Ah, my friend, what a web she weaves. Extreme caution is needed now. We know both women have something up their sleeves. Not a good sign. What do you want to do?"

Hawk shook his head as more information came in. "Wait, it says she has a flash drive with important information. Needs to get it to me straight away. Let's roll."

They pulled over in the back alley and got out of the vehicle, leaning up against it knowing Perkins rig was just beyond in the back. "We can wait here while she finishes. When the unit across the street texts me the all clear, we'll move in."

"Any word from Maggie what is in that flash?"

"Nothing, she must be finishing up at the office and will advise when ready."

"That would mean Abbott had more knowledge than Maggie was aware of."

"Right, and it proves that the bomb was planned for Abbott, not Maggie. Hopefully, that will bring her some closure."

"She was still her good friend, Hawk. Revenge is utmost in her mind right now. I said it before. Mark my words and monitor her closely. I can tell by the information that is being transferred to us, her tone on all of this has shifted. You must be careful. She's already outsmarted too many of us. Including her own father. She's just getting started."

"I know."

"She's on the move, over here."

Perkins pulled away from the curb and around them as they ducked out of sight. "She looked pissed. I wonder what happened."

"Fuck. Something is not right, Zamir. Let's head up to Maggie's place now."

The unit was waiting just outside her door as they checked for explosives. The clear signal was given as Hawk produced a spare key and gained entry noticing the other set sitting on one counter. Those were the ones they knew Perkins had used. Splitting up into groups, they swept the rooms aware of the box on the desk with Abbott's items from her office including the laptop. One of the members took that and exited the flat.

"Clear, Sir, the devices previously inserted by our suspect have been removed. We have several prints to run through HQ and INTERPOL."

"Ok move out. I will lock up. Zamir stay behind. Something is on your mind. What is it?"

"Not sure, I've got a plan forming."

"Where're you headed?"

"To HQ if they let me in again after the headache I gave them yesterday." He was grinning, "You?"

"I'm going over to the team at the Radisson and speak with them. This is coming to a rapid end, I can feel it."

"I agree. You know how to reach me." Zamir left closing the door as Hawk looked around her place satisfied then headed down the stairs, outside and after a quick glance around, toward the Radisson. He knocked at the door and one of the team members opened it.

"I've got a change of plans for you guys tonight."

"Is HQ appraised?"

"Negative."

"What's the deal?"

*** 

$M$aggie left after six o'clock and stopped at the corner to hail a cab when her '*friend*' pulled up. "Hi, I had no idea you were still with me." As she got in pulling the door shut. "Isn't it about time I know your name?"

"Negative, Miss and yes, I'm still with you. Home, right?" She grinned. "Yes, and hurry it I have things to do. Can you speed and get away with not being stopped by the local police?" He laughed. "No Ma'am, they'd stop me. Then I'd be forced to lie to get you out of another mess."

Maggie gasp. "Oh, so Hawk told you about me." He laughed. "Negative, he told me to watch out. You like to get others into situations. We'd better stop there, Miss, you never know who is listening and the shit that could put us both in."

He let that tail off as Maggie pondered it for a second, then leaned further between the front seats. "Well he's a damn bastard and we know it."

They both laughed out loud. A rolling it hurt like hell belly laugh and it felt so damn good to her! But there was no verbal response from the soldier in the front seat.

*Smart guy*, she thought.

Shutting the cab door and waving her new unknown friend off, she entered the front lobby and took the working elevator up to her flat. The box was missing along with the laptop. It was clear that Susan had been there as well as the team right behind. Since the keys were on the counter but nothing else. It was of small comfort. Shrugging shoulders she started to pace. There was important data Hawk needed. But how to get it to him? This had been relayed to his unit but no word on what she was to do had come back yet.

At nine-thirty she changed into her nightgown and robe and was just preparing to call it a night when there was a knock at the door. Peering through the small peephole, relief spread through her body. It was Doug. Opening it, he entered then locked it.

"I didn't want to text. I thought I'd take a chance you'd be okay with me coming this late, are you?"

"Yes, do you have news?"

"Some, but I wanted to see what you have first, do you mind?"

"I was calling it an early night. Come on. My laptop in the bedroom. I've been anxious about you seeing this. It's damn important." He followed behind as she sat at her writing desk and inserted the flash drive. He leaned down, arms around her completely. Maggie opened the documents. Rising, she motioned him to sit. "You will want to take a good look. Go ahead. I'm going to the kitchen and will be back shortly."

She seemed so different, he thought, monitoring her retreat. Zamir was right. He needed to keep an eye on her now.

Hawk looked through all the attachments and shook his head calling out to her. "Maggie, do you understand what this fully means?"

"I do." She reappeared leaning against the side of the wooden desk. "Caren was working with someone. No obvious name. The big question is who? You had no knowledge so it's not the Army. It also means that bomb was meant for her, not as a warning to me. Someone must have gained enough data to move her above suspicion to a threat of some kind."

He removed the flash. "How many copies do you have? Did you clean the drive?"

"One backup in a secure location and yes the drive has been swept totally cleaned. I even logged back on to ensure nothing was left behind. What are you thinking?"

"That I'd better get this transmitted to command now. I'll head to Chepstow and send it from my laptop. How about some company when I'm through?"

"Yes." He stood as she walked him toward the door. "Lock it and go to bed. I'll use my key to get in. I won't be too long." Pulling her toward him, he leaned down and kissed her lips. Exiting, he halted, listening to ensure the lock engaged. Then bolted down the back stairs and out to the Rover while taking out his cellphone.

"Zamir, Maggie struck gold. She's got her hand on contacts, financial webs and more. Abbott was undercover and I'm guessing she was placed by MI5 to monitor Perkins against our knowledge."

"Do you have documents?"

"Affirmative and it's all mighty damning."

"Do you suspect Perkins knows it was removed?"

"No, she may think it was someplace other than the office and laptop. Especially since her fingerprints were all over everything Maggie packed up and Perkins brought to the flat."

"I'll meet you in Chepstow."

Hawk drove off and as he pulled into his driveway, Zamir drove in on the opposite side, driver's side window lowering.

"What's the plan?"

"Abbott's apartment. To see if there has been any activity."

"Are you delivering the flash drive personally to HQ tonight?"

"Nope. Will transmit to the General. He will ensure it's placed in the proper hands. There are many names that will be incriminated and I've no doubt some will be surprising for him to see."

"If my name is on that list it's bogus."

Hawk laughed. "No, my friend, you were not on there. Nor was I."

"Then go and take care of it and I'll swing by Abbott's and check it out."

"Sounds good. Keep me posted. I'm going back to Maggie's later."

Hawk locked the Rover and entered in through the garage doors as Zamir pulled out of the driveway and drove off.

Walking through and into the house, he picked up an alternate phone and rang the General.

"Better be damn good, Hawk, for you to call this late at night."

"Sir, it is. I'm transmitting a large file. I need you to review it immediately while I wait on the line. Then we can discuss it."

"Hang tight, son, I'm in a different office now. Okay, go ahead, send it." Hawk did, then sat in his chair, legs on top of the desk, crossed.

"How did this reach your hands?"

"Maggie."

He released a gruff, "Go on Hawk."

"She took care of packing up Abbott's things at the office today and discovered this on her laptop, deleting it and removing it from all access and history. She saved two copies to flash drives. I have this one. The other is in a secure location. I will lock it up here until you tell me who to turn it into."

"Hawk, this nails several coffins."

"I know, General. What are your orders?"

"Is my daughter home now?"

"She is."

"Good. Is the team still monitoring?"

Hawk omitted answering that with complete honesty since he'd given them the night off, so to speak. But they were in close range if he needed them in a hurry. "Yes."

"Tomorrow at first light I'll fly from Edinburgh to London. To ensure her safety, I want you to go back and stay with her."

"Roger that, Sir."

"And Hawk?"

"Yes?"

"Tell her I'm very proud but forbid her to do anymore." They both laughed.

"I'll be sure to pass that along."

Disengaging from the call Hawk looked around, grabbed his keys and headed back to Maggie's. The drive seemed to take an eternity tonight. Parked in a safe location close by, he took the stairs, unlocked the door, latched it back up and found her sound asleep in the bedroom.

He shed all clothing and slid in next to her and felt the warmth. She did not budge as he gently pulled her onto his chest. Lifting above him she smiled before kissing his lips.

"Are you feeling better?"

He hoped she was aware that was really two questions rolled into one.

"Yes, very well." Moving to her backside as his hands gently began to roam.

"Mind if I remove this?"

"Be my guest."

"Thanks for the invitation." The warmth of their bodies brought them even closer as Doug kissed her, then pulled back slightly. His eyes penetrated through hers asking a silent, yet important question.

"Yes." As her lower lip dropped, quivering, her voice barely above a whisper. "I need you. I need you to take away the rest of my pain in a way only you can."

His touch was tender, voice raspy, "I can do that for you."

Entering her she resisted his slower pace and took over. Taking him along on a steamy ride that brought them to a shuddering climax in just a few minutes.

Maggie knew he understood how she felt. Why she needed it just like that.

Closing his arms around her, she nestled on her side as he nibbled on one earlobe, placing a moist kiss on her neck.

"It seems we both needed something tonight."

"Soldier, that's a sorry ass way to say you missed me. You can do better, work on that. But, I missed you too." He shook his head as that grin she truly loved appeared. "Anyway, how'd you make out?"

"I've been in touch with the General and he is going to London in the morning. The shit's going to hit the fan. I surmise this will all be dusted and done in less than forty-eight hours."

"I knew it was important. I'm glad Pops is handling it from here. He will shake things up."

Doug's cellphone vibrated on the nightstand. Reaching over her he grabbed it, pushed the button to display the message and together they read it; "*Abbott's flat compromised. The team dispatched.*"

"It had to have been Susan or someone from the cell. Good. I hope they're fired up and pissing mad at what they did not find. Still, I wish they left her place alone. Seems so wrong, she's barely been gone a few days."

"Hang on. I have to send a text." She watched as he sat up and typed a brief message to her father copying a name she did not recognize. Setting it down, he then pulled her back up against him.

"Don't you have to go?"

"Nope."

"Ah, I bet Pop told you to be here tonight, right?"

"Partially, I was already coming back, remember? I'm following orders. His and my own."

Rolling over and facing him, his hand snug against her waist the other playing with her long silky hair, she leaned in and kissed him.

"No matter. I'm glad to see you and that you're here."

"I know, little one, now close your eyes and get some rest. Oh, and your father said to tell you he is proud of you."

"What else?"

"Smart ass. That he forbids you to do anymore."

She yawned, snuggling closer to his warmth. "He knows I never truly listen to him." As his hand wove through her hair it soothed her. In seconds she was sound asleep.

# Chapter Sixteen

She was up early feeling the rumpled indentation where he slept. Knowing it was no longer warm when she dragged her body out of the bed and put her robe on over her naked limbs. Still feeling aches and pains, Maggie entered the kitchen where he was sitting on a stool working on his laptop.

"Morning."

"Damn it, Hawthorne, you can't stay over anymore if you can't sleep later than five." He stood, poured her a hot cup of tea then set it on the countertop in front of the stool next to his. "That may take me some years, Maggie. You know how it goes."

She could hear it. His tone was crisp, mind distracted.

Sitting, she snooped. "What's up?"

"Zafir. There is enough INTEL to go in there and clean house. But, my gut tells me they will close up shop and bug out before we get that damn government clearance to enter."

"So, you need someone inside, don't you?"

"Yeah, but who?"

She waited.

"Hmm, good question." Then glanced over at her staring her straight in the eyes.

"What are your plans today? I need to know your whereabouts."

"Just errands; shopping downtown, post office, getting a rental car from the Radisson. Not much. I'll be around for a spell. What time do you head out?"

"Soon, the General is already in London and they're preparing to dispatch soldiers, MI5 and 6 shortly. I'm awaiting orders. This is the part I detest. Waiting. Waiting while they get their shit together because, so many others are involved. It's frigging clear they should give Zamir and I the green light to proceed. We don't need a damn soul to hold our hands."

She was thinking he was referring to her father overseeing this, but he must have realized how that sounded and added lastly, "The General will help to expedite this process. Without him cutting red tape it could drag on for two days."

Maggie got up and maneuvered around the cupboards and refrigerator, then set about making a proper breakfast. She was starved. When it was in the oven slid one hand up over his shoulder and placed a kiss on his neck. "Going to take a shower while that cooks. Just letting you know my whereabouts."

He opened the glass door as she was washing her hair, arms above her shoulders. There was no escaping him in here, she knew, as she squirmed slightly while he nibbled on one perky nipple. "I just heard from HQ. The General is expected in the vicinity at thirteen-hundred hours. I'll be leaving shortly. I have no idea how long I'll be gone. Could be hours or a few days."

The warm water rinsed her hair as she wound arms around his neck drawing their lips together. "Okay, I'll keep my cellphone on and charged just in case. I've re-activated the GPS in the event someone kidnaps me." She grinned slyly as his eyes flashed a silent warning. Oh, she got it. But chose to ignore it. That strong women's intuition warning her to proceed cautiously. He was always keen to see through everything she said. Fully aware he was too intuitive. Suddenly, she knew it was imperative to get him off her trail. As the perfect cover presented itself, and it was right here in her flat.

"I was thinking about taking the box over to the Abbott's this morning. That's my first stop after getting a rental. I'm sure she'll want me to stay for a spell. I expect I won't be leaving there for a while. After that, I'll see how my time looks for the rest of the day before I decide my next direction."

That worked. He seemed to relax. Then his pager went off. Both knew what that meant. Grabbing a towel, he wrapped it around his waist, left her there and toned back a reply.

"I've gotta go."

"Okay." She had stepped out grabbing a towel and dried off.

"Anything you want to tell me before I head out?"

"Nope, I won't tell you to be safe. I know you've been doing this a long time. All the same," she shrugged both shoulders, "I'll still worry about you. Get in touch with me as soon as you can."

He had pulled her close now fully clothed. "Deal." He moved away eyeing her once more before closing the apartment door shut.

Ear pressed to the door, Maggie listened, apprehensive while waiting to hear the exit door click shut. *Fuck*, she thought. *If he even caught a whiff of what I am doing, he'll twist my bloody neck!*

Then she heard it and breathed a deep sigh of relief moving into the bedroom and took out proper clothing. Jeans, green cashmere sweater, a heavier pair of socks and her lower hiking boots. She needed to be prepared just in case. Under her right pant leg around a sock, she attached then tightened the Velcro securing a sheath and very sharp knife. It had been her Pops from way back. Still deadly, but would serve a different purpose now.

Sliding the SIG and extra mags inside the undetectable interior zippered pocket of her Sharif crossbody bag, Maggie dropped in lipstick, cellphone, tissues and a mini water bottle. Holding it by the strap it felt light enough. Glancing around the room she searched for her keys. Where had he put them? Finally located, she grabbed a leather biker jacket from the closet and left with her ticket to gain entrance to Stonefield in her left hand and Caren's box balancing over a right hip. At the Radisson's car rental desk, it took less than fifteen minutes before she had the paperwork for her temporary set of wheels all taken care of.

Maggie pulled up and parked the rental car a short walk from the Abbott's home. Just for a second she closed her eyes, resting head back and contemplated if it was a grave mistake not wiring up. Finally gathering up enough strength and courage, she got out and went around to the passenger's side and took out the box. Walking up the path she stood at the large wooden front door for what seemed like an eternity, then raised a hand and knocked.

"Oh, Maggie, please come in. Caren's dad is at the church talking with the Bishop. I see you have the box with you. Oh, dear. I am chattering away and all with you standing out there on this cold afternoon. Please forgive me and come in."

Maggie hugged her then set the box on the window seat in the living room. "Would you like me to bring this up to her room and you can look through it another time?"

"Yes, dear, that would be best. It's on the second floor. Third door on the right."

As Maggie opened the bedroom door and peered inside, a sudden sadness filled her heart. As she stepped over the threshold, her nostrils flared inhaling Caren's scent as it quickly engulfed Maggie's senses. She imagined everything was exactly the way her parents left it when she moved out years ago.

Setting the box down on a chair by the window, she glanced around at the walls, shelves and all the awards from years of equestrian events. Lots of old pictures from high school and university were displayed all over the place.

One lone tear slid down Maggie's cheek dropping to the beige carpet under her boots. She dabbed the wetness with one lone finger. Then pulled out a tissue and dried her eyes. Tucking it back into her pocket, she looked at her reflection in the large dressing mirror. Just above one curved part of the wooden frame rested a happy picture of Caren and her sister when she had graduated from university.

Maggie touched it softly feeling emotions rage through her. Her thoughts turned to her very own sister and how close they are. If ever she could make a difference it was now. The woman that glared back did not look sorry, sad and scared. Instead, she locked eyes with herself and found strength and determination radiated deep inside. Turning away from the reflection, not glancing back, Maggie closed the door softly and walked back down the stairs to spend a few minutes with Mrs. Abbott.

Back in the living room, Mrs. Abbott had brought out a pot of tea and some cake on a beautifully hand-painted wooden tray. "Maggie," she patted the seat beside her, "Sit with me for a spell. Can I pour you a cup?"

"That'd be nice. There's a chill of fall in the air today. That's a beautiful tray. I know Caren loved painting. Did she do that for you?"

"Yes, we have several pieces she gave me over the years. No matter how much time she dedicated to her work, she always found that painting helped her to unwind."

The irrelevant conversation in its own sense was therapeutic. It was as if Mrs. Abbott was just mumbling out loud to no one. Except Maggie *was* there.

Sipping the tea, neither spoke many words.

"Can I do anything for you and the family?"

"No dear, just bringing that over for me was an enormous help. We're going over to my sister's tonight for dinner and staying the night. It will be good to go out. Are you on leave?"

"I am. The Professor mandated it. I'm off all this next week and already have no clue what to do with myself. It's only Saturday. I wish you would let me help you. Wash laundry, scrub floors, go to the post office, walk your pretend dog. Something."

They both laughed. "Dear, you will still come around and visit, won't you? Maybe your Mum will come when she's here next. I like being with you both."

"You can count on me to check in with you often, I promise." Maggie stood. "I have shopping to do and want to make it to the farmer's market before it closes. My cupboards are bare. I have no idea who's been eating from it. Hasn't been me." Both women stood at arm's length.

"That's okay, Maggie, I'm glad to see you."

"Me too, Mrs. Abbott, please hug everyone for me and I'll be in touch soon."

"I will dear. Mr. Abbott will be here next time. I will make sure." They hugged a few seconds longer before Maggie disengaged from her. Chewing the inside of her mouth to hold back the tears. Once outside she gulped in the crisp air then let it out while walking toward the rental.

Sitting inside the vehicle she turned the key, glanced at the envelope on the seat then up to Caren's bedroom window then nodded several times. Determined. The hour was now. D-Day. Engaging the shift to first gear, she drove the car up the street and headed back to Bristol. It seemed to take hours as her mind formed what she hoped was a solid plan.

A steely calmness enveloped Maggie, reinforcing her intention to have closure. Closure for Caren. Closure for her family. Closure for the cowards that did this. Nothing and no one would stop her. Parking a few blocks from Stonefield, she placed her campus parking block up on the dash as a precaution in the event she never returned to the rental.

Grabbing the envelope, she locked the car, turned, then headed straight for her destiny.

Not too far from Stonefield's main doors she acutely became aware of being watched. Using a trick of her own, a high-powered listening device, she inserted it into her left ear, then listened in on all that was going on around.

"Are you seeing what I am seeing? What the hell is *she* doing here?"

"Shit, I don't know. But this whole situation has turned bad. Inform Hawk now. Zamir is already in position, but I've no confirmation exactly where that is."

"Go ahead and send the message. We can't proceed until we have more INTEL. The General is going to be bull-shit."

"Forget about the General. Hawk's going to be bull-shit."

That was all Maggie needed to hear. With each determined stride, she moved on up the walkway toward the main door. Stood there only a fraction of a second, then knocked.

\*\*\*

When Hawk received the text, he glared at it for several seconds. A vein in his neck throbbed as anger rose. *What in God's name was she doing?*

The General was next to him, watching, and as they squared off, face to face, he knew someone had done something stupid. He knew before Hawk's words came out who it was.

"General, I've got news and it isn't good. We are at a full stop."

He moved closer, hands on hips.

"It's your daughter. She's just entered Stonefield."

"What the fuck is she doing there and how the hell did she get in. Just opened up the front door and closed it behind her?"

"Don't know, Sir." Then Hawk recalled the envelope and overdue accounts and was bloody pissed at himself for forgetting that conversation at his home in Chepstow.

"I do know, General. She's been snooping. Trying to find a way in when she latched on to a pretty good idea and followed it through. I'll save the details for later. But clearly, it worked. Shit, you have to give me the green light now, Sir."

"Who's close enough to pick up a conversation?"

"Zamir's team."

"Contact him now."

Hawk tapped his mic on and spoke. "Ugly Goose, Baker one here, repeat Baker one, come in."

"Roger, Baker One, go ahead."

"Unexpected package has arrived."

"Affirmative, Baker One, no communication established, will advise. Ugly Goose out."

"Roger that Ugly Goose, Baker one standing by."

"General, Zamir monitored her entering and has no further information. His team is gathering INTEL and will advise. We are on stand-by."

"That cheeky girl. Will she ever learn? I'm more surprised than angry she got in that easily. Is she still hooked up to a transmitter?"

"Negative. I already texted communications. They have advised the frequency is dead. She obviously didn't want us to know."

"Damn that daughter of mine. I'm not sure I can help her this time."

"Sir, what are your orders."

"Hawk, at all costs. Do what you will."

"Yes, Sir." Hawk moved out to Zamir's secure location close to Stonefield.

"What the hell is she thinking?"

"Don't you know that's your department, not mine." Both men stared at each other, slight grins appearing.

"She's armed. I had just a few seconds to run a thermal on her. Carrying a handgun, mags and a pretty nasty knife under her right pant leg."

"When I left her, she was naked. I guess I need to check with her every day and see what she will be wearing." Their grins grew.

"Damn feisty wench you got there, Hawk. She may have bested us all. I'm beginning to feel like I want to bring her back to Israel with me. I could use her."

"May heaven shit on your head, friend. No way in hell you'll do that." They laughed. Pulling out the layout of the building displaying they had three points of entry. "Move team three behind the building, two to that rooftop and we can move in."

"What's your plan?"

"Bring in team one. I'll go over it." Zamir got on his mic, "One report to base, repeat, report to base."

*** 

That seemed way too easy Maggie thought. Once inside there seemed to be young women and men alike scurrying in all directions as she saw a face she recognized. "I'm not sure you know me. I am Maggie Cohen from the library. I came to drop this off for Daniel Levy." She reached into her crossbody bag and lifted the flap removing the envelope. He looked suspiciously at her.

"Why didn't you just send it by campus courier?"

Maggie lowered her eyes just as they welled up with tears. "I'm sure you heard my assistant was just killed by a car bomb a few days ago. I found this when I cleaned out her office. She was going to take care of it for me. I," she stammered, "thought I should be the one to do this now."

"Follow me."

Maggie recognized her right away from behind before she even turned around and they were face to face. She had expected her to be here and had a dialogue already formed in her mind. "Susan. Hello. Are you finalizing the story for the paper?"

She turned suspiciously. Maggie could tell she was alarmed by her presence.

"Yes, nearly finished. What brings you here? I must say it's highly unusual to have someone of your position delivering overdue notices."

Maggie wondered how she knew that.

"I have something personal to give to Levy. The man that let me in thought he would be in this direction? Sadly," she continued to buy more time, "Caren was going to take care of this for me but…." Glancing backward looking for where that guy had disappeared, Maggie's stomach lurched as warning bells loudly rang in her mind. She knew she had to get out and get out now.

"Well, you should have thought about your actions a bit more closely. But let me extend our gratitude. You just did us a huge favor." Susan's face said it all. She had indeed fucked up by coming here.

"Now, why don't you just follow me."

Quickly realizing the double meaning behind Susan's statement, Maggie tried to bug off. "If you don't mind giving this to him?" She held it in her hand, "then I can be on my way. Still not feeling up to par yet."

Susan stopped. "You mind if I open that envelope?"

Maggie handed it to her looking at bit confused. "Well, it's personal business between my department and him. Why do you want to see it?"

"Oh, dear Maggie. Let me make this perfectly clear. If you cooperate you may see another day and not end up like Abbott. But if you don't, no one will be able to save you and you'll pray for a swift end."

Her eyes locked with Perkins, face blanched.

"What did you say?"

"You are bright, figure it out."

"I don't understand, Susan, you had something to do with Caren's death? But why?"

"Before I answer that how about you open up that bag and let me have a look inside."

She flipped open the crossbody holding it wide for Perkins to view the contents entirely. "Unzip the top flap." Maggie did as Perkins checked to make sure her cellphone was shut off, glanced at the lipstick and keys then shrugged.

"You really had no idea, did you? I find that hard to believe having heard all the stories how you can't keep your nose out of anybody's business. You're not just the highlight of college meetings and gossip, but the INTEL world as well. How much shit did your General father cover up for you, Maggie? Must have been a lot because your fuckin' dossier reads like Mary Poppins and we all know, don't we, that you are hardly her."

Maggie flinched.

Perkins grin grew as she let out an evil laugh. "Still don't get it, do you? Man, you really are a dumb bitch inside."

There was a pause as Susan ripped open the envelope and looked at the bill. "You came here for this?" Perkins broke out in laughter waving it around letting the envelope fall to the floor, keeping hold of the bill. She was bordering on lunacy as Maggie moved one step back.

"As you see. How could you do this, Susan, have Caren killed? She was just my assistant and of no harm to a soul. Perhaps it was not she you were looking to hurt, but me?"

"No, idiot, this had nothing to do with you at all. Caren was not as she appeared, you know. While you were playing games, other people we were playing you for a fool."

Maggie stood poised to flee, glancing quickly around for the closest exit.

Perkins laughed louder. "You are fucked, my dear woman," as she moved closer. "Come with me. I want you to meet some very interesting people. Who have a keen interest in *you*."

Maggie wished she had kept her device on. But knew something was going to happen. Hoping her father and Hawk had been informed. She followed along as suddenly her blood turned cold. Heart possibly stopped beating. Maggie had no idea. But now she really felt the chilling hand of fear grip her entire being.

"Michaez, look who's stopped in to pay us a visit."

Zafir glanced up while he and other cell members were taping up two younger men with explosive vests. Maggie recognized them. American students. She knew who they were as her heart sank further and hope along with it.

"Susan, what the hell is going on? Explain yourself now."

"She came to bring this bill to Levy." She displayed it, waving it around "She is dense. Ignorant. I did thank her for coming to us."

He handed the duct tape over to Davide to continue and grabbed Maggie by the arm shoving her further into the room. That abrupt and rough movement caused her to openly flinch from wounds not healed from the explosion.

"So, Miss Cohen, Maggie, daughter of the great British Army General Cohen. You are indeed a wanted visitor. A very welcomed visitor indeed."

A violent internal eruption chilled her to the bone. Her body shook as she watched an evil smile appear on Zafir's dark-skinned face.

"Yes, we know who you are now."

Her mouth finally opened to speak. It was dry, words hard to get out. "What do you want from me? I can tell you right now my father will not negotiate with you. Whether it is me or any other person."

"You are, as you, British like to say, full of shit and you know it. He *will* negotiate for *you*. Where is your cellphone?"

"In my bag." She moved her hand to flip the flap as he came forward quick as lightning. But was halted by Perkins' hand gripping his arm. "She's clean. I examined the contents of the bag myself before I brought her in."

He nodded. "Take it out and get him on the phone."

Maggie pulled the cellphone out pushing down the on the button and held it in the palm of her hand, extended toward him.

"No, you call him. When you have him on the line, you tell him I want to talk with him. You tell him it is Zafir."

She spoke verbally to her phone, "Call the General." She had it on speaker remembering that once she turned it on, her exact location would be transmitted by GPS.

Hope renewed.

"Maggie. Where, are you?"

"Dad, I have you on speaker phone. I need you to listen to me. It's not clear what my status is, but I am in a room right now with Zafir and Perkins in Stonefield." She paused, lower lip quivering slightly. "Dad, stand-by, Zafir, wants to talk with you now."

She knew he would know something else was up. Maggie had never in twenty-nine years, called her Pops, Dad.

"Zafir, Cohen. Speak your intent with my daughter. But let me be clear. This is a warning. We will not negotiate with you. We don't have too. As shit smells, you will all be dead shortly."

Maggie bit slightly on her lower lip suppressing a grin feeling her father's strength transferred directly into the room. But quickly squashed by Zafir's next statement.

"It's damn clear to me, General, this will be a long, anticipated eye for an eye. You were the commander during the operation that destroyed my brother. Then sent his battered and tortured body back to Palestine presented to our family in a sacrilegious manner. It's my turn to return the favor. You will not see this daughter of yours again. Except as a desecrated body when it is returned to you as my brother was."

An enormous pause ensued as Maggie's world took a dramatic change and she knew action had to be taken swiftly. Or, this was going to become bloody and deadly.

"I'll hunt you like the dog you are, Zafir, you will never leave this building alive."

"No, I won't. But neither will your daughter."

Maggie stepped back a few feet avoiding his attempt to tear the cellphone away and spoke fast. "General, they have an arsenal in here and are wrapping several men with body explosives. Vests."

That was as far as she got before he knocked the phone and slapped her face. So roughly her head snapped back just as he smacked it again. Blood now oozing from the corner of her right eye. It wasn't bad enough that her body had been badly beaten up by the explosion just a few short days ago, now this. She hurt so much, perhaps death would bring relief.

Then the well of determination overflowed, filling every corner of her being with courage. It was almost as if a light went on inside. Burning bright. Burning Strong. Maggie stood her ground eyeing him with hatred, fighting back. "Is that what you pigs do? Blow up innocent people and beat on helpless women? Do you feel like more of a man now for it?"

She stepped closer as Perkins moved between them, sideways, and her timing was perfect allowing Maggie one whole minute to unzip the bottom of her bag and remove the SIG. Flicking the safety off, she shoved Perkins into Zafir with an amazing strength born out of sheer desperation. It was just hard enough causing both to stumble. Affording her a few precious seconds to act.

Maneuvering the SIG behind her back, Maggie quickly lifted her sweater and tucked it into her jeans. While with the other hand inserted one mag into her back pocket. Then zipped the bottom of the bag.

As Perkins moved away from Zafir, he reached for Maggie and propelled her so hard, she barely caught the edge of a table before slamming into the wall. Shaking her head and managing to steady for only a second, before he descended upon her with such rage in his features, she flinched just waiting for the next blow.

This time he swung his fist with such might, when he hit Maggie's jaw she lifted off the floor and landed head first, banging it twice before weaving in and out of consciousness. Fighting it became so hard as shaky fingers raised, feeling the salty stickiness of her own blood dripping at the corner of her mouth.

Then it happened.

Adrenalin kicked in. Along with that Cohen sense of survival. Rolling to her side, keeping her body facing him, the weapon hidden, she put up a hand and pleaded.

"Stop! What do you want me to do? Help you get out? You know you can use me as a human shield and they will all back off. That I know for sure."

"No, bitch, this is our final mission. We have trained new members, unseen and unknown faces that will continue our cause. We do not need you for a damn thing other than *dead*."

Maggie lost hope.

Then gunfire was heard coming from the next room. She could not quit! Simultaneously, Hawk and Zamir entered their area with lightning speed. The door broke, shattering into splinters as they entered, machine guns poised and prepared to kill. Quickly they accessed their enemies' positions to take them both out if they so much as twitched. The General was just behind them.

"Go ahead, Zafir, make your move. Killing you right now would be my great pleasure. But make it quick. My comrade, Zamir, wants his hands on you himself. His punishment will not be as merciful as mine."

Zafir glanced over and knew when he heard '*Zamir*' who he was – *the hangman*. Death was closing in on him fast.

Perkins stood frozen. Eyes darting toward the closest exit as it suddenly swung open with maddening force as Davide, Levy, and Horowitz entered with AK-47's firing rapidly around the room.

Maggie crawled on her belly not feeling the pain any longer. Then caught sight of Perkins reaching inside her jacket for her piece. Maggie removed the SIG and using the tactical laser quickly lined up the light on Perkins' hand and pulled the trigger. Blood oozed, forcing Perkins to drop the gun, hitting the floor with a thud.

"You bitch!" Perkins screamed holding her hand as a pool of blood formed. Maggie swiftly stretched out a leg and kicked the gun across the room sliding away from Perkins and into a corner beneath some stacked chairs. She'd not get to that without being shot again. Maggie was sure as hell going to make Perkins rued the day she and these bastards killed Caren.

Perkins was up on all fours crawling with the most frighteningly twisted and grotesque face Maggie had ever seen. Coming straight toward her. She leaned back and sent a shot right through Perkins left shoulder. The bullet went clear and clean and lodged itself in a wall behind her.

"You move one inch and I'll give you more pain than you can stand. I'll just keep putting them in you one at a time until you stop. But mark my words, I will not kill you. I want you alive. *You* will pay for Caren's death.

The force behind Maggie's words did stop Perkins's progress as she slid to her side and began to cry. Not one soul gave a damn.

For some very odd reason when she was reacting to Perkins all sound seemed to dissipate like they were alone in this big room. Just the two of them.

Now the resonating noise was deafening!

Clearing from under the table and sliding along the floor on the opposite wall, gunfire was going on all around her. She crouched up to see Zafir reaching to take an extra weapon from Horowitz and shot his left arm and top right shoulder as the AK-47 hit the ground at his boots. He was so stunned. Could do no more than drop to his knees attempting to pick it up when a dirty boot against his head prevented any movement.

"Go for it shit head. Doesn't matter to me when I kill you. Just as soon do it now." It was Zamir who pushed his boot further grinding Zafir's face into the cold flooring.

Just as Maggie saw her Pops knock one of the terrorists over the back of the head dropping him to the ground, she felt it. "Damn it." She hissed as pain seared through her body. She'd been hit.

Never thought about giving up or setting the SIG down to assess her wound, she stayed under cover until she heard, "Clear!"

Maggie glanced around seeing Doug, Zafir, Pops and four other soldiers.

It seemed like it lasted forever. But later she would find out it had been less than three minutes. The sound of boots shuffling grew closer until she was being pulled up and placed on the top of one of the wooden tables. It was Doug.

"I can't even tell you how angry I am with you right now, Maggie. The only one here that is proud of what you did it Zamir, and he's a damn fool."

Maggie glanced over his shoulder watching as Zamir was handcuffing Zafir. She knew that he would be taking this group of men into his custody and they'd never make it out of England alive. They would quietly disappear never to be seen from again and no one at Mossad would twitch an eye.

Zamir nodded, grinning. "I have faith in you, Maggie Cohen. It's a good weapon you carry, and you shot it like a pro. You are your father's daughter and he will be proud of you after he forgets his anger."

She grinned while Hawk probed her left arm, rather roughly she thought, as her eyes watered and Zamir continued. "Unfortunately, Hawk will be a different matter. You will need to give him some time. I've never seen him this pissed off."

She nodded.

Hawk didn't look Zamir's way.

"See, he doesn't turn and swear at me like he wants. I'm sure I'll feel his wrath sooner or later. Until I see you again, little lady, be well." They exchanged smiles.

She watched them leave the room as swarms of MI5 and 6 operatives entered and began their tasks of collecting details. Stonefield was officially under lockdown.

By night's end, they would all be rounded up. Some innocent used as cover, but most were not. Nothing of interest would appear in any newspaper the next day. It would all easily be filed away protected by those in high-ranking positions like her Pops.

She watched loads of things come out of the back room while Hawk worked on her. They found several explosive devices, detonators, high powered powders, manuals and their plan for the next two explosions of which one was to be in London, the other Manchester. It turned into a massively successful joint mission.

"Damn it, can't you at least give me something strong to drink or let me remove my knife? I can gnaw on the damn blade while you probe me like this. It hurts like hell."

She consciously looked down to her right and made sure the SIG's safety was on. It was not, so she flicked at it just as her Pops leaned against the table next to her placing a hand on an uninjured shoulder.

"Your mother would have my hide, daughter, but I'm proud. Your aim was spot on."

"Pops, we both know it's the laser. No brainer. Fine weapon though. I was told before I could keep it."

Her humor brought about a wince as he tied a bandage a bit too tight. Maggie bit back a retort. She could feel it. He was indeed pissed. He'd not said another word to her since telling her how angry he was.

Finished, Pops hugged her. "Hawk, file your report later. I'll leave her in your capable hands. Do what you will. Daughter, I head to HQ. I will talk with you soon. As far as your mother is concerned, I am golfing. You need to stay away for a while to heal those facial wounds. I need my pretty daughter back." He reached up lovingly and touched her swollen and cut lip and battered face. "You decide how to handle that with your mother. She said you are off all next week, that so?"

"Yes, and I will cover you, and Pop, this is the last time I interfere. I promise."

"Daughter, right now I believe you. But in six months or a year, let's have this talk again and see how you did." He kissed her forehead and looked at the wounds.

She'd be fine. Patting her on the back he exited Stonefield with three soldiers in tow.

"Can you walk?"

"Absolutely." She hurt like hell, especially where her hip smacked the floor.

"Okay, head out with Zak." He pointed toward a burly soldier dressed in fatigues. "He will get you further medical treatment. Go."

He was all business right now. She could feel it. Could tell he really was pissed. Sliding off the table he held her by the right arm for a moment looking like words were forming on his lips. Then, his eyes turned cold and hard, mouth clamped shut.

"Zak, move her out. She's prepared to travel. I'll report in once on base." That parting comment seemed more for the soldier than for her.

Maggie was glad the jeep had its hardtop on as she sat in the front placing the seat belt around her shoulder and clipped it in. "Zak, he's really angry."

"Ma'am, it's not a great idea I discuss the LC with you. He's filled us in only briefly on your hand in this mission."

"Ah, I see. But he's pissed, isn't he?"

Zak grinned. "Been on a few missions with the LC and never seen him like this."

Apprehension gnawed at Maggie along the entire drive to the base. She had plenty of time to examine her stupidity over all the years and this one iced it all. But, it had worked out in the end and none of the team members even got shot. She had been the only incident and that's not bad. She thought. But her mind kept replaying the cold, hard look of his eyes when he helped her off the table. This time may be her last in getting involved, but she may have done irreparable damage to her relationship with Hawk.

# Chapter Seventeen

"Miss Cohen, you are cleared to exit the base. We have a jeep and driver ready outside to take you wherever you request."

She was perplexed. Four hours had passed, and he had not come in. But suspected he was debriefing and filing reports. Zamir had stuck his head in, nodded then hastily left.

Outside it was Zak sitting in the driver's seat. The jeep's engine rumbling as she climbed in and shut the door with quite a thud.

"Location?"

"My apartment. Zak, can you tell me if he is still on base?"

"Negative, Miss Cohen."

Crap she thought. "Do you need my address?"

"Negative." He seemed to be all Military bull-shit now as well. It didn't take long to get there as they rode along in dead silence. In less than an hour, she was outside the main entrance of her building. As Maggie grabbed her bag just before shutting the jeep's door, she thanked him and headed up the flight of stairs. As normal that damn elevator was out again. It was time for her to get a new place to live, period. It was time for many things.

In her apartment, she walked around not wanting to go into the bathroom or near any mirror to see her appearance. Knowing full well she'd look as beat up as she felt. Then she yelled into the empty place, "Idiot! You forgot your frigging rental car. She quickly phoned up a cab and ran downstairs awaiting the arrival half hoping it would be her special driver. But it was not.

"Where you headed to, Miss?"

"Stonefield house."

The cabbie nodded asking, "You are aware that area is quadrant off, right?"

Oh, if he only knew, she thought. "Yes, just as close as possible will be fine."

She paid him and walked down three blocks, found it, got in and started it up then returned home. Back inside, her next project was the damn cellphone which had been nearly destroyed. Moving over to her work desk, she logged on her netbook, obtained the number of her cell carrier, and rang customer service.

"Hello, this is Margaret Cohen and my cellphone has been destroyed. I'd like to have a replacement sent immediately and know what my options are for transferring files. It is still on but not operational." Finishing up she'd have it expressed for arrival the next day and then call them back and they would do a file transfer for her. Good that process took less than ten minutes. What now?

She went into the bedroom removing from her bag the Sig and mag placing it in the armoire and locking it with the skeleton key. Setting the key inside a draw under lavender parchment paper, she went to the kitchen and put on the kettle.

Sitting half on the stool with one foot on the floor, the other one dangled as Maggie rested her palm on a small portion of her face not beaten. Sighing sadly while glancing at the phone in the cradle latched onto the kitchen wall. She knew he was really pissed off. He had good reason to not be in touch with her. Perhaps that was it. Finished before it really began. She could break down and ring her Pops, but that might trigger her Mum's keen instincts and open Pandora's box.

That night when she went to bed with still no word, the pit of her stomach was relaying a strong message through her brain.

*"You fucked up big this time, you lost him."*

The telephone was ringing as Maggie glanced over at the clock. It was eight-thirty in the morning. Reading the number, she clicked the talk button right away.

"Sasha, hey, how are you?"

"Fine, Mags, but your Pops called, and the message was very strange. Maybe you can explain it to me?"

"What did he say?"

"That you may need some company and feel all cooped up right about now. What's happened? What did you do?"

This time Maggie felt the sting of those words more acutely than at any other time in her life. Where in the past she would have just laughed them off. But it was what she said, '*need some company.*' that nearly made her burst into tears.

"Can you come over? I am thinking about packing up for a few days. I'm just waiting for my new cellphone to be delivered before I decide where I am going."

"I'm on my way, Mags...."

Maggie opened the door wondering if her Pop had spoken with Hawk and indeed this was it. That he was not going to see her or even ring to check her status.

"Holy shit, you look like bloody crap. What the hell happened to you?"

"Do you mind coming in and not yelling down the hallway?" She closed the door suppressing a grin, after all, it was Sasha. Her longest and dearest friend in the world. One she needed most desperately right about now. "It's a long story, and most of it I can't even divulge. Pop was right. I'm sure glad to see you.

My new cellphone arrived, and I was just packing. Come with me to my room."

"Why are you doing that? Where're you headed? Tell me you are out of danger now?"

"Depends on how you view it, but yes I am."

"Okay, Maggie," she sat on the corner of the bed, "I saw your bike loaded on the back of your rental car. What are your plans?"

"Don't have a destination right now. I was going to just start driving and see where I landed."

"Are you on leave?"

"No. I'm on vacation for the week and possibly the one after as well. I have over four weeks to use up."

"Hmm, I've got an idea. Can I log on to your computer if it's not packed?"

"It's right there, go ahead." Maggie didn't even ask what she was up too. Just stood there at the armoire wondering what to select. Cycling and outdoor gear was a must along with a camera and sketchpad. *Ah*, she silently thought. *I'd love to sit somewhere peaceful and beautiful and draw again.* She'd not done that in a dog's age. Just how long was that anyway? Idle chatter was scattering through her mind and Maggie knew she was hurting more inside than outside. Holding the tears at bay with her friend in the room was becoming a burden she didn't want to bear any longer.

Sasha was suddenly standing in front of her causing a momentary retreat backward. "How about a private home near Dunster with long walks, abundant cycling routes and privacy in all directions? You can cook, sleep, do whatever you want. How does that sound?"

"Great. Who owns it?"

"My cousin. She is in the middle of a divorce."

"Jennie?"

"Yes. She and Rick have agreed to sell the house and part amicably. She's told the realtor that you will be there and to call the home before she has any showings. Will that work?"

"Oh, it does. Have I been there? I cannot recall that I have."

"Nope, you'd remember the coral house."

"Coral?"

"Yeah," she zipped the carry-on than the duffle bag. "Is this it?"

"Yup, I'm going to shop when I get there. Will you come along at least for the day?"

"I will, ready to get headed?"

"Sooner than later. I absolutely am."

Sasha helped her load up the rental vehicle. "When do you get your new wheels?"

"Soon, the insurance company has been contacted by the proper authorities and a check should be coming along in the next two to three weeks. I'll get a new one as soon as it arrives."

"Another BMW?"

"Nope, I want a fresh start. I was thinking about a red and white convertible MG or Triumph. I'm going to start looking while I'm off."

Hugging her, Sasha moved away to her car parked next to Maggie's. "Follow me. We will be there soon, and have you settled in no time. When we arrive, I'll head shortly after and get your staples. Can't have you scaring the living shit out of the locals."

Maggie reached up still feeling the tenderness. Knowing how the bruising would soon discolor her face and she'd have to apply a lot of makeup and wear wide hats to lend a shadow to it.

"Come on, Maggie, get in your car. Let's go."

The sixty-minute drive was beautiful as Maggie drove behind Sasha's Toyota resisting the desire to stop along the way. They drove through the most adorable old stone village of Wootton Courtenay. Maggie fell in love with it and the area instantly. A left just out of the tiny hamlet and they were pulling off the road and into the driveway of the coral house.

"Sash, this is amazing. You are right. It borders between shades of soft pink and coral. Which gives it an air of being a very peaceful place. You said it's for sale. What are they asking?"

"Don't know, but it has two acres. I used to love coming here for breaks of my own. There is a six-mile walk that you will fall in love with. It's close to Dunster and not far from Abbott's place if you want to pop in and visit. The expansive walks around Exmoor National Park are positively amazing. Plus, the real bonus is the trails for cycling and horseback riding. Mags, you will adore this place. Your healing will begin."

Maggie hugged her knowing what she meant to add, *"Both inside and out."*

"I'm so glad you could arrange this."

"Well, I've got my hand on the key shall we go in?"

Sasha took the time to show her around each room going over the security codes, heating system, and hot water boiler.

"Okay, are you all set with how to use the gas fireplaces? Oh, I nearly forgot. Make sure you are out if the realtor has a showing. Their office has your cellphone number."

"I wish you could hang around longer. But, I know you have work tomorrow. I appreciate the supplies, by the way. Now I am all set at least for a week. Maybe by then, I won't look so hideous."

They stood at the door hugging as Maggie watched her drive off waving. So, this was what it was like to have your own home? She started back through the hall to the drawing room and looked around at its expansiveness. She'd turn that into a reading area and library. Then walked out into the sitting room which she thought would become an office. Especially with the amazing views out back of the porch toward the gardens. Her eyes drifted to the field and hills beyond.

A peaceful oasis, yes, but it also was silent. Deafeningly silent as Maggie's insides turned out exposing all her fears. She gingerly smiled as a lone tear slipped down her right cheek. Not dotting it away, she let it fall. She would have that much-needed cry today and then it would all start to be easier. She hoped.

In the event it was muddy with all the rain yesterday, she changed into hard-soled hiking boots. Grabbed a few supplies and ventured to the top of the hill just beyond the border where the field was divided by a lovely old stone wall. Hearing rumble in the distance, she glanced up to the East and saw the storm clouds quickly approaching and knew her hike would wait for another day.

Back inside and up the stairs, Maggie had opted not to use the master bedroom. It seemed too large and she thought it would just swallow her up in its massiveness. Maybe later when she was more comfortable. Instead, she opted for the first of three other guest bedrooms with equally lovely views to the hills beyond.

Unpacking, she checked her cellphone. No messages. So, she finished unpacking and in stocking feet set out toward the kitchen to make a pot of tea. For five days all she did was walk, cycle, and read. Her body was heeling bit by bit. But her mind remained engaged with thoughts of Doug. It finally hit home. He was not coming to find her. Would not ring her. It truly was over. But in the admission of all she had done, getting into things she should not have, she realized something important. She really loved this home and the solitude it brought.

With her savings accumulated to a tidy sum, she made an offer and they readily accepted coming in just under asking price. Her minimal loan was processed by the Royal Bank of Scotland representative. Who did not foresee any delays or issues. For Jen and Rick, they graciously agreed to her moving in now. They would move their belonging around her schedule.

A week later they arrived with hired movers on Saturday morning at seven-thirty and by eight that night, when she returned with many things from her apartment, it really felt more like hers than theirs. She took the two full weeks off to let her arm, bruises, and cuts heal. Then returned at the end of the month.

It was a glorious moment when the realtor slapped a large, magnetic SOLD marker across the fore sale sign. Working through that first week was therapeutic, but Maggie was still recovering. Although it felt good to be behind her work desk. But every so often she would glance across to Caren's darkened one and feel such acute sadness. Then loneliness engulfed because Hawk had not made contact at all. Not even to find out how her wounds were healing.

Her business line rang. "Maggie Cohen."

"Maggie, it's Mum. Just when were you going to tell your Dad and I you bought that home?"

"Actually, I was going to wait until you came down for a visit and I surprised you. But, it appears someone let the cat out of the bag. Was it Sasha?"

"It was. Do you want some company this weekend? I could stay a spell and help you out."

"Nope. I'd like to wait until Christmas. Then I can decide what I want to do. There are a few rooms I'm toying with redecorating. You know what, Mum? I'm thinking about giving up my job here and taking up a small post at the library in Dunster. I certainly don't need the income with my savings, investments and the money Grand-Pops left us."

"Mags, is that a good idea? At least at the university, you are around other people. How will you meet anyone if you are so reclusive?" Maggie knew what her mother was trying to delicately say. She'd like to see her settled down with a husband and kids. Just like her brother and sister. She wanted that too. But truly believed that was not in her cards. At least not right now.

"Mum, I will be around all kinds of people at the Dunster Library, and if it's meant to happen it will. I've got to go now. I have a meeting with Seth to go over my resignation. I'll talk with you soon. Love to you and Pops."

Maggie hung up keeping her hand affixed to the phone and felt it again. Suppressing such a strong need to try Doug's cellphone, she stood and strode into Seth's office.

"One month. That means you are resigning before I retire. How about we keep you as needed to take care of the programs and training?"

"Nope, won't work, I'm ready for this. I've done enough and it's the right time. I'll work with human resources tomorrow to line up co-interviews with your schedule. Then we can all determine if I need to stay on longer." She slid him her official typed resignation. "This will do it." Standing, he moved around as she stood, and they hugged.

"Makeup and time heal external wounds, Maggie, but some may stick around for quite a bit longer."

She patted his hand clutching it for a minute. "I am healing and Dunster and Wootton Courtenay will be my solace. I will like working in that small library. I'm going to begin an after-school story-time for younger kids. Who knows, Seth, maybe I'll start painting again and write for the local press. I'm ready."

He smiled as they both heard the sadness in her voice. "Okay, Maggie, but I will miss you ever so much. I truly hope you find what you are looking for."

"Seth, thank you for all the years, sticking in there and for everything." With love in her heart, Maggie left his office and the building.

Pulling into the double garage glad it was Friday night, she settled onto the loveseat in the newly painted library. Glancing around, she smiled in earnest so happy this was her home and knew tonight, with the winds blowing off the Exmoor hills, the French doors needed to remain shut. Pushing a button on the remote, the gas fireplace came to life.

Sipping on a glass of wine, she heard gravel being kicked up in the front yard and wondered if someone was turning around at the bottom of her road again. Or, if one of her friends were popping in unannounced. A knock sounded at the front door. She got up, walked over and looked through the peephole

It was him.

Hand on the knob, she tried to steady her breathing. Slowly, she opened the door wide enough then stood there looking up into those gorgeous brown eyes she had missed so badly.

"Can I come in?"

She stepped aside allowing him to enter than shut the door. "Come through this way. I was just having a glass of wine. The weather had gotten cooler here. Can I get you a beer or something stronger?"

To them both, her voice sounded uncertain, shaky.

"That would be great."

He seemed on edge as she quickly left him standing there and went down through the long hallway into the kitchen. Without a backward glance, she knew he was just behind.

"This is really nice, Maggie, how many rooms?"

"Four bedrooms, two baths and nine in all."

"Your Pop said you just bought it and had given your notice at the school. Have you sold your flat?"

"Yes, almost right after. It seemed to all fall into place." She poured the amber liquid just as she knew he liked it, straight up and neat. Then she heard a very strange sound.

"Did you hear that?"

He grinned but did not reply. From beneath his half-zipped, very weathered, brown leather bomber's jacket, a tiny, fuzzy head appeared.

"Oh, it's a kitten!"
Maggie reached over placing her hand inside and scooped out the little Oreo cookie. It was all black and white and instantly maneuvered right up under her chin, purring.

"I knew it would be a wonderful fit."

"You remembered?" Her voice was quivering, eyes watering as she turned walking back to the sitting room. He came around the front, halting her progress.

"Yes, you said you were going to be ready to give up your post at the university, sell your flat, buy a home and live a quieter life. You did all of that without me. So, I thought I'd help you out with what was left."

The kitten had moved up to her shoulder as two cute little eyes were peering out at him from beneath Maggie's hair. Which was down and flowing softly in all directions.

"It seems like he has found a safe place to hide."

She grinned. "So, it's a male?"

"Yes, I'm sure you will find a suitable name. In the Rover I have a few supplies, food, a dish and a litter box until he's bigger to go out. Unless you keep him as a house cat."

"Not likely when there are mice to be had out in my fields." They both smiled.

"Can I see the rest?"

With the cat still neatly tucked close, she moved on nodding. "Sure," opening a door, "this is the utility room with my washer and dryer. Off that way is the porch which leads out to my shed." Closing that she moved back through the kitchen stopping and opening the door to her study. "I will work in here depending on what I decide to do next," as they moved onward.

"This is the library and through that entrance the sitting room. The views are wonderful when it's daylight. Come on, I'll show you the first floor."

Up the large, wooden stairway they went. Maggie had decided she liked the large master and was working in the other bedrooms and the bathrooms. "Very nice. You seem to have settled right in. This fits you perfectly."

She grinned. "You may think differently if you saw the exterior color during the day. I've been told it's a toss between soft pink and coral. But it's grown on me and I'm not going to change it."

He smiled. With his drink in hand, they entered the library as she picked up her wine glass and sipped.

"Thank you for the gift. He's perfect."

She sat on a single winged back chair setting the glass down resting it on a coaster. In the meanwhile, the kitten climbed down her shoulder and onto her lap nestling into a ball of fuzz as she grinned completely in love with it already.

"I've got it – Moon, he will be Moon. You know like the cow that jumped over the moon was black and white."

He laughed. "Do you mind if I pull over this hassock and talk with you there? I have a lot on my mind." His voice, deep and penetrating, caused her stomach to bunch up into a knot.

Her whole mood altered from apprehension to one of hope. The air crackled with it. The ambiance of the gas-lit fireplace, the wind howling outside, and the soft lights in the room radiated an intimate feeling.

Sitting in front of her, he folded his hands on his legs. Inches separated their bodies. She melted. He truly was here. Right in front of her now as blue eyes stared into brown.

"I was angry, Maggie, you had lied to me. Then over time, it became apparent that too much of being a hard-assed soldier remained inside. I sorely neglected your feelings over the loss of Caren. You wanted justice. But more than that you wanted to help. Felt driven by it."

"Yes," she whispered.

"You are the most beautiful woman I know. A rich, rare combination of smart, deadly and dangerous. Your Pop tells me you have changed since buying this house. That you really seem ready to lay to rest once and for all your ghosts. Are you?" He gave her no time to answer. "I just sold my house and sign in two days. You just sold your flat and bought this and it seems like a mighty large home for you to be living here by yourself. Don't you think?"

There he paused, as the air crackled. She looked deeply into his eyes and knew. She never wanted to retreat from them ever again.

"I've retired for good. Perhaps I will be brought in for consulting behind the scenes, but my missions are over. My apartment is back to the school's use and I am not teaching any longer since this last mission has been completed."

He stopped, watching closely. Drawing her deeper and deeper into his heart and soul. "I'm wondering," he paused, clasping her hands in his, feeling the warmth. "If there is a chance we can move forward."

Maggie could stand it no longer. Moving the kitten beside her on the chair, she slid onto his lap watching that wonderful grin she loved so much, had missed so badly, appear.

"You always liked to sit this way."

"I'm sure you know. But right now, it's more than that. I'm sorry for deliberately placing all of you in danger. For not trusting anyone including my Pops. I'm not going to nosey about like that again. I mean to spend a quiet life now. Explore more peaceful options."

"I'm sorry too, woman. I would not have had such an adverse reaction, one I had no clue how to deal with, if I was not so in love with you."

She smiled as he continued.

"I never liked to hear people say let's start over. That won't work for us. We've gone through more in a few weeks than most go through in a lifetime.

"What are you saying?"

"Lots. Let me get this all out. It's important. You were so bruised and beaten up I could not stand it, Maggie. It drove me nearly over the edge. I was ready to kill Zafir with my bare hands." He stopped, raising one hand, running fingers through her hair and moving part of it over one shoulder.

"You were never just the General's orders. It started the night you waltzed up and stood between Zamir and me."

She leaned in and kissed him. She knew he had more to say but this needed to be done right now. "Do you need to finish this here? Can we move to my bedroom and talk there?"

He raised both brows, standing, as she tightly wound her legs around his waist. "We can't walk down the altar like this, woman. It will cause more than a scandal."

She had not heard what he just said. She was busy. Very focused now beneath him, removing his shirt. He leaned down and kissed her while unbuttoning her blouse then tossed it to the floor as his eyes drank in the beauty of her skin.

She saw much in those eyes. Love, healing, and her future.

"Why don't you move in?"

"I can do that. Tomorrow soon enough?"

His hands were roaming all over her now. Clothes completely removed, thrown hastily about the room as he parted her legs. A deep moan of desire passed from her mouth into his as their kiss deepened. Then he entered her. Back arching, she took all of him, clutching on for sweet life as they truly merged as one.

Later, bodies covered in sweat, she finally spoke. "Yes, tomorrow would be soon enough. But, tonight you go nowhere, Doug.

# Chapter Eighteen

"Aunt Maggie, tell me again how he proposed. It is so beautiful."

"You are such a little romantic, Abbey, for one so young. Fine. Here it is again. We just returned from a walk through the hillside when we crossed this bridge. Below, like it is right now, thc watcr was rushing from a previous night's rain. He stopped me from continuing to the other side. While pulling something out of a pocket."

Maggie stopped, hearing someone approach.

"Please, go on before the ceremony begins."

"All right, you know you remind me of me when I was your age. Very impatient."

"Aunt Maggie!"

She laughed resisting the urge to ruffle her niece's hair. It was decorated so pretty with spring flowers from their own garden.

"Maggie," he said, "Would you like a full military ceremony, or, a small family-only?"

I thought, "What the heck is he talking about? Did I miss something and he was receiving an award and asking me what would be better after?"

"Then?"

"It took me by such surprise when he started to laugh. Moon had a paw in the brook trying to catch something and he even looked up at us. That's when Doug leaned sideways facing me and held out a beautiful, little, red velvet box with the most beautiful ring I had ever seen. It was his great-grandmothers. He did it right, Abbey. Got down on one knee and asked me to marry him. What's a girl to do? So, romantic. I said yes."

"Ah, Aunt Maggie, I love that story. Now, it's your wedding day and I get to throw flowers ahead of you."

Pops appeared. "Sweet, are you ready? I know he is. If you don't come along now, he will have a team sent in to fetch you. Your sister and the bridesmaids are waiting outside. Your ride awaits, daughter."

"We are ready, Pop."

When the lovely woman at the organ began the wedding song, Maggie stood just inside the massive front entrance of the church as the large wooden doors opened. Glancing up at the altar she could see him dressed in his tuxedo with her brother Kevin, his brother Jonathan and Zamir all standing at his side. If he wanted six kids she'd give him twenty as a giggle weaved its way from deep inside, escaping pink lip-glossed lips.

"Daughter, I don't know what's caused that, but if your feet don't start moving we are going to cause some embarrassment. Just look at all those eyes staring at you. Hurry along before Sasha and Patty come and drag you down."

That worked. Her arm rested in the crook of his while they walked, smiling, down the aisle. She could hardly remember all the words and how long it took. Staring into his eyes had caused her mind to stop working once again. But she sure as shit heard this when it was proclaimed; *"Under the eyes of Almighty God and for all those present, let me now present you Lieutenant Colonel and Mrs. Douglas Hawthorne."*

They had not even made it to the rear of the church before he leaned down and whispered in her left ear, his warm breath causing a delightful shiver up her spine, "I think we should delay our arrival to the reception and start working on those kids right away."

Raising one eyebrow, a soft flush enhanced her face. "Dismiss the driver. We can manage on our own and, oh," her tone now sultry, "because I surely agree."

The End

# About Sandra Waine

The author currently resides in central New Hampshire with her cat, Irene. She enjoy's long cycling rides, photography, hiking, reading, traveling and being active.

## Social Media

Social Media Links:  www.sandrawaine.com

Facebook:  https://www.facebook.com/sandrawaine

Twitter: @slwaine777

Instagram:  https://www.instagram.com/seattlewinenirvana/

www.ingramcontent.com/pod-product-compliance
Lightning Source LLC
Chambersburg PA
CBHW051630260626
47170CB00004B/1116